DR. QUINN
Medicine Woman

The phenomenally successful *Dr. Quinn, Medicine Woman* series has quickly become a part of the lives of millions of television viewers. Its sensitive portrayal of a young woman who sets out for untamed Colorado Springs to pursue her dreams of becoming a doctor underscores the important role women played in the development of a burgeoning nation.

Now, for the first time in print, comes an exciting, all-new story based on this hit television show.

Dr. Quinn, Medicine Woman

The untold story of how Michaela Quinn overcame society's disapproval and the bold frontier in Colorado to become one of the nation's first women doctors.

Dr. Quinn, Medicine Woman: The Bounty

Sully must face an enemy from his past—and help protect the future of Colorado Springs. But when the enemy brings scandal to Sully's hometown, Dr. Mike must find a way to clear her husband's name.

DR. QUINN
Medicine Woman:
GROWING PAINS

Teresa Warfield

BERKLEY BOULEVARD BOOKS, NEW YORK

DR. QUINN, MEDICINE WOMAN: GROWING PAINS

A Berkley Boulevard Book / published by arrangement with
CBS Enterprises, a Division of CBS Inc.

PRINTING HISTORY
Berkley Boulevard edition / May 1998

The Penguin Putnam Inc. World Wide Web site address is
http://www.penguinputnam.com

ISBN: 0-425-16492-6

BERKLEY BOULEVARD
Berkley Boulevard Books are published by The Berkley Publishing Group,
a member of Penguin Putnam Inc.,
200 Madison Avenue, New York, NY 10016.
BERKLEY BOULEVARD and its logo are trademarks
belonging to Berkley Publishing Corporation.

PRINTED IN THE UNITED STATES OF AMERICA

10 9 8 7 6 5 4 3 2 1

For Daddy, who provided the inspiration for Chester.

DR. QUINN

Medicine Woman:

GROWING PAINS

1

Michaela couldn't apply the astringent fast enough to the lesions on her patient's arm. In obvious distress, Eddie Thorton squirmed and rubbed and scratched at the lesions, something he had been doing for the last ten minutes, ever since he climbed onto the examination table and rolled up his shirtsleeves to show Michaela what was troubling him. She had known right away what she was looking at—an allergic reaction to poison ivy. She had gone straight to the cabinet where she kept her herbs and other medicinal mixtures, and had reached for a certain bottle.

"What's that there, Doc?" Mr. Thorton asked, eyes shifting between his left arm, the one she was treating, and the amber bottle and the cloth she held. "What's wrong with my arms?"

Michaela paused briefly in applying the concoction to the

1

lesions—it wasn't like her to begin treating a patient before she gave her medical opinion. The anxiety she felt when she thought of the line of patients waiting outside the clinic had caused her to rush into the treatment. Every morning of this past week people had begun waiting on the front porch of the clinic before Michaela arrived. As the hours of each day passed, more and more patients lined up to see the doctor. She never liked to keep them waiting. But lately, as the number of patients grew, they were forced to wait. After all, she could treat them only so fast.

During the last few days, her anxiety had worsened around this hour—in the late afternoon—when she realized that again she would not finish with the patients until well after dark. She had fallen more and more behind at the clinic: patient records sat in stacks on her desk, waiting to be updated; dried herbs hung from the roof of the back porch, waiting to be crumbled and ground; linens and bandages filled several baskets in a room upstairs, waiting to be washed.

At home . . . well, she'd not spent much time there since the increase in patients began. When she did manage to snatch time at home, it was spent catching up on the everyday things involved in keeping up a home and a family—on cooking and cleaning . . . on caring for Katie, who had become busy toddling around and discovering things, not all of which she should be discovering. Katie had learned to open cabinet doors and to climb the stairs. And her favorite thing was yanking the doilies from the side tables. Unfortunately, along with each doily there usually came a lamp or a vase. Despite being exhausted these past weeks, Michaela had learned to be quick on her feet at home.

"I'm sorry, Mr. Thorton, I usually offer my opinion, then begin the treatment," she said, resuming her task. "You've

2

had an encounter with poison ivy, and your body doesn't like it. Actually, a great number of people are allergic to the plant. I'm applying an extract of grindelia—gumweed—mixed with water and alcohol. The mixture should ease the itching until the reaction subsides, usually within a few weeks.''

"A few weeks?'' he complained.

She nodded. "I'm afraid so. I'll send a bottle of the mixture with you. Soak compresses with it and apply them at night. That should reduce the itching and allow you to sleep.''

He reached over her arm and scratched furiously at the affected areas on his left forearm.

Michaela grabbed his hand, concerned that he might scrape the lesions open. "Scratching will spread the rash.''

He scowled at her. She knew he was uncomfortable, miserable with the need to scratch.

She continued applying the mixture to the cloth, then dabbing the cloth on the rash. Once she had dampened the affected areas on his left arm, she turned her attention to treating the outbreak on his right arm.

"I'll send some crumbled grindelia leaves and flowers with you also,'' she offered. "Steep them in boiling water and drink the tea cold. It also will help calm the itching. The rash may spread more before it finally goes away.''

Mr. Thorton's scowl deepened. "I coulda done without that warnin'.''

"It's my duty to tell you.'' Michaela gave him a sympathetic smile.

"I know it,'' he drawled. "Hellfire, I wouldn't ah come to see you if I thought you didn't know what you were doin' or talkin' about.''

She finished applying the mixture to his arm.

3

Michaela went to her medicine cabinet and sprinkled dried and crumbled grindelia leaves, enough for four or five cups of tea, onto a square of brown paper. Then she folded the paper into a bundle and tied a piece of string around the bundle, securing it. No patients knocked at the clinic door, grumbling about how long they had been waiting and demanding to be seen, although half a dozen had stood there when she ushered in Mr. Thorton. Their tolerance was a relief. They coped with her busyness much better than she did.

She gathered the bundle and another bottle of grindelia extract and handed them to Mr. Thorton. "There you are," she said, withdrawing a little, giving him room to ease down off the table.

"Say. . . . It ain't itchin' like it was." He looked astounded.

Michaela couldn't help a laugh—and a cheerful smile this time. "Wonderful. If the rash is still troubling you after you finish with the tea, I'll give you more leaves."

He smiled back, then he slipped down off the table and made his way to the front door.

Michaela washed her hands over a basin that sat on a stand beneath one of the clinic's front windows. Through the gauzy curtain she watched the heavy traffic on Main Street. It was amazing—lately an almost constant flow of wagons, coaches, horses, and, of course, people. There was no method to the madness, no organization, just a tangled mixture going this way and that way. Inevitably one person got in the way of another, and shouts carried through the clinic window. The congestion began every day around midmorning and didn't ease until nearly dark, around suppertime. Colorado Springs had never been busier.

Mrs. Everly's cow joined the melee, turning right, then

left, then completely around, trying to avoid the horses and wagons coming at her from every direction. Mrs. Everly lived alone on the western outskirts of town and owned several cows; she sold the milk to local boardinghouses and to Hank at the Gold Nugget. This cow was Mrs. Everly's favorite, and the woman made that apparent by tying ribbons and bells around the animal's neck.

Unlike many people who lived in town, Mrs. Everly normally kept her animals penned. So the cow must have escaped. Numerous animals ran free around Colorado Springs, adding to the ever-growing confusion and traffic, and their owners collected them when they were needed. Several boys appeared, trying to coax the cow to them, but she danced skittishly around them, her eyes wide and fearful.

At Bray's Mercantile, located to the left of the clinic and across the street, Michaela spotted Loren batting at several fluttering chickens with his broom, despite a steady stream of customers going in and out of his store. The chickens were again after the corn that Loren had laid out in baskets on the porch. For weeks now Loren had had to chase the chickens away, and today he looked more annoyed than ever.

The broom hit one of the birds, and the chicken squawked and fluttered off, heading toward the barbershop, from which a line of men curved around and encroached on the mercantile steps. One man sidestepped the bird as several mercantile customers tried to approach Loren, one woman with a bolt of cloth in her hands. But Loren was concentrating on getting rid of the other chicken, and that might take some time. The bird was being stubborn, backing off, then returning. Meanwhile, Michaela had more work to do.

She left the window and went to the clinic's front door, meaning to usher in her next patient.

Loren whacked the second bird, knocking it into the air and toward the line of men extending from Jake's barbershop.

The men ducked and skittered around, trying to avoid the claws and flapping wings of the creature that looked like it might come down on their heads. It landed in the bucket of rainwater Jake had collected during yesterday's thunderstorm.

Loren cackled as the chicken flapped around in the water, squawking, not knowing what to do. Served it right.

One of the men plucked the hen out of the barrel; she squawked and fluttered out of his hands. Finally she tore off past the barbershop, trying to settle her ruffled feathers, looking like she'd just been dipped in a pot and readied for plucking. Well, except for her head—she still had that.

"You might not keep your head next time," Loren threatened, shaking the broom in her direction.

Jake's customers laughed at him. Loren shook the broom at them and muttered, "You wouldn't be laughin' if those birds were bothering *you* all the time."

He half hoped those men had to stand in line all day to get their jaws shaved and their hair snipped. Fools, all of 'em. *He* wouldn't stand in a line that long. He'd pick up a pair of shears and take care of the problem himself.

He went back inside the mercantile. There Mrs. Levins plopped the bolt of material on top of the others and glared at him over the heads of the three boys who were rummaging through the candy jars. She expected to be helped the second she thought she needed help. Well, he was too busy these days to fetch things for her right away. She'd have to learn to wait like everyone else.

"A pound of sugar and a pound of coffee," said Mr. McCracken as Loren approached the general counter. He spotted two handwritten lists lying there, orders needing to be filled.

"Could I take a closer look at that watch?" Mrs. Costner asked from nearby, pointing through a glass-topped jewelry case.

Four more customers were lined up behind Mr. McCracken. Mrs. Voss and Mrs. Rice came into town once a month to collect supplies, Loren knew, and they'd probably be patient. Mrs. Perryman had eggs to sell—her covered basket dangled from her forearm—and he was glad, because he was plumb out of eggs. He'd sold out yesterday afternoon, and had had to tell numerous customers that he didn't have any eggs.

"Come on up here," Loren said to Mrs. Perryman as he collected the coffee and sugar for Mr. McCracken. Mrs. Levins dropped the bolt of material on the counter, apparently deciding she wanted some cloth after all.

While Loren was packaging the coffee and sugar, three more customers wandered into the store.

Loren shook his head. Since this morning he hadn't had time to eat a bite or even to visit the outhouse. Soon, very soon, people would have to wait a few minutes while he scuttled off to take care of his private business.

"Can I have some candy?" asked six-year-old Johnny Perkins, his bright blue eyes shining up at Loren over the edge of the counter. Johnny reached his arm up and opened his fist. Coins clattered on the counter.

The boy grinned, and Loren saw that he'd lost a tooth since he visited the mercantile last week. "I got pennies,"

Johnny said. "Mama gave 'em to me. She said I did good milkin' the cow an' gatherin' the eggs."

"Two dollars," Loren told Mr. McCracken as he handed the man the packages. Mr. McCracken paid him, and Loren went to the register to deposit the money.

"How many eggs did you gather?" Loren asked Johnny.

"A whole bunch!" Johnny said, opening his hands wide.

"Aw, I'll *give* you some candy an' you can keep your pennies if you go ask your ma if she's got any eggs she can sell me. I'm short on eggs this week, see, an' you'd be helpin' me."

Where his patience with the boy came from, Loren wasn't sure. He felt anything but patient today, especially since Mrs. Levins was now tapping her boot on the floor, trying to let him know that she'd completely *lost* what little patience she sometimes had.

"Really?" Johnny blurted at Loren. Candy rattled in the jars just down the counter.

"Hey, now, no hands in those jars," Loren warned the two boys who'd commenced to sifting through the candy. "Really," he told Johnny, then turned his attention to looking through Mrs. Perryman's eggs.

Johnny dashed away, and Mr. McCracken went off with his sugar and coffee. Two more people collected goods from Loren's shelves and joined the line of waiting customers. Mrs. Levins tapped her boot louder on the puncheons.

Loren scowled. He'd been this busy for a good month now, from the time he opened till the time he closed. He'd thought things might settle down a bit, but earlier this week he'd seriously started doubting that.

He reckoned he'd have to break down and hire himself some help. At least someone to stand guard out front, maybe with an ax in hand, to keep the chickens away.

8

Business also was booming at the Gold Nugget, and Hank was having a time keeping up with things. He was finding out that running a hotel was a bigger job than running a saloon and managing a supply of liquor and a stable of girls. Running a busy hotel, well, it was a chore. As soon as customers checked out, more customers checked in, which meant that for the last few months, rooms never stood empty for long at the Gold Nugget.

Hank and Jake had opened the hotel together last year, and Jake had helped out a lot until things got busy in town for almost everyone—which meant business was hopping at Jake's barbershop, too. At first, when business picked up and Jake stopped helping at the hotel, Hank hadn't minded much. And he still didn't mind all the time, only when the hotel got real busy. He minded, too, when he had to hire extra workers and pay out extra money, as he'd had to do lately. Hank preferred that his money stay in his pocket, not line somebody else's.

As hard as Hank worked, and as rattled as he'd felt during the last few months, being pulled every which way by people always needing things, he was pretty happy every night when he counted the money and entered figures into the books. Preston Lodge and his resort didn't have anything on him anymore.

A month ago he'd hired two more desk clerks, one for the night shift and one for the day shift. A group of Chinese women now came two days a week instead of one to wash the dirty sheets, towels, and other laundry. Hank had taken to throwing his dirty clothes in the pile, too. What the heck, he might as well get the most for his money.

He'd hired Brian Cooper and Ben Hughes for a little after-school cleanup. The boys emptied rubbish cans, swept floors, scooped up horse dung out front of the hotel (an ongoing problem in front of every business). They washed windows and mirrors around the place for about an hour every day, too. Brian and Ben worked harder than some of the adults who'd worked for Hank in the past. They earned their money.

"There ya go," Hank said, doling out Brian and Ben's coins for the day. "Gonna spend it on anything special?"

"Nope," Brian said, grinning.

Ben pocketed his coins. "School in Chicago."

That raised Hank's eyebrows a notch. "Ya don't say?" He'd always thought Ben would follow in his daddy's footsteps and be a rancher. A person didn't need to go to school to learn how to do that.

Ben nodded. "Sure do. Law school. I'm gonna be a lawyer."

So Ben didn't want to follow in his pa's footsteps. He didn't want to watch over a herd of cattle and horses.

"The way you're savin'," you'll have plenty when the time rolls around," Hank told the boy. Far as he knew, Ben and Brian didn't spend much of their money. Most kids would've taken their money and gone straight to Loren's candy jars. Not these two. Loren had told Hank that Brian and Ben didn't visit the candy jars much.

"Say, remember you told us you'd teach us to play foot ball?" Brian asked Hank.

Hank nodded. "I remember." Dr. Mike's boy got taller every day. One of these days Brian might sprout up past him.

"Still want to?"

"Sure. How about on Saturday, when you ain't got school?" Today was Wednesday. Three days . . . that gave him time to make sure he could get free of the hotel for an afternoon.

"All right!" Brian said. Ben's head bobbed, like he thought Saturday was a fine day for learning to play foot ball.

"Saturday afternoon, out at the school yard. Two o'clock," Hank said. "Bring friends—we'll divvy up into teams."

"We'll be there," Ben said, his eyes bright.

Hank walked with the boys to the front door of the hotel, thinking he'd take himself a cigar break. He did that three or four times a day, leaning back against a post, enjoying his smoke as he watched the happenings on the streets and at different businesses.

As soon as he stepped out the door today, he knew there was trouble. A group of men were huddled together with several horses at one end of the hotel walkway. The men were tipping bottles and placing bets. Hank had been in the saloon business long enough to figure that out with just a glance.

Brian and Ben walked off down the street, and after a few minutes they blended with the traffic. All the main businesses were to the left and on down a ways, in the direction the boys had gone. Because traffic was usually sparse in front of the Gold Nugget, unless a bunch of customers arrived at the same time, Hank had had to bust up two or three races since he and Jake had opened the hotel.

He recognized the men. Yesterday, the group had arrived from up north to visit Preston's resort. They'd found it not just full but overbooked, so they rode into town looking for lodging, ending up at Hank's hotel.

Hank had closed his saloon months ago, when the hotel started eating up so much of his time. But other saloons

11

had gone up around town, which meant a man damn sure had access to liquor if he wanted it. And this group had found it. They'd liquored themselves up good. Two of them jumped on the horses and trotted the animals down the street, then turned them around.

Hank crushed the cigar under his boot. Another race, right up the street in front of the Gold Nugget. Not if he had anything to say about it—and he did!

Months ago, Hank might have gotten in on the betting. But lately, probably because Preston's resort stayed full, the Gold Nugget had attracted some dandied-up people who looked like they might have a good amount of money to their names. If those people had to dodge galloping horses while trying to go in and out of his establishment, they might end up preferring a boardinghouse over the Gold Nugget. Hank couldn't have that. He *wouldn't* have that.

He headed for the group of men. The culprits laughed and called out more bets as the contestants huddled over the horses, getting ready. Someone shouted "Go!" and two horses tore off, kicking up dust in a tangle of flying hooves.

"Hey, you can't be havin' races out here!" Hank bellowed at the men. Not that anyone heard him over their shouts of encouragement. He'd have to get in their faces so they could hear him.

Which is exactly what he did. He grabbed one man by the arm and spun him around. "You can't be havin' races out here! I've got customers who ain't gonna like it."

The man glared at him. *"We're* customers."

"You ain't the only customers."

The man turned away and rejoined his friends.

Hank shoved his way between several of the men, getting their attention. "You can't be havin' races out here!"

12

"Get out of the way, I can't see," shouted one man, and he shoved Hank.

Hank stumbled backward, into the railing on the outside of the hotel's front walkway. He bounced off—in a temper now, not just irritated anymore.

He lurched forward, grabbed the culprit by the scruff of the neck, and flung him.

The man rolled like a tumbleweed. A wagon rattled by, just missing the varmint.

The man's companions didn't notice that their friend had been tossed like a corncob doll into the middle of the street. Some booed and some cheered as the horses reached the end of the short passage, and wagers were won and lost.

The man Hank had flung scrambled to his feet and charged Hank like a mad bull. Forget his fine clothes and lacquered hair. He meant business—Hank saw that in the flash of his eyes.

"Come on," Hank said, crouching and encouraging the attack. He forgot a few things himself, mostly that he was supposed to be a respectable hotel proprietor now, not a rowdy saloon keeper.

The man hit Hank harder than he expected, and Hank stumbled back into the walkway railing again. This time the railing splintered. The man went through it and sprawled onto the walkway.

Hank let out a roar—now the man hadn't just disrupted business, he'd damaged the hotel. For a few minutes his friends forgot about collecting on their bets. They spotted their friend tussling with the hotel proprietor, and they began betting on that contest. The race and the fight were more excitement than they'd counted on during an afternoon in Colorado Springs, and they were loving it.

Across the street, Matthew stepped out of the sheriff's

13

office, meaning to stretch after spending most of the afternoon trying to memorize the faces on the new batch of Wanted posters he'd received this morning.

He spotted the fight on the walkway in front of the Gold Nugget and reckoned he didn't have time for a stretch right now. Colorado Springs had become so busy that lately Matthew usually was forced to choose what disturbances he broke up. Hank was involved in this fight, looking like a mad bear, his hair flying and his eyes blazing.

Matthew raced down the steps in front of his office and headed for the Gold Nugget. By the time he reached the front of the hotel, Hank had punched his opponent several times. He gave him a hard right in the jaw and knocked him clean off his feet. It had been a while since Matthew had seen Hank as angry as he looked right now, or whomp somebody so hard.

"Break it up!" Matthew yelled, approaching the two men. They'd drawn a crowd at one side of the walkway, a few startled-looking ladies among the gathering. A group of men off to the left of the crowd shouted encouragement to one of the men. Matthew couldn't tell whom they wanted to win.

Hank and the man he was fighting either didn't hear Matthew or they ignored him. The man scrambled to his feet, put his head down and charged Hank. Hank dodged him. The man barreled across the walkway and crashed through a front window of the hotel.

Hank cursed and started forward, obviously intending to go after the man again. The ladies screamed. The group of men who'd been shouting encouragement booed.

Matthew stepped between Hank and the shattered window, and pushed Hank back.

"That's enough!" Matthew yelled, and to his relief he saw a spark of sanity return to Hank's eyes.

Hank stopped in his tracks, seething. "You'd better get him outta here, Matthew. An' you'd better tell him an' his friends they can't race horses in front of my hotel!"

Blood trickled from one corner of Hank's mouth. His opponent had gotten in at least one good punch.

"Matter o' fact, ever'body's goin' too fast in the streets these days. I got respectable people comin' to my hotel. I ain't gonna have people run down on their way to my front door." Hank shot a glare around Matthew, at the man he'd just knocked through the window.

"I'll get him," Matthew promised, pushing against Hank's chest, backing him up more. He was sure Hank would try to get past him in a minute, and if Hank did, the fight would be on again.

"An' just what're you gonna do with him?"

"I'll lock him up 'til he cools off."

"That's all?"

"That's about all I can do, unless he aimed a gun at you. We don't have a law against racin' horses in town."

"We oughtta have one!"

Behind them, people in the crowd murmured agreement. The group of men who'd been cheering on Hank's opponent had quieted and now looked worried—they might find themselves in jail along with their friend.

"Do I have to lock you up, too, 'til you cool off?" Matthew asked Hank.

Hank made a sound of exasperation in the back of his throat. His eyes shifted to the left and flared, as if he'd just spotted something else he didn't like. He stomped off, to where a hog was rooting in a fresh pile of animal dung.

"This's gotta stop, too," Hank muttered, kicking the hog.

The animal squealed and ran off, and Hank spun to face Matthew. "How'm I supposed to run a hotel when people are racin' horses out front an' hogs are messin' an' rootin' around on my walkway?"

Matthew didn't know what to say. The men racing the horses hadn't broken any laws. And hogs, and other animals, were allowed to run free in town.

While Hank fumed on about this not being the first time he'd had to clean dung off his walkway and chase off pesky animals, Matthew went inside the hotel to collect the man Hank had been fighting.

He found the man picking shards of glass out of his bleeding palms. Matthew shook his head. He'd lock the man up, then go get Dr. Mike to tend to the troublemaker's hands.

At the clinic, Michaela treated Henry Hughes for his on-going battle with kidney stones, giving him more birch bark from which to make a tea. She advised him, as she had last week and the week before, to drink only one glass of tea a day. The tea would eventually dissolve the stones, but too much would expel the stones intact, causing him more severe pain.

She saw four new patients with a variety of ailments from angina to ringworm, and she treated them all accordingly, mostly with herbal remedies she had learned from Cloud Dancing. Mary Tennessey had a festering case of mastitis, a breast infection, to which Michaela advised applying a poultice of boiled chaparral leaves and twigs; Mary should return next week if the infection were no better. Her nearly two-month-old infant—Mary and her husband had named him Kevin—had a little colic from time to time, but was otherwise fine.

She walked outside with Mary, intending to collect her next patient. Out in the street, the boys had finally cornered Mrs. Everly's cow by herding it against the front of a boot shop located directly across from the clinic. Down the way, Matthew had broken up a fight in front of the Gold Nugget. Meanwhile, the tangled traffic and the endless noise continued on Main Street.

"Madness," Mr. Britton said to Michaela as he sat on the clinic's bench, waiting for the doctor to see him. Mary had stepped off the porch and was waiting for the traffic to slow so she could cross the street.

"People began discovering the mountains and the springs, and it's been madness ever since," Mr. Britton said. Shaking his head, he pointed toward Hank's hotel, and now Michaela saw that Matthew stood between Hank and another man, that Hank had been involved in the fight. "Men were racing horses in front of the hotel. You can't be racing horses in the middle of a busy town."

Mr. Britton played the piano in a local saloon, no doubt earning a small fortune these past months because of the influx of people into Colorado Springs. He was a quiet and levelheaded character, keeping to himself when not at work. Sometimes, when she gathered herbs, Michaela encountered him walking through the forest and alongside creeks and streams. Just the other day he had commented to her that it was far too crowded in town lately. But it wasn't simply crowded; he was right—it was madness. And people *shouldn't* be allowed to race horses in the middle of town.

Michaela folded her hands in front of her. "What can I do for you, Mr. Britton? Would you like to come inside?"

Four or five patients ago she had stopped apologizing for the wait to see her; day after day, the apologies became repetitive and tiring. Besides, the patients seemed to understand.

Mary saw her chance and took it, stepping into the street, holding her bundled infant against her chest.

"I've had a little trouble catching my breath," Mr. Britton said, rising.

Michaela pushed the clinic door open and stood aside to allow him to go in first.

In the time it took Mr. Britton to take one step toward the clinic door, Michaela heard shouts, a curse, then a woman's scream and the screech of a frightened horse. The sounds occurred within milliseconds of each other, and immediately Michaela's stomach tightened and her heart lurched. Before she could turn toward the street and the sounds, she knew what had happened.

Mary and her infant had been run down.

Michaela shot down the porch steps and into the street, dodging wagons, horses, and people as she raced in the direction Mary had gone. Another scream turned Michaela slightly to the right.

She broke through a cluster of people and found Mary on the ground, her left arm at an odd angle as she scooted toward the bundle that had apparently been knocked from her arms. Blood trickled down one side of Mary's face. She screamed again, and then Michaela saw why: a wagon, the driver glancing around at the sights, was headed straight toward the infant.

Distantly aware of the baby's squalls, Michaela dashed for the bundle. She tripped on her skirts, propelled by the horror that the horses and wagon would run over the infant.

She scooped up the bundle, and seconds later the conveyance rattled by. Michaela dodged a horse, then another. She wove her way between wagons back to where Mary had collapsed on the ground.

Michaela uncovered the infant, and with a quick glance assured herself that little Kevin was not physically hurt, just frightened. Mary was a different matter, however.

"Dear Lord!" came Dorothy's horrified voice over Michaela's shoulder. "He looks fine. Here, give him to me." She came around and reached for the baby, folding the brown blanket around his flailing arms and legs. His face was red and crinkled from the effort of crying. Michaela handed him to Dorothy and put her full attention on Mary.

Mary's arm was broken, surely. And the blood trickling down the side of her face must be coming from a laceration somewhere on her scalp. Her face had turned starkly white.

"My baby," Mary gasped, struggling to sit up. "Is he hurt?"

"He's just fine," Michaela assured. "Are your legs hurt? Can you walk? We must get you out of the street."

"Don't you worry, he's just fine," Dorothy said, swaying with the infant, trying to calm him. "I'll take care of him 'til Dr. Mike fixes you up."

Several men had managed to jerk themselves out of their shock and were now detouring traffic around the small crowd that had gathered around Mary and Michaela. Michaela helped Mary get to her feet.

"I'm dizzy," Mary said, swaying against Michaela.

"You might have a concussion."

Sully was there suddenly, scooping Mary up. She gasped as her injured arm dangled. Michaela carefully lifted the arm and laid it across Mary's waist, holding it in place as she and Sully walked toward the clinic.

Behind Michaela and Sully, the gawkers talked: "Somethin's got to be done. There's too many people—the streets ain't safe no more.'' ''A person can't cross the street without gettin' run over!'' ''It's a wonder someone ain't been hit b'fore now.''

Mr. Britton stood on the clinic's front porch, shaking his head as he held the front door open for Michaela and Sully. ''Our quiet town is not so quiet anymore.''

Wasn't that the truth! As Sully placed Mary on the examination table, Michaela thought that Colorado Springs had become rather like Boston—chaotic, noisy, confused, and sometimes even dangerous.

Perhaps it was time to call a meeting of the town council.

2

Another evening getting home late. Another day of seeing little of Katie, Brian, and Sully.

Sully met Michaela in front of the barn. He took Katie from her and helped her down from the wagon.

She kissed him, looking into his eyes to see if he was annoyed that she had been delayed again. "I'm sorry I'm so late. I took Mary home—I didn't want her to be alone—and I stayed a few minutes to caution her husband about things to watch for, signs of concussion."

After carrying Mary into the clinic, Sully had gone back to what he'd been doing, helping build a house. He'd come into town to get a few things from Robert E., and had been close by when Mary and her infant were struck by the wagon.

He smoothed the stray hairs away from Michaela's face, and then he returned the kiss. "It's all right. You were a busy doctor when I married you. I knew what I was gettin' into.''

She almost laughed. ''Not this busy. I hardly have a minute to breathe lately.''

''I know.'' He handed Katie back to her, and he began unharnessing the horse from the wagon.

Katie usually sat quietly on Michaela's lap during the ride home, and today had been no different. But once they got there, Katie always became impatient fast. Months ago she had settled into the routine of eating her supper soon after they arrived home, and she expected no different this evening. She extended her chubby arm in the direction of the house and said, ''Eat, Ma-ma, eat.''

Michaela hugged the baby close. ''I know—you're hungry, aren't you? How is the house progressing?'' she asked Sully.

''Eat,'' Katie said again, insistently this time. She squeezed her fingers together, then unfolded them and reached toward the house. She bounced on Michaela's hip, trying to get her mother's complete attention.

''I'll be along in a while,'' Sully said, giving Michaela a reassuring smile.

Michaela nodded, understanding. Until Katie was fed, they couldn't carry on a conversation; they both knew that, so why try? Babies had a way of demanding that their needs be met.

From the wagon seat Michaela gathered the patient records she had brought with her, hoping to update them after everyone was asleep. If she had stayed at the clinic to update the files, she would have been another hour getting home. Already this was the latest she had arrived home in a long time.

After examining Mary, setting her arm, and stitching the

cut on her forehead, Michaela had convinced her to stay at the clinic until after the last patient was seen. That allowed Michaela nearly an hour to observe Mary for signs of concussion. Afterward, Michaela gathered the patient records and collected Katie from a tired-looking Grace. Then she took Mary home and spoke with Mary's husband. After telling Mr. Tennessey to bring Mary into town if she developed symptoms of concussion, Michaela headed for her own home.

Holding Katie in one arm and the patient records in the other, she walked toward the house. Behind her she heard the harness jingle as Sully continued his task.

Inside the house, Michaela placed the records on the secretary in the main room.

"Hi, Ma," Brian said from where he sat at the table.

Katie wasn't just fidgety now, she was fussy. She was hungry, tired, and understandably clingy. She squirmed on Michaela's hip, and when Michaela boosted her higher, she grabbed her mother around the neck, buried her face in her throat, and worked up a cry.

"I know, I know," Michaela soothed, rubbing Katie's back. "You're hungry, aren't you? Hello, Brian."

Someone had put the roast beef that Michaela had planned for supper in a kettle and started it cooking. Onions and herbs had been added, and the delicious smell filled the house, making Michaela's stomach growl.

Someone also had placed Katie's pewter plate—they didn't dare put a china plate in front of her—on the small tray that attached to her tall nursery chair after Katie was placed in the chair. The tray was made of thick elm, and two deep grooves on the underside fit over the arms of the chair, holding the tray in place in front of the baby. Right now the chair sat beside the table and the tray sat on the

23

table. Smoked ham and corn bread, leftover from last night, were arranged on Katie's plate.

When Katie twisted around and spotted the plate of food, she drew her knees up and pushed against Michaela, trying to get down so she could run to the table. She did the same thing every evening when they arrived home. The one evening Michaela had put her down on her feet, Katie had run to the table and pulled the tray off. Her food had gone everywhere. Michaela wouldn't risk such a disaster again.

"I put the roast on to cook," Brian said as Michaela placed Katie in her chair.

"Thank you, Brian. That's a tremendous help." She had assumed that Sully had started the roast cooking. What a pleasant surprise to learn that Brian had. "Where did you learn to do that?"

He shrugged. "I watch you an' Miss Grace, sometimes Miss Dorothy. I just never tried it before."

Michaela slid the tray onto the arms of the chair. Katie scowled at the fork someone had placed on the tray. She promptly threw it to the floor and began eating tiny chunks of ham, picking them up with her fingers.

Michaela shook her head in amazement. It was uncanny; over the years she had heard again and again from her sisters about what a stubborn baby and child she had been. Katie's stubbornness often reminded her of those stories, of her own childhood willfulness.

As Katie busied herself with eating, Michaela sliced potatoes. Brian had gone back to reading, always occupying himself whenever Katie consumed Michaela's time and attention. Michaela sprinkled salt and pepper on the potatoes, then crumbled dried basil on them. She put the dish of potatoes in the stove's oven, then buttered more corn bread for Katie.

She sat near Katie as the potatoes roasted. Brian was engrossed in his reading. But he wasn't turning pages at a very fast rate.

"What are you reading?" she finally asked him.

"History," he mumbled, sighing. Suddenly he looked haggard, supporting his chin in his cupped palm, his elbow propped on the edge of the table. "George Washington and the Continental Army at Valley Forge and in New Jersey. Miss Theresa says we're gonna have a test on all these dates. So I reckon I need to memorize them. I'm not sure any are gonna stick in my head. I like to read about what happened, but I don't know if I can remember exactly *when* everything happened."

Michaela gave him a sympathetic smile. "I can't even recite the dates when events happened during the Revolutionary War."

He went back to reading.

Katie finished her corn bread, and Michaela helped her drink milk from a cup. She tipped the cup just the right amount so that Katie wouldn't soak the front of her clothes with milk.

Katie grunted, frustrated. Lately she wanted to do everything by herself, including trying to tie her small boots. She usually succeeded only in twisting the laces.

"She has a streak of her ma's independence," Sully had commented the other day while Michaela and Katie battled over who would put her dress on her. Occasionally Michaela let Katie try to dress herself, and her arms inevitably ended up in the neck hole. The episodes usually concluded with Katie shrieking in frustration and Michaela rearranging the dress, then comforting the baby.

Her attempts to help Katie drink and eat usually became battles, too. Tonight, Katie didn't battle her too much over

25

the cup. She grunted, grabbing for the cup once. Michaela shook her head slowly at Katie, and Katie lowered her hands and grinned around the lip of the cup, melting her mother's heart.

Sully came in and took over with Katie while Michaela checked on the potatoes. They were completely cooked. She took the dish out of the oven and placed it on top of the stove. She spooned the potatoes into a serving bowl, then carried the bowl to the table.

After putting the bowl down, she bent over Brian and hugged him. "Thank you for putting the meat on to cook. It looks and smells wonderful."

As soon as she had realized she would arrive home late again, even later than what had become almost normal, she began worrying about how late she would have supper prepared. Too late for Katie certainly. And surely Brian would be hungry, too, although he rarely complained.

When Sully was home, he started supper if she was late. But these past weeks he had been hiring himself out to work odd jobs. In town and outside of town, people were building homes and structures for businesses, and Sully helped with those.

"I should take advantage of the boom," he had told her, although he didn't like the rate at which Colorado Springs was growing. He preferred the wilderness, the quiet and beauty of it, and the influx of people would ruin all of it.

Not only that, but the hordes of newly arrived people would spell trouble for the reservation Indians; as Colorado Springs and other communities grew, people would want more land. And taking land from Indians wasn't regarded as a crime. Michaela had had little time to just sit and talk to Sully lately. Despite that, she was positive he still felt torn between the Indians' dilemma and hiring himself out to help people build.

She knew what drove him: not too long ago she and Sully had fallen behind on their loan payments to the bank, and Preston had threatened to foreclose. Although her increase in patients had increased her earnings, Sully, as the man of the house, felt it was his duty to make certain Preston didn't foreclose. Hunting and trapping—bringing food home—wouldn't prevent that from happening, Sully had told her one evening. He had to work for money, because only money would pay off that loan. Michaela knew he wasn't happy helping people build a community he knew would eventually overrun the reservation land, but she understood his reasons for doing it. She understood his love and devotion to his family.

Brian grinned at Michaela, as he always did when she praised him. "I know you've been awful busy at the clinic."

"Yes, I certainly have been. And you've been very understanding. I appreciate that."

He beamed more, then went back to his reading. She lifted three china plates from a stack in the cupboard and placed them on the table. From the same cupboard, she removed three glasses and set them down near the plates. Then she went after the silverware.

"I've been thinking . . . I may need to hire someone to help me at the clinic," she said as she laid down the last fork.

Brian glanced up, his brows pressed together. "You mean like another doctor?"

Back at the stove, Michaela prepared to remove the roast from the pot. A fork in each hand, she lifted the roast and placed it on a platter. "Not necessarily. I have time to see

27

the patients. I simply don't have time for all the other things—for preparing the herbs, for washing sheets and bandages, for cleaning the clinic and the instruments I use. . . ."

"Katie's asleep," Sully announced as he entered the room.

Wonderful—but not so wonderful. Michaela missed the baby, and often felt that her long hours at the clinic made her short with Katie. She had had time to feed Katie this evening, and that was all. No playing with her, no sitting and just holding her for a while.

"How did you wash her and get her to sleep so fast?"

Sully grinned. "She was fallin' asleep *while* I was washin' her."

"Ma's talkin' about hirin' someone to help her at the clinic," Brian told Sully.

Sully fixed a surprised gaze on Michaela. He knew she was particular about how things were done at the clinic— how the herbs were prepared, how the instruments were cleaned. "That might not be a bad idea," he said gently.

In the past, she had had only Colleen and Andrew—who stayed very busy at the resort these days—help her. Certainly she'd never considered hiring anyone. Until recently, there had never been a need to.

"It will take time to teach someone how things should be done," she said, and suddenly her vision blurred with tears. Now what was wrong with her? One minute she was putting supper on the table, and the next minute she was crying.

"Ma?" Brian said, concerned. "Are you all right, Ma?"

She tried to blink back the tears, but they welled up in her eyes even more. She wiped her hands on her apron, feeling embarrassed. It wasn't like her to cry suddenly.

"I think I'm overwhelmed," she finally admitted, looking at Sully.

He had tipped his head. Now he smiled, not a smile of mockery but one of understanding. "I know," he said.

The two simple words meant the world to Michaela. They meant that he knew her better than anyone in the world, and that he understood and sympathized. He was truly a special person. Knowing how stubborn she could be, he almost always stood back and let her reach conclusions by herself.

He walked around the table, and in a simple, comforting gesture he slipped his arms around her. He didn't pull her toward him—he gave her even that distance, knowing her pride required it.

Laying her cheek against his chest and hearing his strong heartbeat was the comfort Michaela needed. He didn't ridicule her weakness, he simply held her. With her unusual position in the world, that of a female medical doctor, she was forced to be outwardly strong. But with Sully she could display weakness and not worry that he might belittle her for it.

He stroked her hair and the side of her face, and Michaela felt a surge of warmth and love for him. They had not seen very much of each other lately, but what little time they spent together was sweet and meaningful.

After a few minutes Michaela collected herself and wiped away the tears. Sully and Brian were hungry, she was sure, and so was she. Her stomach growled, and she realized that she'd not eaten anything since breakfast.

"Sounds like you're hungry." Sully remarked.

"I am." She withdrew, meaning to collect the bowl of potatoes from the stove and put it on the table.

Sully tugged on her arm, stopping her. "I'll get it. You sit down."

It was a gentle order, one Michaela obeyed. She sat and let Sully serve the rest of the meal. Brian took his books up to his room, then returned to the table.

"Got a letter from Colleen," Sully said, and he paused to pull an envelope from a pocket in his shirt. He handed the envelope to Michaela, who smiled up at him. He knew she loved to receive news from Colleen.

Michaela tore open the envelope, pulled out the letter, and unfolded it. She leaned back in her chair and read Colleen's words, the smile still on her face.

"What does it say, what does it say?" Brian asked excitedly. He bounced a few times in his chair, and Michaela laughed at him.

"It says she received my letter in which I told her how busy I've been at the clinic. She wants to come home soon for a visit. She wants to hear Katie jabber—I told her how Katie can put several words together now. She's doing dissections. . . ."

Michaela paused, reading on silently.

"Oh, no, listen to this," she said, suddenly serious.

Sully finished serving the plates and joined them at the table.

Michaela read from the letter: *"This past month two bodies disappeared from graves in the Denver cemetery, and almost immediately people began speculating that officials and students at the medical school robbed the graves. My anatomy instructor tells me that our cadavers are bought from territorial prisons when a prisoner dies and no family claims the body. Mr. Wayne even made the statement to a reporter from the* Denver Post *and the remark was printed. Still, in public people whisper among themselves if I dare tell them I'm a medical student. I hope the bodies are found soon and the whispers and suspicious looks stop. If not, I fear there may be more trouble.''*

"People don't really rob graves, do they, Ma?" Brian asked, his eyes wide.

"I've known it to happen," Michaela responded. "Before most medical schools began buying cadavers."

"Do you think they did it—the school people, I mean?"

"I'd hate to speculate as it sounds like the people of Denver are doing, Brian."

"But the school needs bodies for students like Colleen. Who else would need bodies?"

"Let's say grace," Sully interjected. Either he was hungry or he didn't think the topic a good one to discuss over a meal. Probably both.

Brian said grace. Then they ate, hardly saying two words among the three of them because they were so hungry.

A slice of apple or cherry pie would taste delicious, Michaela thought. They hadn't had dessert in at least a week. She'd been lucky to get a meal prepared.

"Scrumpt'us." Brian beamed at her.

Michaela laughed. "Well, having supper so late certainly makes us appreciate our meal."

"Sure does," Sully said.

"I think I'll advertise for an assistant in the *Gazette*," Michaela mused, thinking aloud.

"Colleen's your assistant whenever she's home. She won't get her feelin's hurt if you hire someone else, will she, Ma?"

Michaela glanced at Sully. Colleen's feelings weren't something she had considered when she thought of hiring an assistant, and now she felt guilty that she hadn't stopped to consider them.

31

"Write to her an' explain more," Sully advised. "You already wrote that you've been busy. Tell her *how* busy, an' I bet she'll understand."

"I hope so. I don't want to hurt her feelings." Michaela was worried now.

"She knows the clinic has to go on even when she's not here. She'll understand you needin' to hire someone."

"She might wonder why I didn't just ask Andrew."

" 'Cause he's busy with his own patients. Preston's resort's been full every day. He's had to turn people away. I sure ain't seen Andrew around town lately. Write to her, Michaela—she'll understand."

"I will," Michaela said. Doubtless Sully was right. Still, she would worry until she heard back from Colleen. She might even consider not running the advertisement until she received Colleen's response.

After supper, Brian hugged them and went upstairs to bed.

Sully said he would wash the dishes. Michaela fussed with him, saying she could manage the dishes. Really, there weren't that many.

"You're right, there ain't many," he said, and he began collecting dishes from the table.

Fine. If he insisted on washing the dishes, she would find something else that needed to be done, one of the daily chores. She looked for the milking bucket, intending to milk the cow.

The bucket was gone from where it usually sat. Michaela glanced around for it.

"Already done," Sully said, grinning. "Milk's strained an' in the springhouse."

"Sully," she admonished, "I feel like I'm not doing my share."

32

"You're doin' plenty."

He kissed her. "Why don't you go get ready for bed?"

His voice was low and husky, and Michaela saw in his eyes that he wanted to make love to her. She couldn't remember the last time they had made love. He had certainly been patient, more patient than most husbands would have been.

"All right." She blushed a little.

He laughed softly and kissed her again. Then Michaela went off to get ready for bed.

In the bedroom, she washed and changed into a nightgown. She brushed her hair until it was soft and shiny. Then she pulled back the coverlet on the bed and lay down to wait for Sully.

She fell asleep.

3

Michaela woke with a start at dawn. A pink glow was just beginning in the eastern sky, filtering into the bedroom through the windows' lace curtains. Beside Michaela, Sully was sound asleep.

She covered her mouth with the tips of her fingers, embarrassed and frustrated. Apparently he had found her asleep and had chosen to not wake her. Or, if he had tried to wake her, she had been unrousable.

He enjoyed making love in the morning.

But he was sleeping so well, his breathing deep and even, she didn't have the heart to wake him. His days had been long and difficult lately, too.

He must have covered her. She recalled pushing the coverlet to the end of the bed before she lay down.

She smiled at him, watching him sleep, adoring him.

She wondered what she would say to him when he woke.

Good morning, certainly. But an apology was also in order.

Michaela slipped from the tick, her feet touching the cold floorboards. She pulled her slippers from beneath the bedstead and wriggled her feet into them. Then she lifted her wrap from the corner post of the headboard, slid her arms into it, and tied the sash around her waist. Tea sounded appealing. She would brew some, and update those patient records before Katie woke. She lit the lamp on her bedside table and carried it to the bedroom door.

In the hallway her gaze went to the basket of Katie's soiled clothing and blankets, reminding her of how far behind she was on everyday tasks here at home. Her stomach clenched. Once upon a time she had washed clothes and bedding and other items every Wednesday. For the last several months she had spent Wednesdays at the clinic and washed laundry several items at a time, every few days. This past week she hadn't time to do even that. The laundry simply sat there, the pile growing daily. She would be forced to deal with it soon.

She brewed the tea and carried a cup of it and the lamp to the secretary on which she had placed the patient records last night. Once she set the lamp and the tea down, she tied back the curtains on the nearby window to allow the light of sunrise, still faint, into the room. Finally she lit another lamp, one that sat on the fireplace mantel.

Dust had collected on the mantel, also on the lamp and the framed lithographs of her family that were arranged there. The shirt Brian had asked her to mend more than a week ago still sat where he had draped it, over the arm of a nearby settee. Pieces of a dress she had begun stitching for Katie a month ago remained where she had placed them then—neatly folded on top of a brass-handled trunk.

As she sat surrounded by the signs of neglect, Michaela's shoulders slumped slightly.

If the clinic continued to be so busy, she might never mend Brian's shirt, or finish Katie's dress, or tend to the laundry and the dusting. She might continue to see her children for only two hours every evening after arriving home. And she wouldn't blame them if they forgot that she was their mother.

She sank down onto the chair in front of the secretary.

Upon awakening, she had felt well rested and ready to meet another day. But then she wandered out of the bedroom, looked around her, and realized what meeting another day meant. This day doubtless would be as busy and chaotic as other recent days had been.

Suddenly she wanted to slam a door in the face of this day. She wanted to freeze the sunrise. She wanted to stay home and play with Katie. She wanted to mend Brian's shirt and stitch Katie's dress. She wanted to clean and feel proud of the home she kept for her family. She wanted to cook a delicious meal, complete with dessert. She wanted to stay awake long enough to make love to her husband.

Her hand trembled as she brought the teacup to her lips and sipped.

The day overwhelmed her, and it had not even begun, not really.

Brian and Sully had been patient and sweet. But her long hours at the clinic were hard on them—she could tell. They missed her, and she missed them. Her busyness disrupted their family routine.

She cared about people who were sick or who had been injured, and she didn't want to dread going to the clinic and treating patients. Recently, however, the many patients overwhelmed her. She *cherished* her family members, and her close relationships with them would suffer more and more if she continued to work such long hours.

She sipped the tea, hardly tasting it, and thought more as she stared out the window. An orange and red glow now painted the eastern sky. Soon the bleeding colors would draw together.

Her mother had once spat at her that she couldn't be a medical doctor *and* a mother and a wife. Michaela didn't believe that, and she carefully juggled her many responsibilities most of the time. But lately she had dropped several balls and was in danger of dropping several more—several precious ones.

Limiting her hours at the clinic might make the juggling act easier.

For months after giving birth to Katie, she had opened the clinic only two or three days a week. Out of necessity, she had limited her time at the clinic then, and she could do the same now. Only instead of opening it only two or three days a week, she considered opening it every day but Sunday. She would post clinic hours and adhere to them. Loren and Jake, and scores of other local merchants, closed their businesses at a certain time each day. Why shouldn't she do the same?

She could see her last patient at three o'clock, then spend an hour updating patient records and sterilizing instruments. By doing that, she could be home in plenty of time to cook her family a decent meal and spend a relaxing evening with them. She could close earlier on Wednesdays because Wednesdays were supposed to be her wash days. She could close an hour every day for the noon meal, relax for a while, then reopen and see patients until it was time to close for the day.

The tea tasted better and better with each sip as Michaela

stared out the window at the sunrise, the schedule coming together in her head. Presently she rose to go pour herself more tea.

She tipped the teapot and filled her cup with the delicious amber liquid. She scraped a little sugar from the sugar cone, dropped it into the teacup, and stirred the tea. Now and then she took a sip of Sully's coffee. But tea was her favorite drink, and she had it morning, noon, and night. Some habits died hard—and some habits never died at all.

Soon her hand no longer trembled and her stomach no longer felt like a hard ball.

Michaela smiled to herself as a fond memory sprang to mind, that of her sisters Rebecca, Claudette, and Marjorie (of course Marjorie—she had been involved in nearly every quarrel that took place beneath the Quinns' roof) counting the guests who arrived at the Quinn household every Tuesday afternoon for tea. Tuesdays had been set aside by their mother for the Quinn family to receive guests, and there was always a quarrel among the Quinn sisters about how many guests came to tea.

Moments later, when Michaela opened the first patient record, she did so with the smile still on her face, without feeling resentful because her family was being torn apart by the demands of her patients.

In each patient record, she wrote brief notes of the symptoms and treatments she recalled from yesterday. Updating the notes was important; she now had so many patients that she couldn't always recall their past illnesses and treatments from one examination to the next.

She was so engrossed in her notes that she didn't hear Sully come up behind her. She felt something on her neck, and although the touch was warm and soft, it startled her. She jumped and twisted around in her chair.

"Mornin'," Sully said, smiling. The colors of sunrise reflected in his eyes. He wore no shirt, and the sight of his naked chest stirred Michaela.

She blushed, feeling ashamed again, recalling how she had awakened this morning and discovered that she had fallen asleep last night while she was supposed to be waiting for him to come to bed.

"Good morning," she greeted. "Sully . . . last night . . . I didn't mean to fall asleep. I lay down on the bed to wait for you and—"

Shaking his head, he put a finger over her lips and squatted beside her chair. "Ssh. You've been tired. We'll have another chance. Plenty."

"You're so tolerant." Truly, he was.

"I love you," he said simply.

She kissed him, then embraced him. He urged her to stand, then he sat in the chair and pulled her down onto his lap.

She slipped her arms around his neck. "I've reached a few decisions that may help our situation. Would you like to hear them?"

He nodded.

"I want to treat every patient who lines up outside my door, but I realize that I can't. Or that I can't and still spend a decent amount of time with my family. I plan to establish specific clinic hours and post those hours near the front door. I'll close an hour for dinner every afternoon. On Wednesdays, I'll close at one o'clock and come home early. Wednesdays used to be our wash day, remember?"

"I remember."

"What do you think so far?"

He kissed her temple. "I like your decisions."

"I can't treat every patient I want to treat," she said again, gloomily.

"I like it that you *want* to treat 'em all."

"But there are only so many hours in one day."

"Yep."

"The children miss me—and I miss them. I'm surprised they haven't forgotten that I'm their mother."

Sully shook his head. "They ain't gonna forget that you're their ma."

"Sometimes I worry that they might."

"Well, don't. That ain't gonna happen."

"If there's an emergency, an accident or a birth, I'll have to see to the patient, as usual," Michaela cautioned.

"I know."

She laid her head on his shoulder, snuggling with him in the chair. She loved him, the way he understood her, the way he often simply listened to her while she worked through a problem. She slid her hand down to rest on his chest. She pressed her lips to his warm neck.

"Katie's still sleeping," she said, stirring against him.

"Yep." He stared out the window.

"Well, that means we might have a little time. . . ."

"Yep," he said again, but this time the corner of his mouth twitched.

She knew that twitch. It meant he was teasing her.

Raising up, she poked him in the side. "Sully!"

He laughed, shifting his gaze to meet hers. "So how're you wantin' to spend that time, Mrs. Sully?"

She blushed. He knew; he just couldn't resist teasing her and watching her squirm. She ran her fingers through his chest hairs, dipped her head, and looked up at him. "Well, I . . . Perhaps we could . . ." Her fingers danced up to his neck and played there.

He growled at her and grabbed her hand. " 'Perhaps?' You keep that up, an' there ain't gonna be no 'perhaps.' "

Giggling, she nipped at his jaw, working her way to his mouth. She had turned the tables on him. Now he was the one squirming.

He'd had enough, it seemed. With a quick move he rose from the chair with her in his arms, his eyes glazed with desire. And like a pirate making off with his bounty, he headed toward their bedroom.

He had taken maybe four steps when they heard Katie cry.

Michaela closed her eyes, not believing this. They had worked themselves up, and now Katie was awake and needing attention.

Groaning in frustration, Sully put Michaela down.

"I'm sorry," she whispered, slipping her hand into his. They desperately needed some private time together.

He shook his head. "It ain't your fault. It's just how things are."

She gave him a weak smile, then started down the hallway, intent on the nursery.

Sully caught her by surprise, tugging on her elbow from behind, turning her around. His hands rose to her neck, his fingers slipped into her hair as he slowly backed her against the wall.

He kissed the side of her mouth, then kissed her full on the lips. Michaela gasped as his lips nipped their way to her ear. She had stirred his hunger, aroused it, and now he seemed bent on satisfying it.

"Sully we can't . . . not here!"

"How about startin' those hours today?" he said, his voice raspy against her ear.

"I will, I promise," she whispered, breathless.

"I'll make you a sign for the new clinic hours."

She nodded.

He dropped his hands and backed off, his chest rising and falling more quickly than before. His eyes were narrowed and clouded.

Michaela tipped her head back and fought for air. She *wouldn't* fall asleep before he reached their bed tonight. Doubtless she'd think about his ardent kisses and his blazing eyes all day. She would be treating a patient and blush because of certain intruding thoughts.

They stared at one another for a moment. Then Sully smiled and Michaela smiled back. She glanced at the floor, his gaze was so intense, then back up at him. Down the hall, Katie's cries became louder.

Sully laughed, shook his head, and leaned against the opposite wall.

Michaela saw her chance, and fled—although she would have loved to stay and do what they both wanted to do.

A few hours later, Michaela halted her horse and wagon near Grace's Café. Every café table but one was full, and the air buzzed with the conversations of customers. Several weeks ago Grace had hired two Swedish girls to help her take orders and serve food. The girls scurried around now, setting full plates in front of customers and taking away dirty dishes. Before the Swedish girls, Grace had hired a girl to wash dishes and another to help her cook. The dishwasher and the cook were set up with a stove and basins behind several long tables on which they placed clean dishes and full plates of food.

Grace buzzed around the customer's tables with a coffeepot in hand, refilling cups and taking orders. She completed one round of the tables, deposited orders with the cook, then started another round of the tables. She usually spotted Michaela and Katie when they arrived. But not today. She was so busy she didn't have time even to glance up.

Like every other business in town, Grace's Café was flourishing. It had become busier and busier over the last several months. This wasn't the first time Michaela had sat on the wagon seat with Katie on her lap and wondered how in the world Grace found time to care for a baby while tending to her many customers.

Grace was Katie's godmother, and she felt obligated to care for Katie during Michaela's clinic hours. But more and more Michaela felt she should hire someone to look after Katie, to prevent Grace from feeling overwhelmed. Twice before, when Michaela had tried to broach the subject to Grace, Grace had cut her off, insisting on caring for her godchild.

Grace had had Robert E. build Katie a little "playpen," as he called it, something that looked like a crib but was three times as big. The playpen was on wheels and could be rolled around. In it, Katie could play safely during the café's busy breakfast time. After the rush passed, when customers went about their business of the day, Grace always took Katie out of the pen and played with her. But then the noon hour arrived and the café tables filled up again.

Grace said she juggled Katie's care and her customers fine. But she seemed understandably harried of late. And Michaela knew that, like herself, Grace often overwhelmed herself with responsibilities—and didn't realize it until she was nearly in tears.

Continuing to expect Grace to care for Katie was not fair to Grace, Michaela knew, and yet she had continued to bring Katie to Grace during clinic hours because Grace in-

43

sisted that she should. Grace was very attached to Katie, and Michaela cherished their relationship. But seeing Grace so harried and overloaded with responsibilities tore at her.

Michaela glanced down at Katie, who had become accustomed to the wagon rides into town and usually didn't fuss about them. Katie always sat on Brian's lap during the ride to the schoolhouse, and on Michaela's lap during the ride from the schoolhouse to the café or clinic.

Katie was in a playful mood this morning. She pressed against Michaela, tilting her head back and grinning up at her mother.

Michaela laughed. "Would you like to spend the day with Mama, Katie dear?"

Katie reached up and back and tugged playfully at Michaela's dress. She giggled and said, "Mama!"

Affection swelled in Michaela. Katie was often tiring to care for, requiring a tremendous amount of energy. But the joy she brought Michaela was unequaled. If anyone had tried to tell Michaela, before Katie's birth, about the pride and happiness a baby could cause in a parent, Michaela might not have believed the person. She had attended countless births, had seen the love and awe on the faces of new parents. But before she'd had the experience herself, she had had no grasp on the depth of that love.

Michaela hugged Katie. Katie giggled more.

Michaela flicked the reins, guiding the horse in the direction of the clinic. Caring for Katie herself between seeing patients was never easy. But Michaela had managed both before, and would manage both today.

During the dinner break she intended to take at noon, she would write out two advertisements—one for an assistant, and one for someone to care for Katie during clinic hours.

After closing the clinic at the end of the day, she would talk to Grace about her decision. And this time she would stand firm when Grace insisted that she continue to care for Katie during Michaela's clinic hours.

4

With the influx of people into Colorado Springs, the number of telegraphed messages and pieces of mail going in and out of town had doubled. At first Horace spent his days and part of his nights trying to keep up with them. Then, a good month or more ago, he'd decided to hire himself some help—a German boy who learned the telegraph signals at a pretty good clip and could count out American money and change just fine.

Horace fussed over the boy for a few weeks, making sure he got the telegraphed messages right. Finally he felt pretty confident and began leaving the boy alone with the telegraph sometimes, while he delivered mail and messages. A lot of people stopped in the office daily to see if they had mail or telegrams. But a good number of people didn't, and Horace felt it his duty to get the things to the rightful recipients.

The delivery of mail and messages had become a job that took a good amount of time. Horace usually went around town on foot or, if he had a number of packages, he delivered with a horse and buggy. But Lord knew, there were enough horses and buggies on the streets these days!

One morning during the week he hired Hans, Horace had been reading a copy of the *Denver Post* when an advertisement caught his eye. He glanced up from the paper, looking all around the main room of his house, which had been untidy since Myra left. He looked back at the paper, then at the clutter again. Finally his jaw dropped open, and he came up with what he thought was a right smart idea.

He'd order himself a velocipede, a three-wheeled contraption he could pedal around town. A velocipede was smaller than a buggy, so he'd have an easier time getting through the traffic—which meant he could deliver the mail and messages faster. He'd pedal around delivering everything, feeling like nobody could come up with a better idea. He wouldn't have to fuss with harnessing his horse to the buggy, or with trying to lead the horse and buggy safely between the hordes of other horses and conveyances that occupied the streets.

He drew his money jar out from under his bedstead. (After paying off the loan from Preston for a buggy, he'd decided he wanted nothing more to do with Preston's bank, and he'd gone back to storing his money in this jar.) He uncorked the jar and plucked out thirteen dollars and seventy-five cents. He counted the money twice, just to make sure he got it right, then he went off to collect a pair of shears from atop his chest of drawers.

He clipped out the advertisement and circled the velocipede he wanted. He could carry mail and telegrams and small packages in a bag strung over his shoulder and across his chest. Better still, he'd rig a basket to the back of the velocipede and drop the bundled mail and telegrams in it.

At a small desk in the main room he wrote a note, asking that the manufacturer—Morgan and Wright, in a place called Northfield, Illinois—please send the contraption straightaway. Then he packaged the clipped advertisement, the note, and the money all together in an envelope.

Horace sealed the envelope with wax and picked up a pen, meaning to address the envelope. But he'd sealed the address inside, and he wrinkled his face as he tore open the envelope, emptied it, and pretty much started over. This time he addressed the envelope first, *then* dropped the advertisement, his note, and the money inside, *then* sealed everything up nice and neat and safe and sound. Later that day, when he watched the train pull away from the station, knowing it was going off to deliver his order, he smiled real big to himself again.

He'd stood straighter since that day, something he'd not done a lot of since Myra filed for divorce. He'd felt unwanted and unloved, incapable of accomplishing much. The idea of using the velocipede to deliver mail and telegrams made him feel proud of himself for the first time since Myra had taken Samantha and left him.

And then he'd wondered . . . if just *ordering* the velocipede made him feel somewhat better, what else might he do to make himself feel better?

Not long afterward, as he was combing his hair one morning, he paused, as he'd done a lot this past year, to rid the comb of hair. He'd started noticing that his hair appeared thinner every day. Why, in some places he could see his scalp shining beneath what hair was left! He combed a little more, as gently as possible—one couldn't simply not ever comb his hair—then paused with the comb in midstroke. He stood in front of the washstand, staring at himself in the mirror that hung over it. He studied the bedstead and chest of drawers that reflected from behind him—but he wasn't really studying them at all. He was having thoughts, another smart idea.

He recalled glancing at an advertisement in this week's Denver paper about a tonic that restored hair.

He dropped the comb onto the edge of the washstand and scampered into his sitting room to find that newspaper. He read a dozen or more papers a week. He sent all over the country for them—to New York, California, Pennsylvania, and other places—just because he liked to stay informed and because reading newspapers was the best way to do that.

Hunching beside an overstuffed chair, he rummaged through his pile of newspapers and found the latest *Denver Post.* Then he sat in the chair and scanned the paper, trying to remember where he'd seen the advertisement.

He found it halfway down on the right side of page 3: *Princess Hair Restorer, a wonderful new hair tonic, guaranteed to restore natural color, preserve and strengthen hair, promote new growth.* According to the advertisement, the tonic also cured dandruff and scurf, and allayed all scalp irritations.

He didn't have a problem with those things. But since he'd been losing hair every day for a while now, he sure could use something that "promoted new growth." He'd gone a little gray around the temples, too, and the part about restoring natural color sounded good.

He'd seen enough "snake-oil" doctors come through town selling their wares that he was somewhat skeptical. So he thought about asking Jake about the tonic, if he knew whether or not it would work. Jake was a barber, after all.

But Horace changed his mind pretty quick about doing that—he'd been ridiculed by Jake a few times in the past, and he didn't care to experience that again.

He could ask Dr. Mike about the tonic. He could even ask Robert E. if *he'd* tried tonics before he lost all of his hair.

To ask Robert E. such a thing, though . . . well, questions about baldness might be too personal to Robert E. In fact, the possibility of eventually going bald seemed so personal to Horace himself that he doubted whether he could bring himself to ask even Dr. Mike about the tonic. He reckoned he'd just order it and find out for himself whether or not it worked.

A bottle of Princess Hair Restorer was only sixty-five cents. Horace figured that if the hair tonic worked, then he'd feel better about himself, probably at least as good as he still felt about ordering that velocipede. Heck, just making up his mind to order the tonic made him feel better.

So Horace pulled out the money jar again. He cut out another advertisement and wrote another note. When he had everything together nice and neat, he sealed the envelope, remembering to address this one first.

He splashed cologne water on his face. Then, his steps spry, he left his house and headed for the depot, where he made sure this newest order was on a train with the next batch of mail.

As Michaela turned the sign around on the clinic's front door, from Closed to Open, the early train whistled and slowly screeched to a stop beside the depot. And there was Horace, waiting to see what packages got carried off the train. For a good week now, Horace had waited at the depot every morning, although he normally sent Hans down to collect packages.

Ten minutes later, the porter handed several small packages to Horace, who carried them to his buggy. When he returned to the train, wondering if there were more packages, the porter and another man were struggling with a large crate.

"Where's that from?" Horace asked, feeling his legs go jittery with excitement.

"Let's see now. . . ." The porter bent over and poked his head around the far side of the crate, looking for an address. "Morgan . . . Morgan 'n' Wright's what it says here." The porter's voice, coming from the other side of the crate, was somewhat muffled.

But Horace heard him all the same, and he wanted to help the men lift the crate off the car, down the steps, and across the platform, where they could deposit it in his waiting buggy. *If* it'd fit in his buggy. Come to think of it, it didn't look like that crate *would* fit in his buggy.

"Let's lift it up 'n' carry it down," the porter told the other man. And that's what they did, taking the steps very carefully.

Horace shifted from leg to leg, foot to foot, thinking he'd have to go get a regular wagon from Robert E. And in the meantime, until he got back here with the wagon, he'd have to leave the crate sitting on the platform.

He had the awful thought that while he was getting a wagon, somebody might snitch the crate and make off with the velocipede he'd waited on for weeks. And after it had come all the way from wherever that was in Illinois. Heck, he was so excited that it had arrived, he couldn't even remember the name of the manufacturer. Morgan and . . . ? Nope, that wasn't right. Morton . . . ?

"Where're we goin' with it?" the porter asked.

"Uh . . . I'll have to go get a wagon. I brought my buggy, but it ain't gonna fit in it," Horace explained.

"Nope, it ain't gonna fit in no buggy, that's for dang sure," the other man agreed.

"I'll have to leave it sittin' here while I get the wagon."

The men wasted no time setting the crate down. The porter struggled to straighten his back, then scratched his whiskered chin and asked his companion and Horace, "Whaddaya s'pose is in that thang?"

The porter's helper twisted his mouth and shook his head.

Horace said, "A velocipede," tilting his head in a jaunty way.

"A vel-o-what?" the porter asked as he paused in rubbing his chin. His companion's thick eyebrows cocked at a funny angle. They looked like two furry caterpillars all twisted around.

"Velocipede," Horace repeated. "With a wheel in front and two in back."

"Never heard tell of such a thing."

"There's so many wagons on the streets these days, it ain't safe no more. So I'm gonna use the velocipede to deliver mail an' telegrams. It's smaller, so I can get in between all the wagons, go in an' out between 'em. I don't have to saddle it an' hitch it, either."

"Or feed it," said the porter, his interest perking.

"That ain't a bad idea," his companion commented, shifting his eyebrows again.

"Or comb it," Horace remarked. "Or clean up after it."

"Well, if that ain't the dangedest thing!" The porter laughed.

"You pedal it," Horace said proudly, drawing his shoulders back more. "There was a drawin' with the advertisement."

"This oughtta be somethin' to see," the porter's helper said, laughing.

"Reckon I oughtta go fetch that wagon," Horace remarked. He pushed on the crate, surprised at how heavy it was. "Let's push it against the wall of the station, over there." He gave a flick of his head to the left, to indicate where he meant.

So they pushed the crate against the wall, and the porter and his companion returned to the train while Horace went off to trade Robert E. a buggy for a wagon for part of the morning.

Hank was proud of his new hotel with its crimson carpet and fancy chandelier hanging from the lobby ceiling—the thing was bronze and decorated with dangling pieces of cut glass. At first he'd thought the chandelier looked, well, too *female* to be hanging in the lobby. But then he'd reminded himself that this wasn't gonna be a saloon and that the place had to appeal to women, too. After realizing that, he'd even had banquet lamps with flowers painted on the globes put on the tables in each room. Men spent money on their women. Once he thought about it, if the place *didn't* appeal to women, he'd be in trouble.

As busy as he was, Hank always took a breather now and then. This morning he left the desk in the hands of Henry Miller, who usually carried in trunks and showed customers to their rooms. He'd hired Henry not long after the Gold Nugget opened. Henry was quiet but he did his job, and after having been in the saloon business, Hank reckoned that was the best kind of employee—the quiet kind. The cook he'd hired sometimes talked too damn much, and too loudly, her shrill voice carrying from the kitchen into the eating area. Henry called it "the dining area," and Hank was trying to learn to do the same himself, now that his place was attracting a few gussied-up people who looked like they might have more than a handful of change in their pockets.

He had a man fixing the front window today. That character Matthew had hauled off to jail yesterday had coughed up some money, not wanting to spend even a night in jail. Having the money in hand, Hank had decided to forgive him, long as he didn't see his face around the Gold Nugget again. If he did, well, he'd have to *change* his face for him. So Hank had decided he'd get himself a new window and fix the front railing, and that he wasn't so mad anymore. He'd told Matthew to let the man go. Only thing he didn't like about the whole situation was figuring the man and his buddies would head back to Preston's hotel to see if any rooms had come open there. But then Hank chuckled over the thought. Maybe they'd bust a few windows out of that place, out of a room or two, and Preston would lose a little business. An amusing thought.

Hank stepped onto the walkway and walked down a bit, away from the main congestion of town, away from the barbershop—definitely away from the barbershop—and the mercantile. He reached into a vest pocket and pulled out a cigar, running it under his nose and savoring the rich smell of the tobacco before he snipped off the end with his teeth.

He leaned his tall frame against a wooden post, struck a sulfur match on the post, and lit the cigar, closing his eyes as he inhaled, relishing. He was smoking better quality these days, since business had picked up in town, which also meant at the Gold Nugget. He reckoned he and Jake had gone in together on the hotel at just the right time.

Thinking of Jake made him scowl.

Hank had himself an office at the back of the hotel, on the first floor. He'd been sitting at his desk going over the books at about nine o'clock last night. The door slammed open and there was Jake, grumbling about him fighting with that horse racer in front of the hotel earlier in the day. "You'll scare off customers, fightin' with people like that out front!"

If that wasn't the damnedest thing! Here Jake hadn't shown his face at the Gold Nugget in nigh on to two weeks or more. He was too busy at his barbershop to lend a hand every now and then (after Hank had *closed* his other business to run the hotel). But he'd damn sure show up to complain about the way Hank had done something.

Hank had drawn himself up nice and tall behind his desk. "If you ain't gonna help me run the place inside, don't tell me how to run it outside."

"I'm half owner," Jake snapped.

"Coulda fooled me."

Jake glared at him. "No more fightin' out front."

"Tell you what," Hank said. "I'll run this place the way I see fit. You got a problem with that, sell your half to me."

They had a staring match after that. Jake's sour look got worse, and Hank knew what he was thinking. Jake didn't much like the idea of selling his half of the hotel to anyone. Money was coming into the Gold Nugget in a steady stream, filling their pockets, and Jake knew he'd be a fool to sell out.

He'd turned around and huffed toward the office door, nothing more to say.

"I'm doin' so bad runnin' the place, why's it makin' so much money?" Hank had shot at Jake's back.

Jake kept walking.

Now, standing here enjoying his cigar, Hank laughed, remembering. Yep, he'd shut Jake up. He figured Jake wouldn't be back to complain.

Overall, except for too many people on the streets and occasional riffraff who caused trouble, and except for Jake's lack of help and sour disposition last night, life was pretty damn good. Hank was getting older, having to work out hitches in his knees now and then, mostly when he bent down and straightened—although he'd never tell anybody that. But all in all, he was a mighty contented man.

He moved farther down the walkway. He glanced across the street and froze.

Through the cloud of smoke that swirled around his head, he had no trouble spotting the raven-haired beauty who stood on a ladder in a window just across the way. Not a week ago Wayman's Hat Shop had occupied the small building. But not anymore—things changed pretty fast around this town lately. Now the building looked deserted. Well, except for the beauty on the ladder.

A bucket sat on one of the ladder steps, and the ladder itself was splattered with white paint. The woman wore a gray dress that was splattered, too, the sleeves pushed up just beyond her elbows. While the color of the dress didn't appeal to Hank, the way the material hugged the woman's curves damn sure did.

She bent at the waist, dipping her brush into the bucket and delicately drawing it against the rim to wipe off the excess paint. Just about that time, she glanced up, spotted Hank, and gave him a smile that nearly toppled him. Nothing sexually inviting about it—just a smile to greet someone. But how sweet it was. It lit her eyes (he couldn't tell what color they were) and her whole face.

Hank had taken four draws from the cigar. He paid a good price for his cigars, but suddenly this one didn't interest him. He didn't give a damn what he'd paid for it, or that he wasted more than half of it when he dropped it and crushed it under his boot. The lady looked like she could use some help, especially if she planned to paint the whole inside of that building. It wasn't all that big, but Hank reckoned he could take care of a wall or two for her. He could even reach all the high places that she had to stand on her ladder to reach.

Hank straightened his vest as he stepped off the walkway. The sun was already shining on him today, that was for sure. He was getting a new window and was headed toward a beautiful lady—and it wasn't even nine o'clock on this fine morning.

He strode into the empty shop, grinned, and introduced himself to the lady on the ladder.

She took a few steps down. "Cora Reeves," she said, offering her hand.

Ah, a lady indeed. Her voice was like velvet, brushing over Hank in a smooth stroke. He lifted her hand to his mouth and gave it a little kiss. Her skin was soft, and he bet that if he turned her hand over, he wouldn't find a single callus. Which meant she wasn't used to such hard work. Which meant the lady definitely needed a little help here.

"I'm the hotel proprietor," he said, always liking the sound of that.

She arched a fine brow. "The Gold Nugget?"

He nodded.

"It appears to be a very nice establishment."

He always liked the sound of that word—*establishment*. Something dignified and important-sounding about it. "It's acceptable," he said, not wanting to seem like he thought he or his "establishment" was too important.

She liked that—her smile widened.

"Want some help?"

She wiped paint from her chin. He'd be glad to do that for her. Fact was, he might've already done it for her if she hadn't been such a lady and he hadn't worried about offending her.

"I thought about hiring several men. But then I thought I might enjoy doing the work myself. Why, do you know someone who is looking for an afternoon of work?" she asked, as if having second thoughts about doing it herself. "I'll pay well."

Hank grinned. "I know someone who'd do it for no pay, providin' you'd have supper with him this evenin'."

Her brow wrinkled as she puzzled over that, not getting what he meant. When she did understand, she blushed. She glanced down, then back up, smiling.

She stepped off of the ladder (he bet she wasn't much over five feet tall), and rummaged through a nearby pile of things—paper she'd apparently stripped off the walls, a ragged carpet she'd rolled up, a few buckets of paint. She came up with another paintbrush and a bucket of paint, and she handed them to him along with another shy look.

"We have a deal, Mr. Claggerty," she said, smiling again.

And a mighty fine deal it was, too. He'd paint fifty, a hundred rooms with her if that's what it took to keep her smiling.

Before the afternoon was over, he knew where she was from and why she was painting the shop. She planned to open a bookstore here, she told him. Hank wasn't sure Colorado Springs had any need for a bookstore, but he kept that thought to himself. Instead he told her that another pretty lady sure was welcome in this town, was *always* welcome.

Cora blushed over that remark. Then she gave him another dazzling smile.

Hank had a hard time concentrating on painting.

5

The one time Horace had been forced to fix a wagon wheel, he hadn't had an easy time of it. He'd pried the wheel off and then chased it down. And once he fixed the wheel and put it back on the axle, the wagon was lopsided. Myra had looked at him and shaken her head, and Horace had told her how he'd never been good at such things—he was a telegraph operator, not a blacksmith. Luckily for them, another wagon had come along and they'd gotten a ride into town.

He'd received his velocipede—but the wooden wheels had to be fitted onto the frame. It didn't sound so hard. But Horace didn't trust himself to put the velocipede together. He'd paid for it and had waited for it, and he didn't want to mess it up.

After borrowing a wagon from Robert E., after struggling to lift the crate to the wagon bed all by himself, after getting the crate home, wrestling it out of the wagon and plopping it down on his small front porch . . . he'd pried the crate open and discovered that the velocipede had to be put together. He'd sat back and scowled at the pieces, knowing he'd be no good at putting them together, and wondering what he should do.

He had to take the wagon back to Robert E. anyway. Then he figured—no, he *knew*—Robert E. would know how to put the velocipede together so that *it* didn't sit lopsided, the way that wagon had. Horace wasn't about to ride around town on a lopsided velocipede.

So he put the wheels back into the crate and pushed the crate toward the wagon. He worked (really worked) at heaving it onto the wagon bed, then he led the horse and wagon back to the blacksmith shop across town.

"You get that crate?" Robert E. said. He'd been making horseshoes—a row of them sat on a nearby table. A fire blazed in an open stove, and Robert E.'s forehead glistened with sweat as he used a steel rod to place a new horseshoe onto the table beside the others.

"I got it," Horace said, a little sourly. He'd expected to pull the velocipede out of the crate, ready to go.

Robert E. spotted the crate in the back of the wagon, and his brow wrinkled. "Why didn't you deliver it? What's the sense bringin' the wagon back b'fore you deliver it? It still ain't gonna fit'n your buggy. A few hours didn't make the thing shrink any."

"I know that," Horace snapped, and Robert E.'s brows went up. "It's *my* crate—I'm the one I gotta deliver it to. So I did. Then I opened it an' found out it's got to be put together. I figure you'd be a whole lot better puttin' somethin' together than me."

"Uh-huh . . . I see. . . ."

61

Robert E. didn't look excited about putting anything together. In fact, he turned away and headed back to his fire.

"I got some thirty more shoes t'make for the Tennesseys—they bought themselves a whole herd o' new horses," he said. "Then I gotta mend the Gray's buggy. I got harnesses to work on, an' three wagons the people all need by this afternoon. I got 'nough work to keep me busy for a week—even after another blacksmith done set himself up two streets over." The more he talked, the more his voice became a grumble. *I don't want any more work,* was what he was saying.

"Well. . . ." Horace made his way down from the wagon seat. "When do you reckon you could get to it?"

Robert E. eyed him. "What is it?"

"A velocipede."

Robert E.'s face scrunched up. "What's that?"

"It has three wheels, an' a person sits on a seat in the middle of it an' pedals it. He doesn't need a horse to get where he needs to go—he just pedals an' the wheels turn, an' he goes."

Just talking about the velocipede, Horace was getting all excited again. But he knew he'd better simmer down. Robert E. might not have time to put the thing together for days.

"Is that right?"

Horace nodded.

Robert E. looked baffled, and curious. He went back to his fire for a minute, poking around in it, then tossed his hooked rod down and ambled toward Horace. "Show me," he said, and Horace was glad to do exactly that.

Together they pulled the crate forward, then hoisted it down from the wagon seat. They placed it on the ground behind the wagon, and Horace began pulling at the top of the crate, trying to work the boards free. He'd nailed them back down before he'd reloaded the crate onto the wagon. He'd done a pretty durn good job, good enough that they wouldn't give with just a few tugs.

Robert E. scuttled off and returned a minute later with his hooked rod.

He wrestled the hook under one of the boards, gave a yank, and the board popped up, almost catching Horace in the jaw. Horace jumped back.

"Might wanna gimme some room," Robert E. said

Horace took two more steps back, thinking that was a good idea.

Soon Robert E. had loosened all the boards from the top of the crate.

Horace neared the crate again and began pulling out the pieces of the velocipede—first the large back wheels, then the smaller front wheel, then the frame, then the pedals, and finally what looked like a seat. Robert E. lifted his brows high at the sight of the pedals and shook his head.

A page of typed instructions with sketches of the veloc- ipede lay on the bottom of the crate. Horace reached down, trying to get his hands on the paper.

He bent over so far that he lost his footing and would have tumbled headfirst into the crate if Robert E. hadn't caught him by a suspender and yanked him back.

Robert E. scowled and said, "Lemme get it."

Horace stepped back, letting Robert E. reach into the crate to collect the instructions.

Once Robert E. pulled the instructions out of the crate, he began studying them. As he studied, he passed a hand over the top of his head, then rubbed his jaw. Finally he walked off, still studying, toward a beaten-up wooden bench that sat not too far away. He sat down on the bench, reading the directions and puzzling over the drawings, working his jaw one way, then another.

Finally Horace made his way over to the bench, feeling anxious. He didn't like the way Robert E. was studying that paper, like maybe he didn't know whether or not all the pieces *could* be put together, at least not in a way that resembled the velocipedes in the sketches.

"Think you can fit it all together?" Horace asked, sitting on the bench, but not really sitting. He shifted around a lot.

"Yep, I reckon," Robert E. mumbled.

Horace tried to contain himself, tamping down unasked questions while Robert E. studied the instructions. Horace wanted the thing put together right, so he figured he'd better not interrupt Robert E. too much.

Minutes passed.

"Wh-when do you reckon?" Horace couldn't stop the question.

"I reckon I'm gonna try right now. I ain't *never* seen anything like this," Robert E. said, again passing a hand over his shiny bald head.

Horace flinched in surprise. "Right now—really?"

Robert E. looked up at him and nodded slowly. "Right now. You oughtta go on back home or back to mindin' yer machine for a spell. Y'know, so you don't get in the way an' I don't put wheels where there ain't s'posed to be wheels. Or pedals where there ain't s'posed to be pedals."

"Or a seat where there ain't supposed to be a seat?" Horace asked, wide-eyed.

Another slow and serious nod. "It's called a saddle, 'cordin' to the directions."

"A saddle. . . ."

"Yep."

Horace wanted the velocipede put together right. He

wanted it to look like the one in the newspaper advertisement and the ones in the sketches on the page of instructions. He wanted it to look perfect, wanted it to pedal right.

So without another word, Horace went into Robert E.'s livery and found his horse and buggy waiting exactly where he'd left them.

He was horrified at himself. He'd been so excited about the arrival of the velocipede that he'd forgotten the other packages in the boot of the buggy, the ones that came off the train. Shame on him. Shame and double shame. He'd have to deliver the packages straightaway.

Horace headed off in his buggy, fighting the urge to look back.

Sully had been hired to help build a home just south of town for the Blake family. He and Robert Blake had started two weeks ago, digging up an area in which to build the wooden foundation for the house. They'd chopped down trees and stripped bark from the logs. They'd cut beams and planks for the floors, and a few days ago, they'd built the foundation. Finally, this morning they began building the frame. While they worked, Mr. Blake's wife scrubbed laundry not far away, beside a large tent in which the family lived. Their three girls left for school before Sully arrived.

The Blakes had come to Colorado Territory from Virginia, looking for land and a new start, like almost everybody who ended up here. Sully didn't care for some of the newcomers, mostly the ones who came thinking there might still be gold around. The fools panned the streams, and now and then somebody found a small nugget. But mostly the streams around here were all panned out.

Then there were the rich people who came to Colorado Springs to take advantage of the hot springs and the clean mountain air. Most of them had their noses up in the air. But at least they didn't take anything from the land. Sitting in the springs didn't use it up.

People who came looking for a fresh start, like the Blakes . . . Sully couldn't find fault with them. He'd seen Boston, how overcrowded it was, and he knew other eastern cities were just as crowded.

Still, the western migration that had started decades ago and that continued now spelled nothing but trouble for the Indians. Sometimes Sully wondered what would happen when Colorado Territory was completely settled by Caucasian people. More would come, surely, and they'd need pieces of land, too. If they couldn't find land to settle on here, would they look south, to "Indian Territory," land onto which most of the southern Cheyenne had been forced? They would—and then where would the Cheyenne be forced?

It made him angry, thinking about the Indians' fate, wondering what would become of the Cheyenne.

He'd thought about not helping new settlers, about not hiring himself out to build new homes and buildings for businesses.

But he couldn't stop the growth. He was just one man, and the homes and businesses would get built whether or not he helped build them. If he didn't help, other men would. And they'd get paid the money he needed to pay off the bank loan Preston had given Michaela after she had to burn everything in her clinic, even her pa's medical bag. Patients had come down with a mysterious, similar infection after being treated in the clinic. Many of the patients had died, and Michaela had felt she had no choice but to burn everything from inside the clinic—furniture, instruments, curtains . . . *everything*. Burning everything had stopped the infection, but Michaela had had to start over and again obtain the supplies and medical instruments she needed to run the clinic. She'd needed money that she and Sully didn't have. Preston had been more than willing to give her a loan—with interest included, of course.

Sully and Robert nailed more beams together. Once they'd built part of the frame, they tied ropes to several beams and used horses to pull the beams upright. They secured the beams, then built another part of the frame.

The morning went by, and soon Amanda Blake called them over for dinner. Robert was hungry, and he scampered right off. Sully was hungry, too, but he took his time. He straightened and stretched and watched a flock of birds flutter up from a nearby tree. He'd make that sign for Michaela as soon as he reached home.

Thinking of the sign made him think of this morning, of how close he and Michaela had come to making love for the first time in a few weeks.

He recalled her embarrassment at falling asleep last night, the way her face had flushed when she apologized this morning, the way it reddened even more when he suggested they go back to their bedroom and spend some time there before Katie woke. He loved a lot of things about Michaela. But he reckoned he loved the way she blushed most of all. This morning the blush had crept all the way down her neck.

He thought of the way she'd looked in that chair when he approached her from behind, her hair loose and splayed out, the morning sunlight casting a haze on her ivory wrap. Her lips had felt soft when he kissed her, softer than he remembered from yesterday. Her eyes had glowed with morning freshness, and her skin had smelled better than a meadow of flowers. He'd wanted to scoop her up right then and carry her back to their bedroom. But she'd had patient records sitting in front of her, and a pen in her hand, and scooping her up and carrying her away would have been rude.

"You coming?" Robert called from the tent.

Sully realized he was still staring at the tree—and that the flock of birds was long gone.

He'd gone lovesick over his wife, remembering how she looked and felt and even smelled this morning. He still smelled her—and she was a good mile away. He missed making love to her. He missed just *talking* to her.

"I'm comin'," Sully said, and he walked toward the tent. He was hungry, all right. But not necessarily for food. He was hungry for his wife.

Robert E. had the velocipede together, and it was an amazing contraption.

Putting it together hadn't taken long. Of course, he'd ignored everything else he should have been doing. He'd become curious when Horace started pulling the pieces out of the crate, a lot more curious than he'd been when Horace had just talked about the velocipede. He reckoned the Tennesseys would have no choice but to wait on their horseshoes. And those wagons and buggies and harnesses that needed to be mended . . . well, he'd get to them tomorrow and the next day, and probably even the day after that.

Robert E. sat and stared at the velocipede for a time. Then he went back to making shoes, heating the iron and pounding it into the right shape.

He made one shoe, and plopped it on the table with the others. Then he couldn't help himself—he went over and pushed on the velocipede's left pedal. Sure enough, all three wheels turned and the contraption eased forward.

"I'll be," Robert E. said, scratching his head. "Thing really goes."

Horace had been so excited about the velocipede that Robert E. figured he would've come back for it by now. He hadn't snapped at Horace—or at least he didn't think he had. He'd just suggested to Horace that putting the thing together might be easier for him if Horace went away, off to his telegraph office, maybe. And Horace had jumped up to do just that.

Robert E. pushed on the pedal again, and the velocipede moved forward more. The pedals were attached to the front wheel, and he'd figured out that the rider's feet were supposed to rest on the pedals. A body was supposed to work the front wheel by turning the pedals with his feet. Working the front wheel, pedaling it around, made the back wheels work.

Robert E. turned the pedal with his hand for a while, forgetting the horseshoes, distracted by the contraption. He hand-pedaled the velocipede all over in front of his shop, thinking as he did.

This morning, Horace had been real eager for him to get the thing together. Now it was after noon and Horace still hadn't come back to see if he'd gotten it together.

Maybe things had gotten busy at the telegraph office and Horace hadn't been able to get away. Maybe that boy he'd hired hadn't shown up and he'd had to stay and mind the machine. Surely that's what had happened. *Something* had tied up Horace, otherwise curiosity and anxiousness would have drawn him back by now.

Robert E. reckoned he'd pedal the thing over to the telegraph office and deliver it to Horace. Maybe repay Horace a bit for all the mail Horace had delivered to him and Grace in the time they'd been in Colorado Springs.

Robert E. took hold of the "handlebars" that he'd slipped down over a larger bar that ran down, forked, and connected to the front wheel. He swung his left leg up and over the seat, like he was mounting a horse, and settled himself on the seat. Finally he pedaled the contraption out of his yard and into the street. And lo and behold—he couldn't believe it—the thing didn't have a hitch anywhere, even with his weight on it. It went, good as gold, just like a brand-new wagon, only with three wheels instead of four.

He pedaled between and by wagons and horses and people, and the people who spotted him stopped what they were doing to stare at him. He chuckled to himself. He was sure a sight, he figured, pedaling around on the strange-looking gadget.

The faster he pedaled, the faster he went, buildings and houses and people and animals shooting by.

Laughing, he went uphill, toward the main part of town, where the clinic, the mercantile, and the barbershop sat on the busiest corners in Colorado Springs. Lucky for him, going uphill slowed him down. He'd been going at such a good clip, he couldn't have dodged the many wagons, buggies, horses, and people without slowing down.

He put his right foot down, slowing the velocipede even more, and worked his way through the congestion. Once he got clear of it, he breathed easier. He'd never liked over-crowded places, and this part of town was overcrowded a lot.

On the other side of the mercantile the street dipped, then started downhill as it passed houses and other scattered businesses. Farther out, it ambled by the café then approached the train station and the telegraph office. Robert E. laughed to himself, following the road, imagining the look of surprise on Grace's face when he breezed by the café. Her eyes would get bigger than he'd ever seen them.

The velocipede picked up speed as it went down the hill, and Robert E. didn't even have to pedal anymore. The wheels turned by themselves as the thing went faster and faster and faster. He picked his feet up off of the pedals, giving his legs a rest.

He whizzed down the hill, whooping as the wind whistled by his ears and over his bald head. Whenever he went around town, he never galloped through the streets on his horse. Fact was, he couldn't remember the last time he'd let his horse do more than a slow walk. But today . . . today he soared like a bird on the velocipede, laughing and whooping and feeling thirty years younger.

The café was coming up soon. He tore by a house, then another one. He heard people laughing, and he realized they were standing up behind the café tables, pointing his way. But Robert E. didn't care that they laughed at him. He was a boy again, having himself a whoppin' good time.

He spotted Grace by her stove, and sure enough, her eyes were round as saucers. Maybe not saucers—maybe plates!

Then the road curved and the velocipede didn't.

He ran into a sheet that hung from a clothesline. It came down over his head, blinding him. A woman shrieked, a hog squealed, a chicken squawked, a goose honked. . . . People shouted in the distance.

The velocipede crashed into something, and Robert E. shot through the air headfirst. He heard wood crack and splinter. Then the ground knocked the air out of him as he plopped down on his stomach.

He turned over onto his back and pulled the sheet off his head. Dazed, he stared up at the sky, thinking maybe he'd been having *too* good a time. There'd be the devil to pay with Grace, that was for sure. Right about now she was probably telling everybody she didn't know him.

"What're you doin'?" a woman shouted. "Gimme that sheet!"

Robert E. poked his head up and saw Mrs. Everly coming at him from the left, barreling toward him, as big as the side of a barn, her face as red as melting iron.

Something gobbled to his right. He shifted his head that way and spotted a mad tom turkey wobbling toward him, his legs going as fast as Robert E. reckoned they could, as fast as his legs had coming down that hill before he lifted them from the pedals.

The bird was irate, and so was the woman. Robert E. figured he'd better find the velocipede and get to pedaling again real quick.

He scrambled up and away, leaving the sheet behind. The woman was happy with that, but the tom kept coming, gobbling and making other turkey noises.

Robert E. glanced around for the velocipede. He spotted it lodged in the side of the woman's henhouse.

The seat was gone—lying upside down some fifty feet away—and he winced as he wondered what the front wheel looked like.

Robert E. pulled the velocipede out of the jagged hole it had created in the side of the henhouse, and he winced again. Half of the front wheel was gone, busted in two. The other half lay inside the henhouse, just beyond where the velocipede had stopped. A dozen chickens clucked around the piece of wheel, pecking at it, puzzled by it. Robert E. ducked his head and shoulders and made his way through the hole and into the henhouse, hoping the tom wouldn't follow him, hoping Horace wouldn't go mad when he saw the velocipede.

"You're gonna have to fix that!" the woman shouted at him.

The tom tore into the henhouse and headed for Robert E. The hens decided they didn't like *this* intruder and went after the tom, twelve against one. In a flurry of flapping wings and squawks, they ran him out of their house as fast as he'd come in. Ordinarily Robert E. might've had himself a good laugh over that. But the sight of the broken velocipede wheel was no laughing matter.

6

At the café, Grace was taking orders when some of her customers began chuckling, then laughing. She thought little of it until more joined in, and then more, until even the customers whose orders she was taking looked beyond her and snickered. Finally, curious, she glanced around.

She heard a whoop in the distance and then what sounded like Robert E.'s laughter. Only it was different, lighter than normal maybe. People were getting up from the tables and walking toward the road to have themselves a better look at whatever was drawing their attention.

Somebody said, "Ain't that Robert E.?" Somebody else asked, "What's he ridin'?" Finally Grace heard Dorothy say, "Why, it's a velocipede! I've seen advertisements in the papers!"

Grace followed the curious gazes, a nervous twitch starting at the corner of her left eye. Her gaze landed on Robert E., who was flying down the hill on a strange-looking three-wheeled thing.

"Merciful heavens!" she said, jumping back. She whacked her thigh on the edge of a table.

He was almost all teeth, his grin was so big. And the whoops he let out! Why, he didn't even seem civilized. He had his legs cocked up like something was wrong with them. Only there wasn't a thing wrong with Robert E. No, not a single thing—except that he'd gone stark raving out-of-his-mind crazy.

"What in the blazes . . . ?"

Grace tossed her pad and pencil on the nearest table and started after the crowd of people—her customers—who were more interested in Robert E.'s madness than in her food.

She caught another glimpse of him just as he shot off the road. He hadn't turned with the curve—if the contraption he was on *could* turn. Instead, he went bumping and bouncing over the grass. He was headed straight for—

"Mrs. Everly's place," Grace said, wincing.

Oh, Lord, if he didn't break his neck, he'd be lucky.

Actually, he might be lucky if he *did* break his neck. Then he wouldn't have to contend with the fury she meant to unleash on him: *(What'n heaven's name were you thinkin', gettin' on that thing? Comin' down that hill so fast?)*. That was, after she started speaking to him again.

He collected a sheet over his head from Mrs. Everly's clothesline and kept going. When he crashed into the henhouse and went flying, Grace stopped dead in her tracks.

Without catching a breath, she hitched up her skirts and ran for Mrs. Everly's place. Her heart in her throat, she watched Robert E. land on his stomach.

She didn't breathe again until she saw him lift his head, turn onto his back, and spot Mrs. Everly bearing down on him. Then he shot up off the ground and beat a path to the henhouse.

He didn't look injured, and Grace was thankful for that. But anger bubbled up into her throat again, and she muttered as she ran: "Gonna wish he was hurt. Be *sleepin'* in a henhouse. Crazy notions . . . flyin' down that hill like that!"

She'd outdistanced the crowd, reaching Mrs. Everly's henhouse just as Robert E., ducking his head and shoulders, emerged through the ragged hole with the broken wheel in hand. His shirt was torn on one side and long strands of grass protruded from his collar. He'd scraped the side of his face, but that seemed to be his only injury.

"What fool idea got into *your* head?" Grace demanded.

Robert E. glanced up, then almost immediately ducked his head and shoulders, looking sheepish. He eyed the contraption he'd been riding, looked at her, eyed the contraption again. He peered at the crowd coming his way, then back at the thing he'd been riding. Finally he said, "I broke it."

No explanation for the madness, for what the thing was, and for why he'd been flying down that hill on it.

"You *broke* it?" Grace blurted, not believing her ears.

He nodded, hunching to fiddle with the half of the front wheel that was still attached. "Gotta fix it."

"So you can fly down that hill an' almost break your neck again?"

"No. 'Cause Horace ain't had a chance to ride it."

She didn't understand. Why did it matter whether or not Horace had had a chance to ride the thing?

Robert E. saw her confusion. He slapped his hand on his

thigh in frustration. "See, Horace brought it t'me to put t'gether for him, then he went back to the telegraph office. I got it t'gether an' was ridin' it to him. But I can't take it to 'im lookin' like this."

Now Grace put at least part of the puzzle together. "It belongs to Horace?"

Robert E. nodded. His wide eyes could have lit a large room.

"An' Horace had you put it together for him so *he* could ride it?"

"That's about right," he said, shifting from one boot to the other, too many times for Grace to count.

"Only he can't ride it now 'cause you crashed it into this henhouse?"

"That's . . . He's gonna . . . I'm gonna fix it, Grace!"

"I certainly hope so!" she huffed.

She turned away just as the crowd of people arrived in front of the henhouse. The sight of the crowd made her spin back around and glare at Robert E. "No more customers at my tables! They're all here. Fix *that*, too!"

Grace stomped off, intent on returning to the café and getting herself a cool drink of water. Her and Robert E., they'd be laughed at for days, maybe for weeks and months! She wanted to shoot him, she was so furious with him.

But at least he hadn't hurt himself.

Back at the café Dorothy had pulled a small pad of paper and a pencil out of her skirt pocket. She'd sewn pockets into four of her dresses, the everyday gingham ones she wore around town, and the pockets were handy. She carried paper and pencils, and a little change just in case she found herself wandering around town searching for a story and decided she needed to visit the mercantile because she had a sweet tooth.

Her interest, like everyone else's who had been sitting at Grace's tables, had perked when Robert E. came flying down that hill on the velocipede. She'd immediately wondered where he'd gotten the thing. If he made it. How fast it could go. If he'd spent much time learning to ride it. And when questions began buzzing through Dorothy's head, the journalist in her knew that she needed to pull out her paper and pencil and get to work.

A few people other than herself had seemed to realize what Robert E. was riding. But old-timers and people who rarely picked up a newspaper or a book didn't. Word was, according to the Denver and St. Louis papers Dorothy got, velocipedes were catching on. People kinda liked the idea of not having to hitch a wagon to go somewhere—of course, that was, if only one person needed to go. But then, that wasn't necessarily true. She'd seen advertisements in the St. Louis newspaper for a velocipede that two people could ride, complete with two sets of pedals. A pretty remarkable thing.

So Dorothy had scribbled notes about how Robert E. came tearing down the hill, going fast as a bird, maybe even faster. On the velocipede he'd been like a child in front of the candy jars at the mercantile. Dorothy didn't suppose she'd forget the look of boyish excitement on Robert E.'s face anytime soon, or the way he'd whooped and hollered with joy, having too much fun to contain himself. She lowered her pencil, feeling she ought to pay attention to Robert E. and the crowd that was barreling down the hill to have a closer look at him and the velocipede.

As the sheet came down over Robert E.'s head, Dorothy said, "Oh no," and took a few steps forward. He slammed into the henhouse and she gasped, thinking he'd surely hurt himself. Good thing the velocipede kept going but he didn't. Robert E.'s flight through the air was what saved him from getting hurt.

Dorothy scribbled more notes, trying to look at her pad and keep an eye on the Robert E.-velocipede situation at the same time. Robert E. seemed fine; he got up and ran to peer into the henhouse at the broken velocipede. Maybe he suffered just a scratch or two. Dorothy didn't figure he'd gotten up off the ground without at least that.

Mrs. Everly and the turkey tore after Robert E., and the scene suddenly became funny. Dorothy laughed, watching, still trying to take notes. At first she worried about trying to decipher them later, when writing the article. But she quickly laughed that thought off. Shoo! She felt so entertained by Robert E. and the velocipede, she figured she wouldn't forget much about how things happened.

The hens dealt with the tom turkey, chasing him a good fifty feet beyond Mrs. Everly's property, and Robert E. dealt with Mrs. Everly, who appeared rather upset, probably over the hole in the side of her henhouse. She went off shaking her head, then Robert E. came face to face with an irate and obviously embarrassed Grace. She glanced nervously at the people still rushing toward the henhouse, then at Robert E., then at the customers, then at Robert E. again as she tried to scold him in a discreet way.

He looked sheepish, and although Dorothy was still giggling over his ride down the hill and his encounter with the henhouse, and then with Mrs. Everly and the turkey, she felt rather sorry for him now. He'd been having himself a grand time. Then he'd forgotten to turn and look where he was. Worse than up the creek without a paddle. He was at the bottom of the hill with a broken wheel and an irate wife. In a few words, Robert E. was in a pickle of a mess.

Shaking her head again and trying to control another giggle, Dorothy took more notes. ''Robert E.'s Adventure,'' she'd call the story. And my, oh my, what an entertaining story it would be.

Jon Voss and Henry Hughes walked into the telegraph office laughing and wiping tears from the corners of their eyes. Minutes earlier, they'd arrived at the telegraph office, which had a good view of Grace's Café and the hill beyond, just as Robert E. came flying down the slope on the three-wheeled contraption. Jon had stood and gaped, not believing his old eyes. But Henry had known what the thing was. ''A velocipede!'' he'd sputtered. ''Robert E. on a velocipede!''

Henry whooped with laughter, and Jon jumped and swore when Robert E. crashed into the side of the henhouse. They'd both laughed at the turkey and Mrs. Everly coming after Robert E., then at Robert E. coming out of the henhouse with the velocipede seat and broken wheel in hand.

''Funniest thing I ever *did* see in my life!'' Henry said as they entered the telegraph office.

''Like Robert E. was eight years old again,'' Jon remarked. ''Had me a shepherd dog when I was a boy that I hitched to a little wagon my pa built special for me. That dog, he was givin' me a ride one day an' he spotted some cats and shoo! there he went. Funnest ride I ever had. I recollect whoopin' just like Robert E. Got any mail t'day, Horace?'' Jon sidled up to the counter and glanced at the telegraph operator.

''What's that thing called again?'' Jon asked. ''That

thing he was ridin'? Somethin' that ain't no more, that's for sure!" He cackled at his last remark.

"Nope, no mail, Mr. Voss," Horace said before Henry could answer Jon. "Robert E. was ridin' somethin'?" Horace wasn't one to meddle in other people's conversations. But the mention of Robert E. and then of Robert E. riding something had perked Horace's ears. It had made his knees go a little weak, too.

"*Was* he? He sure was! Came flyin' down the hill on it. Shoulda turned, but didn't." Jon shook his head, laughing more.

"Crashed into Mrs. Everly's henhouse," Henry added. "Went flyin'. Had to run from Mrs. Everly an' her tom turkey."

"Then Grace," Jon said, hooting.

"Yeah, then Grace."

"An' she looked as mad as old Tom!"

Horace didn't like the sound of things. Robert E. riding something, flying down a hill on it, crashing into Mrs. Everly's henhouse. . . .

Had Robert E. put the velocipede together and decided to ride it himself?

Business had just slowed down at the telegraph office. Hans would come shortly. Horace had planned to go back to Robert E.'s shop when Hans arrived and see how Robert E. was coming on putting the velocipede together, or on not putting it together.

"Any mail or telegrams for me or my wife, Horace?" Henry asked.

"The thing Robert E. was ridin'," Horace said, leaning over the counter. "Did it have three wheels? No horse?"

Jon guffawed. "*Two* wheels now. How Robert E. got outta that without a few broken bones, I don't know."

Horace gulped.

"No mail, Henry," he said, ducking under the counter and racing to the door of the office. Robert E. had ridden the velocipede and crashed it into Mrs. Everly's henhouse. It had two wheels now instead of three and . . . Horace thought he might be sick.

He dashed out of the office.

Jon and Henry stared at the door for a few seconds. Finally Henry scratched his temple. "What do you reckon Horace has to do with that thing?"

"I sure don't know," Jon said. "Must be somethin' important. Horace don't leave his machine much 'cept to go home an' sleep."

The men emerged from the telegraph office and watched Horace running toward the café, kicking up dirt, his long spindly legs occasionally tripping him up.

"Got something to do with that three-wheeled thing," Henry observed.

Jon grunted in agreement.

They were curious about Horace's behavior, but neither man thought of running after Horace. He was going too fast, and he looked like he might run over anything, or anyone, that got in his way.

Just past the café Horace spotted Robert E. dragging the broken velocipede up the hill, and he spun his legs more and flew up the hill after him. People pointed at Robert E. and laughed, but most of the crowd had returned to the café tables after Robert E. sullied up and refused to answer their bombardment of questions. Now Grace was contending with the questions and having a hard time trying to shrug off the embarrassment.

"What did you do to it?" Horace demanded, catching up to Robert E. The velocipede looked like the sketches, except that the front wheel was broken and Robert E. carried the saddle.

Robert E. was just about out of breath from dragging the velocipede up the hill. It wasn't a light thing! He winced when he saw Horace. "I was bringin' it to you. Had myself an accident."

Horace snatched the broken wheel from Robert E. "I ain't even got to ride it, an' it's ruined!"

"It ain't ruined. I can fix it."

"It shouldn't need fixin'. I just got it!"

"Well, it does," Robert E. snapped, snatching the broken wheel back. "An' if you don't lemme fix it, you ain't never gonna be able to ride it."

"You can't ride it again," Horace said, pouting. "After you fix it, I mean."

Robert E. glared at him. "I wasn't plannin' to."

"You already did."

"I'm gonna fix it! Right now." Sweat had broken out on Robert E.'s forehead. "Stop snappin' at me. I already got snapped at from Grace, an' I'm sure she'll snap at me more later t'day."

"Good," Horace said. "You shouldn't've been ridin' it."

"I *know* that."

"I'll pick it up in a few hours."

Robert E. twisted his mouth, considering. "Might take longer than a few hours. Might have to make a new wheel."

"*Three* hours?" Horace asked hopefully.

"A day or two. Look, Horace, I'm real sorry."

Horace huffed. A day or two. . . . He'd just gotten it!

He didn't give Robert E. a chance to say anything else. He turned around and walked back down the hill, concentrating on keeping his knees from buckling.

7

Closing the clinic at four o'clock wasn't easy.

Michaela had written out the new clinic hours on a piece of paper and tacked the paper to the front door. Three patients remained waiting on the front porch at four o'clock, the impatient Mrs. Levins among them. If any of the three had lived far from town or had an emergency, Michaela would have seen them before she closed. But they didn't, and she saw no reason why they couldn't return the following morning. She would see them first thing when she opened, she told them.

Mr. Eisenbein and Mr. Sloan were content with that, and they went on their way. But Mrs. Levins was flabbergasted at being put off. She stamped her foot and glared at Michaela.

Michaela told her that while she would love to have around-the-clock clinic hours, she couldn't manage them.

"I would like to see my children for a certain number of hours each day," she said. "And I cannot give patients adequate care if I do not occasionally rest and eat a proper meal."

Mrs. Levins kept fussing, and finally Michaela had to close the clinic door and leave her on the porch.

Katie was sleeping, which allowed Michaela time to tidy the clinic, wash the instruments she had used, and update the records of patients she had seen today. She had never sent patients away before and told them to return the next morning, and while doing that troubled her somewhat, she felt good about accomplishing the other things and about leaving the clinic at a decent hour. Brian would be shocked when she arrived home long before dark.

On her way out of town, Michaela went by Grace and Robert E.'s home.

Robert E. wasn't home yet, and Grace was not in the best of moods. She told Michaela about Robert E.'s soar down the hillside and his crash, and about the laughter and questions she had endured the rest of the afternoon.

Michaela fought a smile when she thought of Robert E. flying down the hillside on Horace's velocipede. Something told her that the last thing Grace needed was laughter from someone else, especially from one of her best friends.

"An' why didn't you bring Katie to me today?" Grace asked, putting the unpleasantness of her afternoon behind her for the moment. She took Katie from Michaela and gave the baby a big kiss on the cheek. Katie giggled.

Michaela took a deep breath. All day she had prepared what she wanted to say to Grace, how she would explain her decision.

"It's not fair of me to expect you to care for Katie and mind the café. We're alike in a sense—I take on responsibility after responsibility and don't realize I'm over-whelmed until the water is closing over my head. I placed an advertisement for a nursemaid with Dorothy today. She'll print it in this week's *Gazette*.''

Grace sat in a rocking chair, arranged Katie on her lap and began playing peek-a-boo with her. Katie giggled when Grace covered her eyes, then uncovered them. Grace said, ''Your mother's a stubborn woman.''

Michaela released the breath she had been holding. Perhaps Grace wasn't angry with her. She couldn't tell just yet.

Grace continued to play peek-a-boo with Katie, this time encouraging Katie to hide her eyes. Grace hid *her* eyes again, then it was Katie's turn again.

''You'd better bring her to see me often,'' Grace said.

Michaela smiled, a smile of relief and affection. ''I will, I promise. We could even have you and Robert E. to our homestead for supper every few weeks.''

''We'd like that,'' Grace said, hugging Katie. She glanced over Katie's head at Michaela. ''We'd like that a lot.''

So it was settled. Michaela would hire someone else to care for Katie during clinic hours. And Grace wasn't angry, as Michaela had feared she might be.

''Now that the mess is over an' done, thinkin' of Robert E. flyin' down that hill on that thing *is* funny,'' Grace remarked.

''It sounds like it was a funny sight,'' Michaela said.

Grace smirked, then giggled. ''I reckon he won't have to sleep out'n the shed tonight.''

''He'll appreciate that, I'm sure.''

''I'm sure.'' The women laughed. Grace shook her head. ''But I'm still mighty sore at him. He's got to fix that

87

woman's henhouse an' Horace's velocipede. *Then* I might not be so sore anymore."

Already she wasn't all that sore. Michaela could tell. When Grace was irritated, her eyes glittered and she set her jaw. She might even be feeling slightly sorry that she had complained about Robert E.

Cora Reeves had gone off to Mrs. Harrow's Boardinghouse, where she was lodging, to clean up. She wanted to don a dress that wasn't splattered with paint, wash her face, brush her hair . . . do all the things women did to spiff up. She would meet Hank in the hotel dining room at seven o'clock, she'd told him, and that sounded just fine to him. By that time, most of the supper crowd would be cleared out of the dining room. He'd have a corner table set, all nice and cozy, just for him and his lady friend.

While Miss Reeves was gone, he decided to spiff up a bit himself. He washed, put on clean clothes—trousers, shirt, collar, and vest. He combed his hair and tied it back, then he splashed rum water on his neck and jaw. A last glance in the mirror assured him that he looked fine—better than fine actually, *dandy*—and then he beat a path downstairs. He didn't think he was keeping Miss Reeves waiting, he didn't really think she'd even arrived yet. After all, women always took more time cleaning up than men did. He just wanted to be downstairs, positioned behind the lobby desk, glancing at the books, looking like a genuine hotel proprietor, when she walked in.

Supper was a treat. Miss Reeves was cultured, one of those Michaela Quinn-from-Boston women. She wore a sky blue dress all done up with lace that made her look soft and womanly, and her hair shimmered like silk in the lamplights. A few smiles, and a few glances of her glittering blue eyes, and Hank was a goner.

She was a widow (so it wasn't *Miss* Reeves, it was *Mrs.*), and her husband had had a prosperous mail-order watch business. She'd done some traveling with him, had enjoyed the theaters in Chicago, Pittsburgh, St. Louis, and other cities. She had always loved to read, she loved books and antique furniture, and so when her husband died (She'd said what had killed him, but Hank couldn't remember. All that mattered was that he was gone, leaving poor Mrs. Reeves all alone.), she had decided to open a bookstore. She loved the mountains, and she'd wanted to nestle herself and her bookstore somewhere in them. So here she was, not too far from the vision of Pike's Peak and the healing qualities of the hot springs. And not too far from Hank, which was mighty fine with him—she was a vision herself.

"You love the mountains, I know some places that'll take your breath away," he told her.

Cora clapped her hands and suggested a picnic sometime in the next few days. And although picnics had always seemed too womanish to Hank, he agreed to this one. He actually looked forward to this one. Just him and Cora Reeves, somewhere alone in the mountains.

She asked him something while Hank's thoughts were wandering, and to his embarrassment, he had to apologize and ask her what she'd said.

She smiled. "You must be preoccupied with this new hotel. You said it hasn't been open for very long. What did you do before you opened the Gold Nugget?"

"What did I do before . . . ?"

She nodded. The question rattled him. He wasn't about to tell this fine lady that he'd been a saloon keeper. He heard himself say, "I owned a hotel in Missouri." Where that came from, he didn't know. But it sounded good, so he stuck with it. "Nice establishment. But I heard how Colorado Springs was growin', so I came here."

It was a big lie, but with luck, he could pull it off. Like him, and like most people, he imagined Mrs. Reeves concerned herself mainly with what was happening now. Sure, everyone was curious about the past. But they didn't get caught up in it. In fact, she probably wouldn't ask any more questions about what he'd done before he opened the Gold Nugget.

But enough people around town still knew him as Hank the saloon keeper, and that made him nervous. If Cora Reeves encountered the wrong person, he'd be in a pickle of trouble. The lady might not have anything else to do with him. She might not want to picnic with him.

He'd corner Jake and Loren first thing tomorrow, maybe even Robert E. and Grace, and Sully and Dr. Mike—and he couldn't forget Horace—and he'd request that if they encountered Mrs. Reeves, they not tell her he'd been a saloon keeper.

Building and overseeing the Gold Nugget had made him feel respectable. Now he wanted more respectability, in the form of a lady by his side.

"The day after tomorrow," Mrs. Reeves said, leaning forward slightly.

He raised his brows.

"For our picnic."

"The day after tomorrow," he repeated.

She smiled again, and he smiled back, feeling like he was floating on a cloud. Right up near the gates of heaven, a place Hank Claggerty had thought he'd never get close to.

.   .   .

At home Michaela enjoyed a calm supper with her family. Brian had studied the Revolutionary War battle dates in the wagon on the way to school this morning, but he still wasn't sure he had scored very high on the test. He wouldn't know until tomorrow. At first he seemed quiet and worried. Then he grinned at Michaela and told her he was glad she had come home earlier this evening, because he'd missed her.

After supper Brian wanted to show Michaela and Sully a new game he had learned at school. He went outside and returned a short time later with a bucket half filled with twigs. Brian assured her that he would clean up any twigs he dropped in the house.

He piled the twigs on the floor, then dropped down onto his stomach and tried to pull one out without disturbing the others. He did it, but accomplishing the trick wasn't as easy as he made it look, as Michaela and Sully soon found out. Sully jiggled the other twigs when he pulled his out, and Michaela toppled the entire pile. The three of them had a good laugh over that. Katie decided to copy her mother—she scattered the twigs with her chubby hands, then laughed with delight, obviously thinking the game was about messing up the twigs.

The second round of the game went somewhat better for Michaela. She didn't topple the entire pile this time, just half of it.

"After all the surgeries you've done, you'd think your hands would be steadier," Sully teased.

She made a playful face at him.

A little later he showed her the sign that he had started making for the clinic. So far only the word *Clinic* was burned into the wood. He intended to put *hours* after that, then drop down and list the times Michaela wanted to open and close.

While she was dressing Katie for bed, she told him about Mrs. Levins' tantrum when she informed the woman that she would have to return in the morning. "I'm afraid some patients won't like the new hours," Michaela said. "But at least I won't feel so tired and overwhelmed."

Sully went to rock Katie to sleep while Michaela and Brian washed the supper dishes.

Brian told her about the new girl who sat in front of him at school. "Prettiest girl I ever saw," he said.

Michaela smiled and thought to herself that in the space of two weeks this was the third "prettiest girl he had ever seen."

They soon finished the dishes and Brian went up to bed.

Yawning as another busy day caught up with her, Michaela began putting a few things in order: the wooden blocks and rag dolls Katie had played with earlier, a few twigs Brian had missed when he gathered up the twigs and took them back outside. She tossed the twigs out the front door, into the grass.

When she returned to the main room, her gaze fell on the sign Sully was making for the clinic. Smiling, she picked it up and ran her hands over the letters he had burned into the wood. For her . . . for the clinic. Burning the remaining letters into the wood would take hours, hours she knew Sully could hardly spare right now. He sacrificed the hours to make the sign because he loved her. The thought warmed her.

As if knowing she was thinking about him, Sully slipped his arms around her waist from behind, pulling her back against him. His touch was warm and welcome, familiar.

He brushed the hair aside from her shoulder with his chin and kissed the side of her neck.

Her smile widening even more, Michaela tipped her head back to rest on his shoulder.

"I say we go to bed," he said, his voice soft.

Hers was just as soft. "I say that's a marvelous idea."

He took the sign from her and placed it on the cushioned settee. His hand slid down around hers, and he tugged, urging her in the direction of their bedroom. His eyes were bright, his smile suggestive. Michaela's heart beat faster. She no longer felt as tired as she had.

In the bedroom he already had the lamp lit and the coverlet turned down.

He kissed her, a mere brush at first, as his hands rested on her shoulders. The press of his fingers drew her closer. Even without the press she would have gone. All day she had longed for such closeness with him, such intimacy.

She reached down and slid her hands beneath his shirt, up his sides and over his chest, feeling the warmth of his skin, the strength of him. She became bolder whenever he aroused her. Not all of her shyness had fled since their wedding night, but she had become more confident of herself; she knew what he liked, knew how to touch him.

He shed the shirt. His kisses became more urgent. His fingers found her bodice buttons and began undoing them.

His hands froze when he reached her waist. His head lifted from her neck, and she could tell he was listening, like a deer alert to danger.

"What is it?" she asked, breathless. Their window was open. His eyes had shifted that way

"A wagon."

Seconds later she heard the wheels grating, the harnesses clinking, the entire wagon rattling. Someone was tearing toward the homestead. From a distance shouts of ''Dr. Quinn!'' carried on the cool breeze.

Michaela began redoing her bodice buttons. She heard Sully heave a sigh of frustration.

She wished she could will away the person approaching the homestead. But she couldn't, and she couldn't ignore a medical emergency. She could think of no other reason why someone would be approaching the homestead at this hour, shouting for her.

Michaela finished the buttons while Sully slipped back into his shirt.

Their clothing in order, they left the bedroom and headed for the front door of the house.

Outside, they waited for a minute on the porch, catching intermittent glimpses of lantern lights as the rattles and shouts grew louder.

Finally the wagon broke through a line of trees. Michaela recognized Benjamin Hughes, all of thirteen years old, standing in front of the seat. She had treated his father at the clinic yesterday afternoon. Was Henry passing his kidney stones? Several weeks ago she had told him what to expect, that passing the stones would be painful.

Benjamin almost didn't rein the horses soon enough. For an instant, Michaela wondered if the horses and wagon would crash into the porch. Sully apparently thought the same. He grabbed her hand and pulled her down the porch steps. They stood beside a corner of the house and waited.

Benjamin managed to stop the horses and wagon just short of the porch. He twisted toward them, not taking the time to get down, and Michaela now had a good look at his face. His appearance and look of pure panic told her he wasn't bearing down on her because his father was passing kidney stones. His clothing and skin were smudged with soot. His huge eyes said he had never been more frightened in his life.

"Fire! At the barn. Pa inside!" Benjamin's shouting and his fear had left him short of breath. "Trapped inside! Got him out. Part of the barn fell. Beam came down. You gotta come!" He was looking at Michaela, his eyes pleading with her.

"I'll get my bag," she told him. Her feet were already moving her toward the porch.

Sully was right behind her. "I'll wake Brian an' tell him we're goin'. You might need some help with this one."

He was right—and she was grateful. The circumstances and Henry's condition sounded grim. Not to mention that Benjamin was in no state to be in control of a wagon and a team of horses.

Inside the house, Brian was coming down the stairs. Benjamin's shouts had awakened him, and he was on his way to see what the excitement was about.

"I'll sleep on the cot in Katie's room in case she wakes up," he said, after Michaela told him about the emergency and that she and Sully were going with Benjamin.

She had her medical bag in hand when she kissed him good-bye on the cheek. He was priceless, her son, not questioning the fact that both she and Sully were going. He simply did what he could to help.

Sully took Benjamin's place at the reins, and he walked the horses toward town. Benjamin panicked again, saying they needed to hurry, that Sully should run the horses.

But the horses were lathered with sweat, and Sully had to coax them even to walk. "They won't reach the ranch if he runs them," Michaela told Benjamin. "They're exhausted now."

"I know, I know." Benjamin threw his head back and

looked at the sky. He gulped air, then lowered his head into his hands and sobbed.

Michaela put her arm around him. He apologized between sobs.

"No, don't," she said. "It's all right."

In town, Sully roused Robert E., who hurried to get fresh horses for the wagon. He'd take care of Benjamin's horses, he told Sully.

With the fresh horses, they reached the Hugheses' ranch within twenty minutes, although Michaela knew that to Benjamin the time seemed like an hour. The air grew heavy with smoke. Michaela unrolled clean bandages for Sully and Benjamin to tie around their heads, covering their mouths and noses. She tied one around her head and breathed easier.

They spotted the ranch house and, in the distance, what had been the barn. It was now a wreckage of smoldering timbers with part of the frame still standing upright. A bucket brigade was still going, extending from the barn down to the creek that ran through the Hugheses' land. Flames still burned in patches.

Michaela spotted Eleanor Hughes huddled over a figure that lay on the ground. She tapped Sully and indicated that they should head that way.

As they drew closer to Eleanor and the person Michaela assumed was Henry, Benjamin's shoulders slumped more and more. He whispered a prayer, only half his words audible, and Michaela pressed his head more tightly against her shoulder.

As soon as the wagon began slowing, her fingers closed around the handle of her bag. When the wagon stopped, she let go of Benjamin, preparing to jump down and hurry to Henry. But she waited for Sully to set the brake, and then she waited for him to jump down and reach up for her.

She felt they weren't moving fast enough. And then she realized that it didn't matter how fast they moved, that Henry Hughes's time on earth was running out. How well she knew by now that no matter how much knowledge and skill she amassed, she couldn't make a person live longer than He intended for him or her to live. Throughout every treatment, throughout every procedure and surgery, she kept that fact in mind.

As Michaela approached Henry, Eleanor Hughes glanced up and smiled, startling Michaela. Then Michaela realized that Eleanor *knew*. Henry was conscious and talking to her, but he was badly burned and she had reconciled herself to the fact that he would die.

A glance at Henry, and Michaela knew there was little hope, little that she or that the finest doctors in the world could do.

Most of Henry's clothing had been burned off. Someone had brought a blanket to cover him. His hair was gone, half of his face was charred, and his breathing was difficult. Which meant that his lungs had been burned. With the lungs burned, the prognosis was usually bleak.

Henry wouldn't need her services much longer. Certainly kidney stones were the least of his concerns.

Sully brought the wagon, and he and another man moved Henry into the back of it. Benjamin sobbed harder. He was blaming himself. Apparently he had knocked over a lamp in the barn, igniting some dry hay. He had tried to beat the flames out, and then his pa had come to help and the fire had worsened. A flaming beam had fallen on Henry, trapping him and burning him severely before Benjamin could lift the beam and pull his father out of the fire.

Benjamin rode in the back of the wagon with his father while Eleanor Hughes sat beside Michaela and Sully on the wagon seat.

By the time they reached the house, Benjamin's sobs had died down. Henry had been talking to him, and while Michaela had no idea what Henry had said, his words had comforted Benjamin enough that he was able to help carry his father into the house and upstairs to his parents' bedroom.

There Michaela explained the grim reality to Henry and, as she expected, he already knew. She could set his leg, broken by the falling beam, bandage his burns, and give him laudanum. But there was little else she could do.

She detested this feeling of helplessness, of knowing she was about to lose a patient.

She had to force herself to look at Henry and Eleanor as she spoke to them. "When the lungs are burned," she said, clasping her hands nervously in front of her, "the outcome is usually. . . ."

"I'm dyin'," Henry rasped.

Michaela nodded.

Benjamin sobbed again. Michaela reached for her bag.

"I don't want no laudanum," Henry said. "The only pain I'm feelin' is in m'leg an' it ain't s'bad. I don't wanna be drunk. C'mere, Ben."

Benjamin gathered himself and approached the bed. He sat on the edge of it while his mother sat on the other side. Henry told Benjamin his plans for the ranch, how he wanted to see it grow, how Benjamin should look after his mother because she was getting on in years.

Michaela could never keep a dry eye whenever a dying patient began expressing last wishes and desires, dreams he hoped someone else would work toward in his place. She excused herself—although the Hugheses were beyond hearing her—and she and Sully left the room.

Out in the hallway, Michaela sank down on a wooden settee. Sully tried to comfort her by putting his arm around her and drawing her head down to his shoulder. But Michaela resisted. She had shed many tears on his shoulder, and they would come again, on cue, if she placed her head there. No matter how many patients she treated, no matter how many gruesome things she saw, death always saddened her. She knew that would never change.

Presently Eleanor came out into the hall and told Michaela that she should go home if she wanted to, that there really was nothing more she could do. But as a concerned individual more than as a doctor, Michaela stayed.

Sully went to help put out what was left of the fire, and Michaela dipped drinking water from the well into a bucket. She carried the bucket and a dipper out to the men.

She returned to the house and fixed tea for Eleanor. When Henry was thirsty, she helped him lift his head and drink. She comforted Benjamin in the hallway when he broke down again.

Henry wanted to watch the sunrise, so she tied back the window curtains for him. Finally, with Eleanor clasping Henry's hand and with Benjamin seated in a chair near the foot of the bed, she closed Henry's eyes shortly after he took his last breath.

Minutes later, Michaela gathered her medical bag and went downstairs.

Outside, Sully held the reins of a horse for her, waiting to take her home and comfort her. She went to him. He helped her mount, then he swung onto another horse that waited nearby, and they rode toward home.

Most of the way, Michaela cried quietly.

8

At home, Brian had Katie up and dressed, and was feeding her oatmeal when Michaela walked into the house.

He looked frustratedly at Michaela—Katie kept smearing the oatmeal in her hair—then his face went pale. Michaela's eyes felt swollen from crying, and she was sure they were red.

"You all right, Ma? Mr. Hughes . . . ?"

"Died just after sunrise."

Brian's face scrunched up. He dropped a spoonful of oatmeal on the floor. He and Benjamin Hughes had been friends for several years. Brian had been at the bedside when his own mother died, and he knew so well the pain of losing a parent. Surely that thought was going through his mind.

"Ben," he said.

Michaela open a cabinet drawer and pulled out a spoon. She stooped beside the table and scooped up the oatmeal. "In time, he'll be fine, Brian," she said, rising. "Give him time."

Brian nodded, his expression suddenly long and sad.

Michaela set the spoon of oatmeal on the table. She kissed Katie on the forehead, dodging her messy hands, and sat in a nearby chair.

"I'll finish here if you'd like," she told Brian. He was such a huge help to her lately, starting supper, dressing Katie for the day, feeding her.

He nodded again and handed her the spoon he had been using to feed Katie. "I didn't wanna just give her the bowl. I'll go help Sully with the horses." He was already dressed for school. Well, no wonder—it was nearly time for them to leave.

Michaela felt exhausted. She had had no sleep, and she felt dirty. Her clothing smelled like the fire. Her hand trembled as she scooped oatmeal into the spoon and raised the spoon toward Katie. "You'll be a little late for school today, Brian. I have to change clothes and freshen up."

He stopped a few steps from the front door. There he turned back. "Maybe you should stay home today, Ma. Y'know, an' sleep. You look like you were up all night with Ben's pa."

She managed a smile. He didn't exactly mean that she looked awful, just that she looked exactly as she felt—exhausted. "I have too many patients to think about staying home today, Brian."

"But you can't do 'em much good if you feel bad yourself, can you?"

He was right, of course. But to think about not opening the clinic today. . . . Why, yesterday she had told three of her patients to return today, including the impatient Mrs. Levins.

Katie grunted, wanting the bite of oatmeal. Michaela realized that she was still holding it in midair, that she probably had been for nearly a minute.

She gave Katie the bite, then returned the spoon to the bowl to scoop up more oatmeal. As much as she loved Katie, even if she did stay home today, she would get no sleep. She would have to mind Katie until this afternoon, when the baby took a nap.

"Please, Ma?" Brian said. "Please think about stayin' home?"

He didn't plead for his benefit, because he craved time with her. He pleaded for her benefit, because he was concerned about her.

His thoughtfulness touched her. "I'll think about it," she told him. He smiled and went outside.

She fed Katie the remaining oatmeal, suddenly realizing that besides dressing and feeding Katie, Brian had cooked Katie's breakfast. He was becoming quite self-sufficient. Maybe he'd been capable for some time, but until recently he had not had the opportunity to be independent. He had helped her care for Katie before, but she certainly hadn't known that he knew how to cook oatmeal.

When Michaela tried to wash Katie's face, the baby dodged the washcloth. But she held her hands out to be washed, calling them "tick-y."

She meant "sticky," and, tired as she was, Michaela couldn't help a smile.

She washed Katie's hands, then removed the tray from the arms of the chair. She placed the tray on the table and lifted Katie out of the high chair.

Katie was happy to see her. She wrapped her arms

102

around Michaela's neck and tried to blow bubbles on her shoulder. Rubbing Katie's back, Michaela carried her to the bedroom.

There she closed the door so Katie couldn't escape the room (Katie had not yet learned how to turn a doorknob) and placed her on the braided rug. Katie wouldn't stay there for long, but at least Michaela could keep an eye on her while she changed her clothing.

In the few minutes it took Michaela to change, Katie pulled a medical book off the bedside table, chewed off a corner of Colleen's latest letter, and yanked the coverlet nearly off the tick. Michaela shook her head in amazement. Babies were so *busy.*

She fastened the last button at her neck, then picked up Katie, rescuing the coverlet, and sat with her in the rocking chair near the window.

Michaela's buttons fascinated Katie. They glinted in the morning sunlight, turning a rainbow of colors. As Michaela rocked gently back and forth, Katie tried to catch the buttons. Watching Katie, smiling at her delight, Michaela wondered how she would keep her heavy eyelids open all day at the clinic.

She didn't know when she nodded off. She heard Sully's voice, and her eyes popped open. She realized that she had fallen asleep while sitting and watching Katie.

"Brian's right," Sully said, lifting Katie. "You need to stay home today an' sleep."

Michaela shook her head. "There's Katie. . . ."

"No. I'll take her to Dorothy. She's said she'd be willin' to watch out for Katie now an' then. I'll tell her about last night. She'll keep Katie today—she's been wantin' to, anyway."

"What about you? You're exhausted, too, Sully. You must be."

"I'm all right," he said, standing with Katie in his arms. "I'll sleep tonight. The Blakes an' their girls are livin' in a tent. We keep workin' steady, we'll have their house up in two or three weeks."

"What about my patients, Sully?" Michaela still wasn't sure that staying home today was the right thing to do.

"I'll put a note on the clinic door sayin' an emergency kept you out all night. People'll hear about the fire an' Henry Hughes, an' they'll understand."

"Looks like she's dressed to go," Brian said, entering the bedroom. He and Sully exchanged looks, and Michaela realized that they had been conspiring to get her to stay home today.

"She's stayin'," Sully said.

Brian bounced down on the tick. "Really, Ma?"

She gave him a playful glare. "I don't think I have a choice."

Sully grinned. "Maybe you don't. Here, Brian. Take Katie an' go feed the chickens some corn. I'll be along."

Katie didn't object to going to Brian. She loved her brother, and she loved to feed the chickens. She heard the word "chickens" and wanted to run out to the barnyard, fill her hands with dried corn, toss the corn on the ground, and laugh when the chickens pecked it up. Brian set her on her feet and took her by the hand. He mentioned feeding the chickens again, and Katie squealed with excitement, pulling him toward the door.

Once Katie and Brian had gone, Sully pulled Michaela from the chair and began undressing her. She stopped him—she could undress herself, she told him.

104

"I ain't too sure about that this mornin'," he remarked, teasing her.

"Well I can," she said smartly.

He and Brian had convinced her, and they didn't need to tell her again that she should stay home today. After she had fallen asleep in the rocking chair, the bed, even with its coverlet in disarray, looked inviting.

She shed her dress, draping it over the back of the rocking chair instead of hanging it up in the wardrobe. Sully gave her a surprised look. She always hung her dresses up promptly. She never draped them over the backs of chairs or over trunks, the way her sisters always had when they all lived together on Mount Vernon Street in Boston's Beacon Hill. But this morning she was truly exhausted, and she would hang up the dress when she woke.

Sully laughed at her, still teasing her, and she was tempted to toss a pillow at him. She picked it up and held it as if she meant to. But it looked inviting, too, and she decided to lay her head on it instead.

Her eyelids felt so heavy, she could not keep them open. She smiled when Sully bent down and kissed her. Then she drifted off into the heavenly softness of the pillow.

A billy goat had decided to join the chickens in raiding Loren's corn bins.

Yesterday afternoon Loren had run the goat off along with the chickens, whopping him with his broom and muttering at him. Loren couldn't knock the goat into the air with his broom and hope he'd land in the bucket the way that bird had the other day, but he sure gave it a good try. He'd given the goat a real good whack on the rear, and it had screeched and run off.

Loren had half expected the thing to turn and come at

him with its horns—billy goats were usually mighty stubborn, after all—but it kept going down the middle of Main Street, dodging the traffic just like everybody else.

Today the bothersome creature was back.

Loren caught the goat with his head in the bin. When the goat sensed Loren's presence, he twisted and tried to wriggle his head free without dehorning himself.

Loren saw his chance and he spanked the goat good with the handle of his broom. One, two, three, four licks. The billy goat would think twice about sticking his head in that corn bin again, Loren thought with a satisfied smirk.

When he finally wrestled his horns free, the goat was plenty mad. Too mad to think about going off down the road and forgetting the corn bins. Today he meant to stand his ground, hold the hill, keep the castle. Today he pawed the ground and lowered his head and came at Loren with his weapons. The war was on.

Yelping, Loren turned and skedaddled. He rounded the potato and onion bins that stood on four tall, solid legs.

The goat rammed the bins, once, twice, a third time, trying to get at Loren. The stand creaked, then keeled over.

Onions and potatoes hit the porch planks and rolled everywhere, tripping up Mrs. Levins as she walked out of the mercantile. The woman dodged onions, then her feet got tangled and she crashed down on her bottom.

Ordinarily Loren might have had a good laugh over the snooty, impatient woman crashing down on her behind. But he still had a mad billy goat trying to get at him, and the potato and onion bin didn't stand in the way anymore. The goat had a straight shot at him.

The goat charged and Loren ran, diving off the side of the porch. He hit the dirt with his legs still going. He scrambled back onto his feet and ran across the street, not knowing where he was headed until he spotted the sheriff's office. Matthew . . . Matthew had to help him.

He charged into Matthew's office and slammed the door behind him.

Matthew was giving his one prisoner a meal, sliding it just inside the cell door while the prisoner stood near the barred window.

"Matthew, Matthew!" Loren sputtered, standing with his back to the door. "You gotta help me. He's after me! He's comin'!"

Matthew pulled on the cell door until it clicked shut. Loren was a sight—his hair ruffled, his normally white apron rumpled and filthy, as if he'd been rolling around in the dirt. Matthew had never seen Loren Bray soiled. And the look on Loren's face. . . . He was scared of something. Of someone.

Why someone would be after Loren, Matthew couldn't figure. But here was Loren, obviously running from someone, shivering like a scared rabbit with a hound close on its fluffy white tail.

"He's comin' here?" Matthew asked. He figured he'd get the culprit and ask more questions later.

Something, or someone, banged on the office door.

"It's him," Loren whispered, in a panic now.

Matthew rounded his desk, opened the middle drawer, and pulled out a loaded revolver. Whoever was after Loren was about to land himself in a cell 'til the circuit judge came through, which might be a good month from now.

"Hey, now," said Jacob Skeeter, Matthew's prisoner, coming up off his bunk. "If somebody's 'bout to start shootin' up the place, you got to let me out."

Right. Two days ago, Jacob had knocked Billy Sloan in the back of the head, stolen his horse, and left him for dead.

107

And he thought Matthew should let him out of the cell if somebody was threatening to start shooting? Not on his life. Matthew meant to let the circuit judge deal with Jacob Skeeter.

Matthew tossed Loren a ring of keys. "Go open the door to that empty cell."

Loren didn't balk. He scampered off to do as Matthew said.

Another bang on the door, about halfway down. Somebody was ramming something against the office door—because they'd probably seen Loren come in here. Still, it didn't sit right with Matthew that the culprit would try to bang down his door. Why didn't the man just open it?

"C'mon, lemme outta here," Jacob said, his face pressed against the bars. "I'll help ya out. You kin depu-tize me right quick."

"Shut up, Skeeter," Matthew ordered.

"Hey, you ain't got no call to talk to me that-a way. I jes' offered to help, is all."

Another slam on the door. This time Matthew heard wood splinter.

"That's enough," he said, as Loren turned the key in the cell door. "Fool's gonna break the door down."

Matthew yanked the door open, ready to confront the bold offender. Loren yelled, "No, don't let him—"

A goat plowed into Matthew, its head lowered. It knocked him sideways into the desk. Then he spotted Loren and went for him.

Jacob yelped, then cackled. "God-durn *goat*! Watch 'im, now. He might have a gun!" He cackled again.

Loren moved as fast as Matthew had ever seen him move. He maneuvered himself into the cell and pulled the door shut, locking himself in. Then he took a few steps back and laughed.

The goat charged the cell bars. He rammed them twice. Loren laughed again, which seemed to infuriate the goat even more.

The crazy thing turned and started tearing up the office, charging the desk, scattering papers, shredding things. He broke a glass and knocked four rifles from their rack.

Matthew caught the goat by the horns and wrestled it to the floor, not an easy task.

"Time to come out, Loren," Matthew said between clenched teeth. "I need to lock this thing up 'til somebody claims him."

"Good idea!" Loren agreed.

"Hoo, hoo! Gonna put a goat in jail!" Skeeter was loving this. "If that ain't the damnedest thang!"

Seconds later, Matthew heard keys rattle and then a key click in the lock.

"Now, you hold onto him," Loren said, sounding scared again.

"He ain't goin' nowhere."

"Check him for guns!" Skeeter said.

God, Matthew wished he'd shut up.

Loren eased out of the cell and past Matthew and the goat. "I'm goin' back to clean up his mess."

"What mess?" Matthew asked.

"Onions an' potatoes, an' Lord knows what else. I'm tellin' ya, Matthew, we've got to do somethin' about the animals in town. I can't have 'em eatin' the vegetables I'm tryin' to sell."

"I know, I know."

Matthew had to push and pull the goat into the cell. He wasn't a willing prisoner. The goat rammed the door before

Matthew could get it completely closed, trapping his horns. The goat wriggled free. When he backed up to charge again, Matthew pulled the door shut.

The goat hit the cell door. Matthew stood back and watched, rubbing his chin. He hoped that thing would get tired soon and lie down. Or maybe the goat's owner would miss him soon, hear where he was, and come and get him.

Jacob Skeeter was rolling around on his bunk, about to pop, he was laughing so hard.

Matthew glared at the man. "I'm gonna put him in with you if you don't shut up."

Now that the excitement was over, Matthew fully realized what he'd just done. He'd just locked a goat in a jail cell.

He shook his head, feeling stunned. This was the first time he'd arrested an animal.

9

Dorothy discovered that Robert E. was uncooperative as far as the story about him and the velocipede was concerned.

When she approached him in the blacksmith yard, he looked busy, melting down this, pounding that . . . appearing serious as he worked. Well, she wouldn't keep him for long. She had just a few questions for him.

He glanced over and saw her, and promptly lowered whatever it was he was working on. "Afternoon, Dorothy. What can I do for you?"

She had her pad of paper and her pencil in hand, and she was tickled that he was asking her what he could do for her.

"I have a few questions, Robert E.," she said, stopping right where she was. She wasn't going any closer to the flames in that iron barrel. The fire was blazing hot. She didn't know how he could stand to be so close to it. Maybe he was used to it.

"I'm writin' a story about your velocipede," she explained. "I was wonderin' where you came by it. If you made it or ordered it, or just where it came from. And *why* you decided to make it or order it."

His expression went sour almost immediately. He stared at her for several seconds, then his lips clamped and his eyes narrowed. "Did Grace send you over here t'ask me those things?"

His sudden surly mood took her by surprise. She knew he'd been embarrassed over his accident with the velocipede, but he didn't have to get sour with her.

"Why no, I—"

"I don't wanna see anythin' printed about all that happened yesterd'y," he said, returning to his barrel of fire. "Bad enough Grace won't hardly talk t'me. She wouldn't like seein' somethin' printed in the *Gazette* about it."

"It'll just be a story to entertain people. I—"

"Entertained 'nough people yesterday," Robert E. snapped.

"Not ever'body saw what happened."

"Thank the Lord for that! Now you aim to tell ever'body who didn't see it what happened? I don't see the sense in doin' that, 'cept to rile Grace more."

Dorothy cocked her head. Grace apparently was still real angry with him, so angry that Robert E. didn't even want to talk to her about what had happened. He didn't want to chance her printing anything at all about his adventure on the velocipede.

She lowered her pad and fingered a long-handled cattle brand that lay on Robert E.'s worktable. "Me, Grace, Dr. Mike, Loren . . . we're all so busy anymore it doesn't often occur to us to take a few minutes an' have fun. You did that yesterday, Robert E.''

"Yep," he said, shaking his head. "Right into Mrs. Everly's henhouse. Now I got to spend this evenin' fixin' it up. Grace was mad already. When I didn't fix Mrs. Everly's henhouse yesterd'y evenin', she was cookin' more. I got to fix it t'night, an' that ain't gonna be fun, that's for sure.''

"How many times since you've been married has Grace lost her temper with you?" Dorothy asked. It was a personal question, but the answer might make him be reasonable about answering her inquiries about his velocipede.

He guffawed. "More than I can count. More than I *wanna* count.''

"An' she always cools off after a few days.''

Using the end of his iron hook, he lifted something from the fire. He scowled at Dorothy. "Yep, she does. So I figure I'll give her a few days.''

"But Robert E., I don't have a few days. I start printin' this week's *Gazette* tomorrow!''

"An' durin' those few days I'll fix the wheel to Horace's contraption an' stay away from the café. Maybe after a while people'll stop laughin' an' Grace can hold her head up again.''

"*Horace's* contraption?" Dorothy's brows had shot up in surprise.

"Yep. Thing b'longs to Horace. He couldn't get it put t'gether himself, so yesterd'y he brought it to me. I ran him off so I could put it t'gether in peace. Horace can get on a person's nerves.''

"How did you end up ridin' it?"

Robert E. scowled again. "Curiosity gets a body into all kinds o' trouble.''

Dorothy recalled how Horace had sped past the café yesterday and up the hill after Robert E., who by then had the broken pieces of the velocipede in hand and was walking back toward the main part of town. Everybody knew that running uphill was no easy thing to do, but Horace hadn't even looked out of breath. He'd obviously had a mission, and that was to catch up with Robert E. At the time Dorothy had thought that Horace was just curious about the velocipede, and worried about Robert E. She'd resumed scribbling her notes, thinking Grace, who was headed back to her café, looked too riled to answer questions about Robert E. and the velocipede.

But now she knew . . . she was putting the puzzle together. Now that she thought of it, Horace hadn't looked too happy. In fact, he'd looked downright angry. And no wonder—he'd taken the dismantled velocipede to Robert E. to put together and then, apparently, gone back to the telegraph office while Robert E. worked on the thing. Why, Horace probably hadn't even seen the velocipede in one piece before Robert E. crashed it into the henhouse.

My, oh, my, oh, my. . . . No wonder Robert E. was uncomfortable with the subject and with her questions. He didn't have just Mrs. Everly and the tom and Grace mad at him—Horace was mad at him, too.

"Curiosity ain't such a bad thing," Dorothy said gently, feeling sorry for Robert E.

Robert E. shook his head. "It is when a person lets it get the best of him."

"Why, if not for curiosity, we wouldn't have printin' presses, or lamps, or—or velocipedes."

"An' that'd be just as well."

She smiled sympathetically. "Everybody meets up with trouble once in a while."

"Well, I met up with a whole lot of it yesterd'y. Now I'm diggin' my way out."

She felt really sorry for him now. He'd ruined Horace's velocipede and ruined Mrs. Everly's henhouse, and he had three people mad at him. If she was in that much trouble, her shoulders might slump and she might sound under the weather, too.

"Everything passes, Robert E.," she said. "Can you fix the velocipede?"

"I've gotta give it a good try, now don't I?"

She nodded. "I suppose you do."

A long spell of no talking went by. He heated and banged and shaped.

Directly, Dorothy said, "You sure looked like you were havin' fun." She didn't laugh. She figured he'd heard enough laughter for a good while.

He pondered that while staring into the fire. Then he surprised her—he chuckled. "Yeah, I sure as *shootin'* had fun."

She smiled, happy to hear him laugh.

As she walked away from the blacksmith's shop, she tucked her pad and pencil into her dress pocket. She didn't suppose she'd get any questions answered today by Horace, either. Maybe she'd let tempers cool off for a week or so, let Robert E. get the velocipede and the henhouse fixed. Then she'd come back around to gather up more facts.

As she headed back toward the *Gazette* office, across the main part of town, she happened upon another story. Only this one was still in the making.

People had gathered outside the sheriff's office, laughing, talking, and pointing at the door.

When Dorothy approached the crowd and asked what was happening, Eddie Thorton told her that Matthew had locked up a goat. When he said it, the people around him laughed. Dorothy reached into her pocket for her tablet and pencil. She had a feeling she needed to take notes.

The animal had been eating the vegetables on the front porch of the mercantile, Eddie said. Loren spanked the goat with his broom, the goat charged him, and Loren ran for Matthew's office with the goat close on his tail.

Exactly what happened once Loren and the goat got inside, nobody seemed to know. But they did know that Matthew had the goat locked up in a cell. Loren had gone back to the mercantile, and Dorothy supposed that's where he was right now, conducting business as usual.

Matthew appeared outside his office door, raking his fingers through his hair, looking exasperated. His trousers had a rip in one thigh. Dorothy jotted a note about the trousers, wondering if the goat had caused the rip.

"Hey, Sheriff, did that outlaw give you some trouble?" someone asked. Another man said, "Looks like ya might've had a time lockin' up that bandit!"

More laughter rose from the gathering, and Matthew raked his hair again.

He raised his hand, palms out, to try and quiet the crowd. "Anybody know who that critter belongs to?"

"Didn't get a good look at it myself," a woman said. "Don't think too many of us did." People around her mumbled agreement.

"Could belong to just about anybody," Eddie remarked.

"If anyone comes up missin' a goat, tell 'em to come an' see me," Matthew told the crowd.

"You ain't meanin' to keep him in there 'til somebody claims him, are ya?" Eddie asked.

Matthew cocked his head. "What else am I supposed to do? Merchants are havin' a time with loose animals anymore. Mr. Bray doesn't stock corn an' potatoes to feed people's animals.''

"You got a point there," Eddie said.

Dorothy was busy writing notes. Between Mary Tennessey getting hit by that wagon, Hank's fight with the horse racers, Robert E. and the velocipede, the fire at the Hugheses' ranch last night, and now Matthew locking a goat in jail for eating Loren's corn, she had some writing to do for this week's *Gazette*. She wondered if Brian would be willing to help her. But Hank had him helping at the Gold Nugget for an hour after school every day. And for the last month Brian had felt like he was needed at home more because Michaela was so busy at the clinic.

Oh, that reminded her—the reverend had mentioned to her this morning that Michaela had posted a note on the clinic's front door about new business hours. In the past, Michaela had never really set times for opening and closing the clinic. Dorothy had seen the lines of patients waiting outside the clinic every day during the past several weeks and had wondered how Michaela was dealing with the busyness. She hadn't seen much of Michaela lately, and the line of patients every day was probably why.

All around town it was the same, lines extending clear out of Jake's barbershop, no vacant rooms at Hank's hotel or at boardinghouses around town. New houses were going up on the outskirts of Colorado Springs, and new businesses were coming in. Rumor was, somebody planned to open a dry goods store out near the *Gazette* office. Dorothy thought that would be a good thing, because Loren had been running himself ragged lately. She'd heard talk of a bookstore, and that excited her. But with all the other excitement recently, she hadn't had time to investigate who planned to open the bookstore.

Matthew said he'd tie the goat behind his office if he had to, that he didn't plan to make a habit of locking up animals in the jail—he wasn't running a barnyard. People would have to start taking responsibility for their animals, for making sure they were penned or tied up if they wanted to keep them in town. Colorado Springs was growing, and the loose animals were a nuisance.

Not many people in the crowd disagreed with Matthew about that. Dorothy scribbled notes fast and furious, hoping she recorded everything he said.

Behind her a horse screeched and a man cursed. Dorothy turned to have a look, and spotted a hog running loose in the street, trying to dodge the horses and wagons.

When she turned back, Matthew was shaking his head, looking even more exasperated. He backed up, turned around and went into his office.

"He's right," Eddie Thorton said, "they're a nuisance."

Dorothy wrote notes about the hog and the wagons, ending with Eddie's comment.

Back in his office, Matthew pondered the goat for a while, wondering what to do with him. He had no idea whom the goat belonged to. When there hadn't been so many people in town, he might've known whose animal it was.

The goat watched him, ramming the cell bars now and then, while he put his office back in order. He fixed his desk—darn creature had given it a good shove. He gathered what papers were still in one piece, smoothed them out, and piled them on the desk.

"Looks like somebody had themselves a brawl, Sheriff," Jacob Skeeter said from his cell.

Matthew did his best to ignore the man. He collected the

shredded papers; scowled at a few of the pieces, recognizing them as things he needed to keep; and threw most of them in the rubbish can. He picked up the rifles and put them back in order on the gun rack. Finally he swept up the broken glass.

The goat smashed into the bars again. Sooner or later, he might break a horn doing that.

"Hee-hee," Skeeter laughed. "That ole boy's plenty mad. Looks like he's gonna stay that way fer a while. Been in a few jails in m'life. Ain't never seen no sheriff lock up a goat."

Matthew worked his jaw, getting more and more irritated. If Skeeter didn't shut up soon, they wouldn't have to wait for the circuit judge. Matthew would bury him alive in the cemetery.

"There I was, starin' at this ugly ceilin' an' this ugly place. An' then, *bam*, in came the old man. Then that goat!" Jacob cackled again. "Gonna make fer an interestin' stay in this here jail, 'at's fer sure!"

"He ain't stayin' long."

"Ooh-hoo. Wanna see ya get 'im outta there. That'll be a fight worth watchin'."

Jacob was right, as much as Matthew would like to stick a gag in his mouth to shut him up. That billy goat didn't look like he meant to calm down anytime soon. Matthew intended to leave him in the cell until he did. His thigh still smarted where the goat had knocked him into the desk. He wouldn't give the goat a chance to charge him again.

Matthew got things back in order, then went outside to escape Jacob's laughter and comments about the goat. He sat in his chair on the porch and kicked back, watching Main Street. His two deputies were out checking on a few things, and since he had a prisoner in jail—two, actually,

Matthew thought, scowling—he had to stay close.

Directly, he heard Skeeter hollering: "Ya better git in here, Sheriff. Ya ain't gonna like this—ya sure ain't! Hey, Sheriff Cooper, come see what yer billy goat done!"

Matthew didn't want to. Whatever the goat had done, it couldn't be anything good, not considering the way Skeeter was eating it up.

When Matthew opened the office door, the smell hit him and he cursed, knowing what had happened. Skeeter didn't seem to mind the smell. He was about to split his gut laughing. Of course, Skeeter wasn't the cleanest person himself, probably didn't bathe but once a year, maybe less. He probably couldn't smell the mess. He'd probably just seen what the goat did, and started laughing and hollering.

Matthew had to clean up in the goat's cell, and that meant he'd have to go in there.

The goat rammed the bars again. Matthew threw a pewter cup at him. At least nothing was in the cup. Matthew wished there'd been hot coffee in it.

Matthew grabbed himself a rope and approached the cell, thinking he'd open the cell door, grab the goat, and tie him up. Only things didn't work out that way. The goat got loose in the office again and splintered one side of the desk before Matthew could rope him.

Of course, Skeeter thought it was all hilarious, and he had himself another cackling fit.

Matthew's original plan had been to take the goat out back and tie him up. But he was sick of Skeeter laughing at him and taunting him about the goat, so his plan changed.

Skeeter stopped laughing real quick when he realized what Matthew meant to do. "Wh-what're ya doin'?" he asked as Matthew pulled the goat toward Skeeter's cell.

"Givin' you some company for a while, loudmouth."

Skeeter backed up. "Huh-uh. Nope. Naw, ya ain't! I don't want that goat in here. Take 'im on outside!"

He said more, objecting, his voice getting louder. He commenced to hollering when Matthew put a key in his cell door to unlock it. Matthew pushed the goat into Skeeter's cell and slammed the door shut.

Skeeter skedaddled under his bunk where the goat couldn't reach him. But not for lack of trying. By then that goat was madder than a hornet, and he tore up the tick on the bunk trying to get at Skeeter, at anybody.

Skeeter cussed and whined and scooted back against the wall. And there he stayed until Matthew collected the goat an hour or so later. He reckoned Skeeter was done taunting him about the time he was having with the goat.

Matthew dragged the goat out of the office and around back, where he tied it to a post. He had plenty of bruises where the goat had gotten him with its horns, so he jumped back real fast when the goat charged him again.

His boot hit something slick and his feet went out from under him. Next thing he knew, he was sitting in a pile of fresh horse dung.

He cursed the goat again, for about the hundredth time. He'd cursed more today than he had in the rest of his life, and he was real glad Dr. Mike couldn't hear him.

Back inside the office, he washed up as well as possible. Skeeter was quiet—he didn't dare do any more taunting. Wise man, Matthew thought. After he'd landed in that pile of dung, if Skeeter started again, he might turn around and shoot him.

Not long afterward, one of the deputies returned. Dan Cox walked in the door and immediately put a hand to his nose. "What in the . . . ?"

"I fell," Matthew said, getting up from behind the desk.

"I know it ain't your day to mind things here, but I need you to stay while I go home an' change clothes."

"Please stay," Skeeter said, cautiously approaching his cell door. "He's goin' crazy! He's gonna let that goat kill me!"

"Aw, shut up," Matthew snapped at Skeeter. "It served you right. If you'd shut up the first time I told you to, you wouldn'ta had to hide."

"I ain't got nowhere to sleep."

"That's 'cause you wouldn't shut up. Sleep on the floor."

"It's cold on the floor!" Skeeter whined. "I'm arrested, but I still got rights."

"I'll stay," Dan said, his gaze shifting back and forth between the two men. It finally settled on Matthew. "I don't know what's goin' on, but it sounds like Skeeter's tried your patience."

"Skeeter an' that goat that's tied up out back," Matthew said as he grabbed his hat and headed for the door. "Tell you what, if ole Skeeter there gets mouthy, put that goat in the cell with him. You'll get some respect."

Skeeter shrank back from the cell door.

"I'll tell you about the goat when I get back," Matthew told Dan just before he left.

Matthew rode out to his homestead, changed clothes, then returned to town. He stopped at the café to pick up a meal for Skeeter. He scowled when Jon Voss asked if he was getting a meal for the goat, too. Then he realized he had to feed the goat, and he told a startled-looking Grace that he needed another meal. She knew where it was going, and she didn't look too happy about the fact that he'd be feeding a goat her good food. He apologized, then took the food and went to the jail.

The goat stared at Matthew like he wanted to kill him, despite the fact that he had food and that goats were *always* hungry. Matthew couldn't feed the goat by himself. He moved close enough to dump the food on the ground where the goat could reach it, and the thing charged. Matthew jumped back.

He finally got Dan to help him. Matthew grabbed the goat by the horns and held tight while Dan dumped the food on the ground where the goat could reach it once Matthew let go of it.

He'd wrestled with that goat so many times since the thing had charged into his office, he felt like he'd been fighting a couple of bulls. He was sore all over and his head hurt—and he'd forgotten all about getting *himself* a plate of food.

10

Michaela slept until nearly one o'clock that afternoon.

After she rose, she had a cup of tea and a biscuit. Then she gathered up the basket of Katie's soiled clothing and bedding and any other dirty articles she could find. To the side of the house, near the barnyard, she had a washtub and board set up.

She enjoyed the peacefulness of the homestead while she worked, listening to the chickens cluck, the hogs root, the cow's bell jingle. She hoped patients hadn't lined up at the clinic this morning, and that Mr. Eisenbein and Mr. Sloan weren't angry that she hadn't been at the clinic this morning to see them. Sully had been right—she had needed to sleep. She wouldn't have been able to hold her head up past nine o'clock this morning. She almost hadn't held it up past eight o'clock.

She hung the clothing and bedding on the clothesline. In the barn she picked up a woven basket and went to the garden, where she pulled up carrots, onions, and potatoes. She dipped water from the well and washed the vegetables. In the smokehouse she cut down a chunk of venison.

Inside the house she hummed while she chopped up the vegetables and the meat. She put everything together in a kettle, then added water, herbs, and salt and pepper. She started a fire in the stove, and soon the stew was simmering, filling the house with delicious smells.

She peeled and sliced apples, and made pie dough, using two forks to break up a chunk of lard and mix it with flour. The mixture looked like cornmeal when she finished with it. Four teaspoons of water dampened the flour and shortening enough that it stuck together when she pressed it with her fingers. She rolled the dough into a rough circle, humming again, enjoying herself and her afternoon at home.

The dough folded in half easily, allowing Michaela to pick it up and put it in the pie plate. She layered apples, sugar, and ground cinnamon until the layers nearly reached the top edge of the dough. Then she sliced a lemon and squeezed the juice over the apples. She made another circle of dough for the top crust, and sprinkled water along the outer edge of the bottom crust. Water made the bottom and top crusts stick together at the edges. Colleen had shown her that trick shortly after she began learning to cook, and it worked well.

She was trimming the excess dough from around the edge of the pie plate when she heard a wagon approach. Through a front window, she glimpsed Sully and Brian on the wagon seat. Katie sat on Brian's lap, clapping her hands together. Michaela put the pie in the oven, wiped her hands on her apron, and went to the front door to greet her family.

She didn't know how Sully had gotten through the day without a minute of sleep last night. He didn't look tired, but Michaela knew he had to be. She reached for Katie, who was already reaching for her, just as Sully jumped down from the wagon. Brian followed him on the other side.

Months ago Katie had learned to give kisses, open-mouth kisses. She kissed Michaela's cheek over and over, at least five times, before Sully reached the side of the wagon to kiss her. Katie continued the kisses, laughing at herself.

"I think she's glad to see you, Ma," Brian said.

Michaela laughed. "Yes, I think so."

"Amanda Blake kept her while me an' Robert worked on the house," Sully said.

That surprised Michaela. "Not Dorothy?"

Sully shook his head. "Couldn't get an answer when I knocked on the *Gazette* office door. So I got to thinkin' Amanda Blake's real civil an' their place's neat. Her girls are in school all day. I asked her if she minded. She didn't, said she appreciated me helpin' Robert with the house."

"Yes, but he's paying you to help him," Michaela said, still enjoying Katie's kisses.

"I think Amanda wants out of that tent an' in a house."

"That's understandable."

"Ma, I think I've got twenty dollars saved now," Brian blurted. He was studying some coins he held in his hand. He had a serious, thoughtful look on his face, and Michaela realized that he had been trying to remember how much money he had saved in the box under his bed.

He had earned some of the money by helping Dorothy write articles for the *Gazette*, and some when he helped her print the newspaper on days when her arthritic hands bothered her. But most of it was money Brian had saved since

Hank had hired him and Benjamin. The Gold Nugget was doing quite well—of course, what business in town wasn't, right now?—and Hank had been generous.

"That's wonderful, Brian," Michaela said.

Sully inhaled deeply. "Something smells good."

Michaela beamed. "Venison stew. And I have an apple pie in the oven."

He kissed her again. Then he kissed Katie. "I'll unhitch the horses an' be in soon."

The mention of stew and pie drew Katie's attention. She waved her arm at the house. "Eat, Mama, eat."

"All right, angel. Stew. . . . Do you want stew?"

Katie loved stew. She bounced up and down on Michaela's hip. She was excited now. In another minute or two, she would become impatient. Michaela walked toward the house, Brian at her side.

"Ma, do you reckon Ben'll be all right?" Brian asked, suddenly serious.

"With time he will. After your ma died, it was a good month before you smiled again. Matthew was angry at the world. And Colleen . . . well, Colleen felt lost, deserted."

"But you were there for us. Ben ain't got another pa lined up."

"Maybe he'll have another pa in the future," Michaela said. They were on the porch now, and Brian opened the door and held it for her, her little gentleman. "Most people remarry—like Sully did."

She took Katie straight to her high chair and sat her down. Brian picked up the tray and worked it onto the arms of the chair while Michaela went to the stove to dip out a small bowl of stew for Katie.

"The hardest thing for Benjamin will be learning to not blame himself," she continued. "He feels like the fire and his father's death are his fault. They're not. Accidents happen, and people die. Even knowing that, death isn't any easier for me to deal with now than it was when I was a girl trotting behind my father.''

She turned back to the table with the bowl of stew in hand. Steam rose from it. She would have to blow on each bite and check the temperature before she fed Katie.

"I've blamed myself for deaths, Brian," she said, sitting. "After patients die, I always wonder if there was another treatment or surgical procedure I could have tried. When I misdiagnose an illness . . . that leaves me with terrible guilt. I experience the same guilt every time something goes wrong or I realize I've missed something. I've learned to put the guilt aside and go on. We cannot change what is done—that is what Benjamin will have to tell himself and live with.''

Brian pulled out a chair and sat down. "I want to go see him.''

Michaela reached for his hand. "Don't crowd him. He'll be back at school. And he'll be back at work with you at Hank's hotel. Henry will probably be buried tomorrow. I'll close the clinic for a while and we'll attend the service together.''

He nodded, then slumped back in his chair. "I'm sad for him.''

"I know," she said, squeezing his hand. "Because you've had the experience of losing a parent suddenly, just like Benjamin.''

"I'm gonna go help Sully," Brian said, as if wanting to put his mind on something else. That was probably the best thing he could do.

Michaela nodded. Her gaze followed him until he went out the door.

"All right, Miss Katie," she said, stirring the stew. "Would you like a bite?"

Katie made a popping sound by pressing her lips together, then opening them quickly. She patted her tray. " 'Tew, Mama?"

"That's right—yummy stew."

Michaela scooped a potato into the spoon along with a little broth, and she blew on the stew to cool it. She dipped the tip of her forefinger into the broth to check the temperature. Satisfied that it was cool enough, she offered the bite to Katie. Katie gobbled it up, then made the popping sound with her mouth again.

Sully and Brian came inside from tending the horses just as Michaela gave Katie the last bite of stew in the bowl. Katie had slowed down and was starting to lose interest. She had twisted around twice, and then, after Michaela had straightened her, she had slid her bottom forward in the chair, positioning her chin on the tray.

"Looks like she's finished," Sully remarked, going to the wash basin. When Katie became full, she was easily distracted and she began playing in the chair.

"I think you're right," Michaela said, dropping the spoon into the bowl.

Sully brought a damp cloth from the basin while Brian washed his hands. As usual, Katie fussed when Michaela washed her face, trying to dodge the cloth. Michaela washed Katie's hands, then the tray on which Katie had mashed a potato.

A few blocks with letters burned into the wood solved the problem of boredom, at least for a while. Michaela guessed that she probably had ten minutes to eat, ten minutes of Katie playing with the blocks and not trying to twist her way out of the chair.

Sully dipped the stew while Michaela took the pie out of the oven.

He and Brian were hungry; there was little conversation during the meal. Sully had begun to look tired, and with each bite of stew, he looked more tired. As he ate a slice of pie, Michaela wondered if he might fall asleep in his chair.

He excused himself from the table, saying he was going to get water to heat for a bath. Brian went to help him bring water in.

They returned minutes later with two buckets of water each, as Michaela was lifting Katie from her chair.

She took Katie to the settee, and she sat on the floor in front of it and played with the wooden blocks and the toy wagon Sully had carved for Katie. She and Katie filled the wagon bed with blocks, dumped it, filled it again, dumped it again. . . . They did that four times before Katie became bored with the game.

She snatched up one of her corncob dolls and tried to take off the dress Michaela had made for the doll. Michaela had sewn tiny ties onto the dress, to hold it together. A good ten minutes went by before Katie realized that she could loosen the dress by pulling on the ties. Once she had undressed the doll, she wanted to dress it again. Michaela knew Katie would undress and dress the doll at least three times; she liked repetition.

Between the blocks, the wagon, and the dolls, Michaela entertained Katie while Sully bathed in the little room just beyond the kitchen area. When he emerged from the room, his wet hair slick and dark, he look refreshed but still tired.

He took Katie from Michaela, which gave her a chance to wash the supper dishes. Brian had gathered and stacked them, then settled himself at the table with a book.

A collection of Emerson's writings, Michaela saw. She asked him about the book as she began washing dishes.

"Miss Theresa let me borrow it," he said. "She thought I would enjoy it."

"And do you?"

He nodded, then went back to reading.

Sully had made himself comfortable in a chair opposite the settee. He entertained Katie with a string and wheel, holding the string horizontally and making the wheel spin on it. He had carved a groove all around the center of the wheel and then had greased the groove.

The spinning wheel fascinated Katie, having an almost hypnotic effect. Soon she laid her sleepy head against her father's chest and closed her eyes.

Smiling at the sweet sight, Michaela dried the dishes and put them away. She almost toppled a glass in the dish cabinet. She spent a few minutes rearranging that shelf so there would be no danger of any more glasses nearly crashing down on anyone.

"Ma, look!" Brian said in a loud whisper.

Michaela glanced at him, then followed the motion he made toward the chair where Sully and Katie sat.

Father and daughter had fallen asleep.

Whenever they had a prisoner, Matthew and his deputies took turns spending the night at the jail. Tonight was Matthew's night.

Things had quieted down since he'd tied the goat out back, thank God. Skeeter had finally stopped pouting and had eaten his meal. Then he'd stretched out on what was left of his tick and, after tossing and turning for a while, had settled down.

An hour or so after nightfall, Matthew lay down on the

131

cot he kept behind his desk. Exhausted, he quickly fell asleep.

Something jolted him awake. He sat up on the cot, rubbed his eyes, and looked around. He'd left a lamp burning, so the office was dimly lit. Skeeter had sat up, too, and he had a fuddled look on his face.

"What're you doin', Skeeter?" Matthew asked, thinking Skeeter had made the noise.

"Not a dang thang. Tryin' to sleep. What was that?"

"What'd it sound like?"

"I don't—"

Thud!

The goat again. Matthew knew it as soon as he heard the noise. It was the goat ramming the side of the jail.

Skeeter screeched, and then he was at the cell door, trying to press his face into it. He moved so fast, Matthew never saw him jump off the bunk and run. He was just there all of a sudden.

"Someone's bangin' on the wall back here!" Skeeter said.

"It's that goat tryin' to get you again," Matthew grumbled.

"Eeee! He's crazier 'n you!"

Matthew swung his legs off of the cot, stood, grabbed a coil of rope, and made his way to the door. He'd tie the goat up for the night if that's what it took to get some sleep.

Outside, he rounded the corner and saw the goat butting its head on the side of the building. Matthew grabbed the goat by the horns and wrestled with it, trying to get it on the ground. He succeeded, but he went down into a squashy pile. The smell of dung drifted up around him, and he cursed worse than he'd cursed all day.

Matthew wrapped the rope around the goat's legs, front

and back, crisscrossing it. Then he tied the rope off and pushed the goat away from him.

"There," Matthew said, getting up. "Maybe you won't cause any more trouble tonight."

Maybe was right.

Back in the office, Matthew stripped down to his underdrawers. His clothes smelled so awful, he opened the office door and deposited them on the porch. Then he returned to the cot, lay down, and went back to sleep.

11

The next morning Brian shook Matthew awake. He couldn't figure why someone had put his shirt and trousers out on the porch—or why there was a goat tied up behind the jail. Brian had heard the thing bleating and he'd walked around the building, tracing the noise to the goat. It was tied up like a calf about to be branded. Curious, Brian had gone around to the front porch, and there he'd found the shirt and trousers

Although it was Saturday and he didn't have school, Brian had come into town for the day with Dr. Mike. He planned to visit with Matthew for a while, then help Mr. Bray at the mercantile, if Mr. Bray would let him. Brian didn't see why he wouldn't—Mr. Bray was awful busy and could use the help. And then this afternoon, he had other things to do.

"What? *What?*" Matthew grumbled as Brian shook him.

He opened his eyes; it was a second or two before they cleared and Matthew recognized him.

"Brian . . . what're you doin' here?" Matthew rubbed his eyes. He tried to sit up, and his face scrunched like something hurt. He rubbed his thigh.

"I just came to say howdy. Say, d'you know there's a goat tied up like a calf ready for brandin' out back?"

"Yeah, I know."

Brian watched Matthew rub his thigh some more. "You got a cramp?"

"That goat's the only cramp I've got." Matthew didn't sound happy.

"Why's he tied up like that?"

"He wouldn't quit buttin' the back of the jail."

Brian studied Matthew, trying to figure this all out. "Is it your goat?"

Matthew slowly brought himself up to sit on the side of the cot, his face twisted. "I don't know who he belongs to. He was gettin' into Mr. Bray's vegetables, so I took charge of him. No, that ain't right. I didn't really have *charge* of him 'til I tied him up."

"You gonna leave him that way?" Brian asked, worrying about the goat. It had stared up at him, making him feel sorry for it.

"I'll untie him pretty soon. But he starts that buttin' again, he'll find that rope wrapped back around his legs."

Brian realized that Matthew had on only his underwear. He'd never seen Matthew in his office in just his underwear. Anybody could have walked in—Matthew never locked the door.

Matthew stood and stretched, rubbing his ribs, then his thigh again, like he was working out kinks. Brian watched him, trying to figure out why Matthew wore only his underwear. Then something dawned on Brian: "Are those your clothes out on the porch?"

"Yeah," Matthew said, swatting at Brian's head. "You've got a hundred questions, an' I ain't in the mood for 'em right now, little brother. I need some coffee an' some food. That's what you can do. . . ."

He pulled open a desk drawer, dug around in it, then handed Brian some money. "Go to Grace's an' get me an' Skeeter some food," he said, jerking a thumb over his shoulder at the man locked in the cell. The man was just waking up. His bed was torn up, and Brian wanted to ask Matthew about that, too. But he reckoned Matthew was about sick of his questions.

"All right," Brian agreed. He couldn't help himself, he had to ask just one more thing: "You're gonna untie him soon, really? He looks sad. He ain't gonna hurt nothin', Matthew. I like goats."

Matthew groaned, frustrated. "I'll untie him soon, I promise. Now go on, Brian."

Brian went.

But outside he stopped and had another look at the goat. The big eyes stared up at him again, begging him. Jack Archer had had a goat once. He'd called him Chester, and Brian had played with the goat a lot. Then a storm had washed Chester down into the creek, and Brian and Jack dug a hole and buried him the next morning.

Brian petted the goat on the side of the face. The goat didn't flinch, wasn't at all scared of him.

"I bet you're stiff," Brian said, eyeing the rope wrapped around the goat's legs. "Sounds like he's had you tied up for a while. You can't even move your legs. I'll call you Chester if you don't mind, Chester the Second. Kinda like Preston Lodge the Third, only you can't be the third 'cause there's only been one Chester so far. So you'll have to be the Second.''

Brian knew he shouldn't—he figured Matthew would get spitting mad at him—but he untied the knot in the rope. Then he unwound the rope, freeing Chester's legs. He left the rope around the goat's neck because it tied him to a nearby post. He didn't want Chester to run off, something he'd probably do, since he was surely scared of Matthew now. If *he* was Chester and somebody had tied him up like that, he'd want to run from them as soon as he got loose.

Chester was wobbly at first, trying to get to his feet. Once he had all four hooves on the ground, he shook his head, like he was trying to clear it. Brian petted the goat again, on the side of its face and down its neck. Chester was no trouble—Matthew didn't know what he was talking about.

Brian shot a look around the corner of the jail to make sure Matthew wasn't standing there watching him. Then he dashed off to get breakfast for Matthew and his prisoner.

When he returned with two plates of food, Matthew was hot around the ears.

''Why'd you untie that goat?'' he demanded as soon as Brian walked into his office.

Brian didn't care that Matthew was mad. He figured he'd done a good thing. '' 'Cause he needed to be untied. He ain't gonna hurt nothin', Matthew.''

''Yes, he will. I've got bruises all over to prove he will. He might've hurt you. That stupid goat's dangerous.''

''Chester the Second ain't stupid an' he ain't dangerous!''

''How do you—? *Who*?''

Brian put the plates on Matthew's desk. ''Chester the Second. Jack Archer had the first Chester.''

Matthew shook his head real quick, like he was clearing

something from it. He narrowed his eyes. "You know that goat? You know who he belongs to?"

Brian shrank back. "No. I named him Chester the Second 'cause there can't be a third when there's only been one so far."

Matthew studied him, his eyes still squinted. "You got along with him that good when you went out there?"

Brian nodded. "He let me pet him."

"He didn't try to butt you?"

"No."

"Sheriff, long as we got that goat, we might oughtta keep this brother o' yer's around," Skeeter said.

"That's the first sensible thing I've heard you say," Matthew told his prisoner. "Brian, I ain't had no luck dealin' with that animal, an' nobody's claimed him. I'll *pay* you to feed him once a day until somebody does. I don't wanna get near him again."

Brian already had a job at Hank's hotel. But feeding Chester the Second every day wouldn't take long. He'd even pet him for a while—somebody needed to. Even animals needed to be loved.

"Right now I want you to do somethin' else for me," Matthew said. "Run over to the mercantile an' ask Loren if he's got any clothes that'll fit me until I can go home an' get more. I was wrestling with that goat last night an' . . . well, just go ask Loren, would ya?"

"Sure," Brian said, and he ran off to take care of the second errand.

Dorothy was too busy writing articles to keep Katie for Michaela the next morning. Michaela always opened the clinic on Saturdays, especially since she began acquiring so many patients.

Dorothy said she certainly would keep Katie if an emergency arose. Meanwhile, Michaela should sit and visit for a while and have a cup of tea. . . . This was the first time Dorothy and Michaela had seen one another this week, other than in passing. So Michaela and Katie stayed and visited.

Dorothy had been engrossed in writing an article about the goat Matthew was holding in jail. Michaela had been at home all day yesterday, so she had heard nothing about the goat. Dorothy told her what she knew: how Loren had chased the goat, how the goat had chased him, how they had ended up in the sheriff's office, how Matthew had locked up the animal and later asked if anyone knew whom it belonged to.

It was quite funny, the thought of a goat chasing Loren and then of Matthew holding the goat in jail for plundering Loren's vegetables. But Loren and Matthew probably weren't laughing—this wasn't the first time this week that Loren had had to chase an animal away from his vegetables. And it certainly wasn't the first time this week that Matthew had dealt with a problem involving animals.

"Has anyone spoken with Jake about holding a town meeting?" Michaela asked Dorothy.

"Why, not that I know of."

"I think I will today."

Dorothy laughed, a little nervously. "If you can get in the barbershop. I've never seen so many people needin' haircuts an' shaves!"

She had a point.

"I'll have to get in," Michaela said. "We haven't had a meeting in more than a month. It's time to have one."

Dorothy sighed, looking doubtful. "Gettin' people t'gether for a meetin' . . . now, that'll take some doin'. Nobody's hardly even seen Jake for sev'ral weeks, he's been so busy. The rev'rend, well, I reckon he could get free. But Robert E.—Oh, did you hear about Robert E. an' Horace's velocipede?''

Michaela nodded. ''Yes, from Grace.''

''Oh, no—a bad one to hear it from. She's pretty mad at Robert E.''

''I think she's calmed down now. She's still irritated with him. But now she sees a little humor in his crash,'' Michaela said. ''Unless something more happened yesterday to irritate her further.''

''I don't think so. It was funny, Michaela,'' Dorothy said, shaking her head, grinning. ''I was sittin' at a café table, like most ever'body, when Robert E. came flyin' down the hill. He was laughin' an' hollerin'. He was havin' himself a fine time.''

Dorothy giggled, remembering, as Michaela leaned forward slightly, Katie on her lap, trying to imagine Robert E. flying down the hillside on a velocipede. He was normally so quiet, and he kept to himself most of the time, both at home and at his shop.

''He won't hardly talk about his ride an' the crash. I tried to interview him yesterd'y.''

''If everyone is angry with him, you can't blame him for not wanting to talk about it,'' Michaela remarked.

''I know,'' Dorothy said. ''An' I'm gonna hold off printin' anythin' about the accident 'til Grace an' Horace calm down. Or at least until Robert E. has a chance to fix that henhouse an' the velocipede.''

Michaela thought that was a good idea.

''Robert E. doesn't like ever'body bein' mad at him, but just before I left the blacksmith shop, he laughed an' said, well, he *had* had a good time flyin' down that hill.''

"Until he ran into the henhouse," Michaela said, laughing.

"Right," Dorothy said. "I couldn't believe he didn't hurt himself."

Michaela rose with Katie in her arms. She had to open the clinic, especially since she hadn't opened it at all yesterday.

Dorothy followed her downstairs.

"Oh, the rev'rend told me there'd be a little something out at the cemetery this afternoon for Henry Hughes," she said as they passed the printing press. "One o'clock, I believe. That was an awful thing, that fire. I rode out to have a look at the barn. There ain't nothin' left."

"It was nearly gone by the time Sully and I arrived," Michaela said. "Brian worries about Benjamin."

Dorothy opened the front door for Michaela and Katie. "Poor boy. We all have our times with grief. I just wish it didn't come to young people. I wish it waited 'til they were grown."

Michaela wasn't sure that anyone grieved easily, no matter their age. She stepped out onto the porch, and turned back to Dorothy. "I'll see you at the cemetery this afternoon?"

Dorothy nodded. She hugged Michaela, saying she wanted to see her more often like this—over a cup of tea, maybe—but she understood that Michaela was busy.

"Not too busy for a cup of tea and conversation every now and then," Michaela said.

She set Katie on the wagon seat while she climbed up.

Once they were settled, Katie nestled down between her legs, Michaela drove to Robert E.'s shop and livery.

She left the wagon and horses with Robert E. for the day, as she always did unless Sully needed the wagon. She

141

handed Katie to Robert E. and was climbing down herself when she spotted what must be Horace's velocipede parked beside the stable. Only the front wheel was missing. And, of course, Michaela knew why. The image of Robert E. flying down the hill leading to Grace's café, laughing and having such a wonderful time, must have been a sight. Just imagining it, Michaela had to fight a smile.

She had seen a velocipede before; someone had had one in Colorado Springs when the traveling circus came a few years ago, if she recalled correctly. Brian and Sully had tried to ride it. People had laughed at the odd-looking contraption. And then the circus had gone, taking the velocipede with it. Now there were more people in town, people who obviously had never seen a velocipede, which explained their amazement.

One of her sisters—Claudette?—had mentioned in a letter a few months ago that velocipedes were becoming the rage in Boston. Some people were dangerous on them—particularly on the two-wheeled ones that required good balance and skill. Without the proper instruction and practice, accidents happened. Claudette had written that several schools advertising velocipede lessons had opened around the city, and that there was talk of requiring velocipede riders to take the lessons. Not a bad idea for Colorado Springs if velocipedes caught on here.

Michaela kept all of that to herself for now, choosing not to say anything to Robert E. about velocipedes. At least not until he fixed Horace's, and certainly not until Horace and Grace were a little happier with Robert E.

Patients were waiting at the clinic when Michaela arrived with Katie on her hip. Mr. Sloan and Mr. Eisenbein were waiting, along with Mrs. Harrow, who occasionally had trouble with asthma. She and Mrs. Perryman sat on the porch bench, talking. They didn't seem to mind when Michaela announced that she would see Mr. Sloan and Mr. Eisenbein first, since she had had to turn them away the other day.

Michaela apologized to the gentlemen for not opening the clinic yesterday. But they had heard about the fire at the Hugheses' place, and Mr. Eisenbein shook his head at her. "None of that," he scolded. "How can you doctor during the day after you've doctored all night? A person must sleep."

She wished all of her patients would be so understanding.

Inside the clinic she placed Katie inside the wooden play fence that Sully had built last year. It was wonderful, very useful, containing the busy Katie while Michaela tended to patients. Katie loved the play area. As soon as Michaela put her on her feet inside the fence, Katie toddled to her box of toys, an assortment of rag dolls that Dorothy and Grace had stitched for her, and small solid wheels and blocks that Sully and Robert E. had carved and sanded down for her. The toys would occupy Katie for quite some time. They always did.

Michaela examined all four patients who had been waiting when she opened the clinic. Katie began throwing her blocks out of the pen, trying to get her mother's attention, and between patients Michaela spent a few minutes talking to Katie, trying to interest her in different things. Doing that enabled her to see even more patients before Katie began fussing.

Michaela managed to treat Mrs. Rice for gout and stitch Mrs. Reeves's thumb. She had heard that a bookstore would be opening in town soon, and she was delighted to meet Cora Reeves. Mrs. Reeves had fallen while trying to reach a high shelf, and had sliced her thumb on a nail that protruded from her ladder.

When Michaela emerged from the clinic with Mrs. Reeves, Irene Garratt and Reverend Johnson were waiting. Mrs. Reeves was grateful for the stitches, and she offered to entertain Katie on the porch while Michaela saw Mrs. Garratt and Reverend Johnson.

After seeing the reverend, Michaela was forced to take a break and tend to the baby. She played with Katie for a few minutes, then put her back in the play area and gave her half of a hard biscuit. It, too, would occupy her for a while.

By noon, Katie was fussy. She had been as patient as she intended to be, and actually had been extremely patient for a toddler.

Michaela went outside to post a note on the clinic door that she would reopen at two o'clock. Normally she would reopen at one o'clock, but the cemetery service for Henry Hughes was at one o'clock.

Hank was waiting on the clinic porch, a surprise since he rarely came to see her—he had been known to stitch himself up after a saloon fight. Doubtless he wouldn't like it that she couldn't see him right now.

"I have to close for two hours," she explained. "I have to feed Katie, and there's a cemetery service for Henry Hughes at one o'clock. Is this an emergency?"

"Nope. Fact is, I ain't needin' medicine or nothin'. Brian's probably goin' to that service, huh? That's a bad deal for Ben, losin' his pa."

"I'm sure Brian will be there, yes." Why was he waiting on the clinic porch if he didn't need medical attention? Surely not simply to talk to her. She and Hank had absolutely nothing in common, and they never just had a conversation. There was always a reason.

"What can I do for you?" Michaela asked.

"Mrs. Reeves . . . I saw her over here earlier."

"Yes . . . ?"

"Did she mention me?"

Michaela didn't understand why he was asking her about Mrs. Reeves. "No. I examined her, I treated her, and she watched Katie while I saw several other patients. A very nice woman. A bookstore will be a wonderful addition to Colorado Springs."

"So . . . you didn't say anything 'bout me runnin' a saloon a few months back?"

"Why would I?"

He shrugged. "Just thought she might've asked questions about people 'round town."

"She didn't."

He nodded slowly. "That's good. Do me a favor? If she ever does ask anything about me, don't tell her I ran a saloon."

Before he had hired Brian and Benjamin, Michaela had not thought much of Hank Claggerty. But he had been kind and generous toward the boys, and she didn't mind doing him this favor, although she wondered at his reason.

"All right," she said.

He straightened his vest, brushing off dust and smoothing wrinkles. Was Hank Claggerty trying to become respectable?

He leaned toward her a little, and he spoke in low tones. "I'm tryin' to clean things up a bit."

He already had, as far as she was concerned, by opening the Gold Nugget and closing his saloon. During the past few months he still hadn't been the most pleasant person. But at least he was trying.

He must be sweet on Cora Reeves, Michaela thought as he thanked her and stepped off the walkway.

She posted her note on the door, smiling to herself despite the fact that Katie was now crying inside the clinic, demanding her attention. Miracles did happen—especially if Hank Claggerty had decided to "clean things up a bit."

She took Katie to the back room of the clinic, where they ate cold ham and bread.

With food in her stomach, Katie seemed to feel better. She was playful again, jabbering syllables at Michaela—some intelligible, some not. She was playing with sounds, learning to put them together. Michaela had seen many babies develop, and the jabbering was part of speech development.

"Come along," she told Katie after she had washed her face and hands. "We're going to see Jake—and my, will he be glad to see us!"

Of course, she was being sarcastic about Jake being glad to see them. He was never glad to see her, or didn't seem to be. She forced Jake to take his civic duties seriously. She knew, too, that he thought women should be seen and not heard. If he had things his way, she would be parked in a house day and night, cooking and changing Katie. She wouldn't have a clinic, and she certainly wouldn't have a seat on the town council.

Michaela held Katie's hand and let the baby walk through the clinic and out the front door. Then she stooped down and lifted Katie into her arms. "Too many wagons and horses for you," she told Katie. "Too many people who don't look where they're going. Too many people who are in a rush."

A minute later, she and Katie approached Jake's barbershop.

The line was not so bad today. Only four men were waiting for haircuts or shaves. Michaela excused herself past them and entered the barbershop.

A man was tilted back in the barber's chair, and Jake was shaving his jaw.

"Good afternoon," Michaela said, announcing her entrance.

Jake glanced up, his eyes narrowing when he saw her. Whenever she entered his shop, she always drew an apprehensive look from him.

"What d'you want?" he asked, not bothering to greet her. He went back to shaving. "I'm busy here."

"I see that. We're all busy lately. Mayor Slicker, I'm sure you've noticed the increase in the town population and traffic. . . ."

"I've noticed."

"A wagon hit Mary Tennessey a few days ago. Her arm is broken, and she required stitches on her forehead. Fortunately, her baby was not injured. But either one of them could have been seriously hurt—or killed. I've seen other near accidents, too. And loose animals are causing problems for Mr. Bray and other merchants."

"Dr. Mike, don't you have a line outside your clinic?" Jake asked irritably. "Don't you have patients to look after?" He was trying to get rid of her.

"Not at present," she said. "We need to have a town meeting to discuss the problems caused by the sudden growth of Colorado Springs."

Jake glared at her. "Nobody's got any time for a meetin'."

"I'm certain the council members will find time."

"Well, *I* ain't got time."

She fixed a determined look on him. This was exactly the reaction she had anticipated. "Then perhaps you should resign as mayor. The townspeople need a leader who cares."

"I care—I just ain't got time for a meetin'! An' you're holdin' things up here," Jake said, waving the razor he held toward his waiting customers.

"Then I'll call the meeting and issues will be discussed and voted on without you. We'll also discuss asking for your resignation."

He took a deep breath and blew it out, a heave of exasperation.

She was bullying him. But sometimes that was the only way to deal with Jake. He was resentful of the fact that she had become such a strong leader in the community. He knew that people listened to her, that she was respected and admired by many. He knew that he couldn't ignore her, not if he wanted to retain the office of mayor.

"All right, Dr. Mike. Call a meeting an' tell me when it is. I'll be there."

"Thank you."

Michaela fought a smile of satisfaction, not wanting to grate on Jake's nerves anymore. She had accomplished what she came here to do.

"How are you feeling, Mr. Ackerman?" she asked. She had just recognized the gentleman in the barber's chair. Nearly a month ago, she had excised a bunion from Jedediah Ackerman's right great toe. He hadn't returned to the clinic, so she had assumed he was doing well.

He raised his hand to lower Jake's razor slightly. "Gettin' 'round real good, Dr. Mike," he said in a muffled voice. He was tipped back in the chair, and he had to look down over his chest and stomach at her.

"I'm delighted to hear that."

Jake was glaring at her again. She really was holding up his business now.

"It's nice to see you," she said to Mr. Ackerman.

"Nice to see you, too, Dr. Mike."

" 'Bye now," Jake said.

She forced herself to smile at him. He didn't like her, and she didn't always care for him. But they somehow managed to be civil to each other most of the time.

She eased Katie a little further up onto her hip and left the barbershop. Katie rubbed her eyes, yawning.

As they crossed the street, Katie laid her head on Michaela's shoulder. It was time for the baby's nap. Michaela would put her in the perambulator she kept in a back room of the clinic. Katie would fall asleep in it during the walk to the cemetery.

Halfway to the cemetery, Michaela met Dorothy. Katie was already asleep. She had curled up on her blanket and laid her head on the little pillow Michaela had made for her.

"I'll print your clinic hours in the *Gazette*," Dorothy offered.

"That would be wonderful. The hours are working out well, so far."

Dorothy took over pushing the perambulator. "The oddest thing happened this mornin'. I interviewed the woman who's openin' that bookstore. Well, it didn't start out as an interview, but it turned into one. I went to her shop to have a look around—a bookstore in Colorado Springs is excitin'. Then I thought I oughtta do an article about our newest citizen who's bringin' such a fine thing to our town."

She pushed the perambulator around a hole in the road. "I interviewed her an' was on my way back to the *Gazette* office when Hank stopped me."

"Let me guess," Michaela said. "He wanted to know if you told Mrs. Reeves that he used to run a saloon."

Dorothy's brows went up. "How'd you know that?"

"Because he asked me the same thing shortly after *I* saw Mrs. Reeves at the clinic. I opened the door to post a note saying I would return at two o'clock, and there was Hank." Michaela smiled. "I think he's taken a fancy to our newest citizen."

"But he can't *hide* somethin' like that. Somebody'll spill it sooner or later."

"True. But apparently Hank thinks he *can* hide it from Mrs. Reeves. He's made some improvements in his life— closing that saloon, for one—and he wants to make more."

Dorothy looked utterly amazed. "He told you that?"

Michaela nodded. "Not in those words, but that's what he meant."

"That's wonderful. But Michaela, if a person judges you by your past. . . . That ain't right."

"I'm not saying it is. And after meeting Mrs. Reeves, I'm not sure she would do that. But Hank apparently fears that she might."

They entered the cemetery. People were already gathered around an open grave. Michaela saw Brian with a group of his friends—all of whom were probably Ben's friends, too. Eleanor Hughes wore black, and a veil shadowed her face. And there was Ben, close to his mother's side.

"I wonder if Hank's gone all over town tellin' people not to say anything to Mrs. Reeves," Dorothy said.

"If he came to us, he probably went to others, too."

"That's what I'm thinkin'."

They reached the gathering. Brian approached and said hello to Dorothy and hugged Michaela. Then he rejoined his friends, at least five of them, who were solemn and quiet. Horace stood near a tree, almost in his own world, as Michaela and Dorothy joined Grace and Robert E.

Just as the reverend began urging everyone closer, Sully arrived. He whispered to Michaela that he had stopped at Robert E.'s shop this morning and that Robert E. had told him about the cemetery service this afternoon.

Loren had arrived, too, which didn't surprise Michaela; Loren had been fond of Henry Hughes. Henry and Loren had shared many conversations over coffee at the mercantile. Michaela wondered if the mercantile was closed or if Loren had someone minding it for him.

Reverend Johnson opened the service with a prayer. He delivered a short message about loving and cherishing friends and family members because you didn't know when they would be taken away. Although Henry's passing saddened his loved ones, Henry had gone on to a better place, the reverend said.

Eleanor Hughes wept openly, although Benjamin didn't shed a tear during the service. But his bloodshot, swollen eyes told Michaela that he had cried for many hours before.

After the reverend's words and the final prayer, people began expressing their sympathy to Eleanor. Benjamin joined his group of friends for a few minutes, shaking each one's hand like a young gentleman.

A handshake wasn't enough for Brian, however. He hesitated, then pulled Benjamin into a hug. Benjamin didn't seem to mind—he appeared to relish leaning his head on Brian's shoulder for a minute. In fact, Brian was the first to pull away.

"Ain't that somethin' how those boys all came out here on their own?" Dorothy remarked to Michaela.

Michaela nodded. Very touching. Watching Brian hug Benjamin made her feel extremely proud.

12

Yesterday morning Brian had found out that Mr. Hughes's service was this afternoon. He'd thought about telling Hank that Saturday afternoon might not be a good time to teach him and his friends how to play foot ball because everybody would feel gloomy after the cemetery service. But the more Brian thought about that, about everybody feeling gloomy afterward, the more he figured they'd need something to cheer them up.

So he never went to Hank and canceled. Instead, he'd arranged for all the friends to meet at the cemetery. After the service, they'd go to the school yard and wait for Hank. Everybody had thought Brian was right about needing something to cheer them up after the service for Mr. Hughes.

Jack Archer had brought a bag of marbles, and while the

group waited, they played "follow on" on the path leading to the school.

They each chose a marble, and Jack shot his first. The boys watched the marble roll out and stop. Then Brian shot his marble and let out a whoop when it rolled past Jack's. Paul Steerforth was next, and his marble knocked Jack's clear out of the way, but it didn't pass Brian's, and that was good news for Brian. Rick Humphrey's marble did, though.

Brian said, "Aw!" and sat down on the grass to watch the other boys roll their marbles down the path.

Andy Blythe's marble didn't go too far, not even close to Jack's. Charlie Hall's hit Paul's and Brian's, and went another foot. Gary Hamilton won the round when his marble rolled on by everybody's.

The boys fetched their marbles and started over. Paul won the second round, Jack won the third, and Brian won the fourth.

"S'pose he's comin'?" Paul asked Brian, squinting toward the main part of town. He squinted like that in the classroom, whenever he had to look at something a little ways off. Brian thought maybe Paul was having trouble seeing things. Seeing him do it today, he made up his mind to talk to Ma, ask her if there might be something wrong with Paul's eyes.

Brian was sure Hank was coming. Hank was pretty civil anymore, and Brian had reminded him on Thursday that he'd said he'd meet him and his friends to teach them to play foot ball.

"He'll be here," Brian said. "Maybe he got tied up at the hotel."

"Well, somebody better cut 'im loose then, or he'll never git here," Jack said, and he fell over on the grass, laughing at his joke. Brian and the others laughed, too, although Brian didn't laugh as hard as everybody else.

"Don't s'pose he's already been here, do ya?" asked Gary, making marks in the ground with a stick.

"Nope," Brian responded. "He said two o'clock."

"Ben looked like he'd been cryin' a lot," Rick said.

Everybody agreed, nodding and mumbling things.

Brian said, "I know how I felt when my real ma died. Pretty awful."

Andy frowned. "Yep, Ben's feelin' bad, an' he will for a while." Andy's brother had died last year from an infection in his throat. Brian remembered because Dr. Mike had tended Willy Blythe, and she'd cried off and on for nearly a week after he was buried. Nobody—none of the friends gathered here right now, anyway, had seen Andy for a good three weeks after that. He'd holed up with his ma, who'd had a *real* bad time dealing with losing Willy.

"Reckon we oughtta give Ben a week, then go out an' see him?" Gary asked.

"Shoot, maybe two weeks," Andy advised.

Jack pulled his knees up to his chest and settled his forearms on his knees.

Beside him, Charlie got up. "C'mon," he said to anybody who was listening, "let's go catch frogs and grasshoppers."

"Yeah," Brian said. "We can feed 'em to the fish in the stream. We can see the school from down there. We'll see Hank when he comes."

So that's what they did. Brian, Jack, and Charlie raced down to the stream, while Paul, Rick, Andy, and Gary walked. Jack won the race, but Brian caught the first grasshopper. He tossed it into the water and the boys watched a fish dart to the surface and nab it.

They had a contest to see who could catch the most grasshoppers. Andy won, catching twenty-three. The fish in the stream had a good afternoon snack while the boys waited for Hank.

They were getting tired of waiting, Brian could tell. Rick and Andy kept looking back at the schoolhouse. Gary said he'd told his ma he'd be home in about three hours, and he figured he had maybe an hour to go now. Jack didn't have anything in particular to do, so he was all right. But Charlie and Paul . . . they had plans to go fishing with Charlie's pa, and after a few more grasshoppers, they headed back toward town.

Gary plopped down on the bank and waited a little longer, then he apologized to Brian and shuffled off, his shoulders sagging with disappointment. Brian didn't blame him—he was mighty disappointed himself. Rick mumbled that he'd better get going, and then he did just that, and Brian didn't blame him either.

Brian sat on the bank, plucking grass and tossing it in the water. "You two should go on, too. Hank ain't comin'," he told Andy and Jack.

"I'm real sorry, Brian," Andy said. "It ain't your fault."

Three more blades of grass hit the water. "I know. But you might as well go on."

"I'll see you at school Monday. Maybe at service tomorrow." Andy was talking about the church service—tomorrow was Sunday. And he'd said "maybe" because his family didn't come into town and attend service every Sunday. They lived some three miles out. Andy had walked all the way into town to meet Brian and their friends this afternoon—he'd walked three miles just so he could go to Mr. Hughes's service and then learn to play football. *Three miles* on foot, and Hank hadn't shown up.

"Nope, I'm the one who's sorry," Brian told Andy. He felt really bad about Andy walking all that way for nothing.

"I had fun playin' marbles an' catchin' grasshoppers," Andy said, trying to make Brian feel better.

Brian forced a smile for Andy. "Me, too. If you wanna wait around town another hour or two, I'll ask Dr. Mike to take you home in the wagon."

"I might do that. Right now I'm goin' to the mercantile to get some candy." Andy reached down and grinned as he jingled the change in his pocket. A minute later, he went off toward town.

Jack lived in town, so Brian didn't feel bad about him coming out here to wait for nothing. They caught more grasshoppers, tossed them into the water, and watched the fish get them.

Directly they caught a bullfrog and watched it swell up, making a bubble under its mouth. Colleen hated the sight of bullfrogs. Once Brian had caught one and put it in her bed. He knew when she found it, 'cause she'd screamed to raise the roof—and he'd laughed until he thought he wet his britches. Brian told Jack about putting the frog in Colleen's bed, and they had a good laugh.

"C'mon," Brian said, getting serious again. "I'm gonna go see Hank."

"Maybe you oughtta wait," Jack suggested. "You're kinda hot right now." He meant that Brian was in a temper.

"Not really. I can't get too hot—it was nice of him to wanna teach us. But I wanna go tell him that he forgot."

Wanting to do that probably wasn't too nice of him. But when Brian thought again of Andy walking all the way into town, thinking he'd be learning to play foot ball this afternoon, and then getting disappointed, he felt irritated all over again.

So he and Jack walked to town. They could see the buildings from the bank of the stream, so they didn't have far to walk.

"Say," Jack said as they shuffled along, "did you hear about Robert E. an' that three-wheeled thing?"

Brian laughed. "The way he smacked into Mrs. Everly's henhouse?"

"Yeah! My ma was down at the café when it happened. Saw the whole thing! Said Mrs. Everly's ole tom about had Robert E. for dinner."

"Wish I could've seen that!"

"Mrs. Everly went after him, too! Ma said the thing Robert E. was ridin'—"

"It's a velocipede," Brian said. "I rode one once when a circus came to town."

"Whatever it is. It b'longs to Horace. Ma said Horace was mad at Robert E. for breakin' it."

Brian picked up a stick and threw it, just to see how far he could. "I bet Robert E.'s hidin'!"

"*I'd* be hidin' if ever'body was mad at me," Jack said.

They reached the buildings of town, and they beat a path for the Gold Nugget

"Hello, Mr. Miller," Brian said as they entered the lobby. Henry Miller stood behind the counter, his head bent down as he scanned something on the desk.

Then he glanced up. "Oh, hello, young Mister Owens. How are you this fine afternoon?"

Jack smirked. Brian elbowed him, trying to make him be quiet. He liked Mr. Miller, and didn't want Jack to make fun of the man. Henry Miller was tall and thin, mostly arms and legs, like Horace. He could look real serious and stern when he wanted to, but he usually had a smile for Brian. He was from back East somewhere, and he'd been raised a lot like Dr. Mike had been raised—to have a lot of manners and respect for people, and to talk just right.

"I'm good," Brian told Mr. Miller. "Is Hank around?"

Mr. Miller had a nervous habit of twisting his left earlobe, something he commenced to do now. Jack turned around to hide his smirk, and Brian shot a scowl at his friend.

"I'm afraid not," said Mr. Miller. "He went off for the afternoon with his lady friend."

"His lady friend?"

"Yes. From across the street. You know, Mrs. Reeves, who plans to open a bookstore soon. Mr. Claggerty met her Wednesday afternoon while she was painting the inside of her shop. They're picnicking this afternoon."

Mr. Miller was full of information, more than Brian wanted to know. Hank had forgotten about him and had gone off to picnic with Mrs. Reeves. Brian had met Mrs. Reeves yesterday afternoon when he'd helped Hank move some things into her shop. He liked her. But Hank had promised to spend the afternoon with him and his friends, teaching them to play foot ball. He wasn't supposed to be picnicking with Mrs. Reeves.

"Thanks, Mr. Miller," Brian said, turning away from the desk.

"Should I tell Mr. Claggerty you called on him?"

"No, thanks."

Brian trudged toward the front door, Jack joining him along the way.

"Ain't that just a fine thing," Jack whispered, sounding put out. "Got himself a lady friend an' forgot all about us!"

Brian wondered if Hank had forgotten, if he had decided to leave him and his friends waiting at the school yard while he picnicked with Mrs. Reeves. If Hank had gotten busy at the hotel, with a bunch of customers or something, well, that would have been different—Brian's feelings might not have been so hurt.

"Are you all right, Mister Cooper?" Henry Miller asked.

Brian turned back and made himself smile at Mr. Miller. He didn't want Mr. Miller to worry about him. "I'm fine," he assured the man. Then Jack opened the hotel door, and he and Brian stepped outside.

"I wouldn't be so nice about things if I was you," Jack told Brian. "I'da left Hank a message all right—that I wanted to meet him out back of the hotel." Jack danced around beside Brian, balling up his fists and punching at the air. He thought Brian ought to box with Hank.

Brian shrugged. He didn't like scrapes the way Jack did. Jack was always getting into them, then having to sit on the school steps during recess. Sure, Brian ought to meet Hank behind the hotel for a boxing match. Jack wasn't thinking about the fact that Hank was three times as big as Brian. Or about the fact that Brian didn't like to fight.

"I ain't gonna bother with it," Brian said, irritated at Jack now. He walked faster, leaving Jack a little behind.

"Hey!" Jack called. "I ain't the one that forgot about you, that went off with a girl instead."

Jack said the last like going off with a girl was a disgusting thing. And that irritated Brian even more than Jack's remark about how he'd have left a message for Hank to meet him out back of the hotel.

"Girls ain't bad," Brian said. "I'm goin' to the *Gazette* office to see if Miss Dorothy needs any help."

Jack grunted. He never understood why Brian liked to write articles for the newspaper, and why he liked to help Miss Dorothy print the *Gazette*. Jack liked to shoot marbles, catch grasshoppers and frogs, and fight—and when all that was done, Jack was done.

"Reckon I'll see you tomorrow morning at church," Jack said.

"I reckon so."

Jack scooted past Brian, heading for the mercantile. He probably had a little change in his pocket, like Andy, and now that he'd run out of things to do, he meant to spend it. If Brian hung around the mercantile, he'd probably see Jack get booted out by Mr. Bray in less than ten minutes. Jack liked to fiddle with the things on Mr. Bray's shelves, anything and everything, and Mr. Bray ran out of patience real quick with Jack Archer.

But Brian had made other plans. As he'd told Jack, he meant to go see if Miss Dorothy needed any help. Helping her might take his mind off of Hank going picnicking with Mrs. Reeves instead of meeting him and his friends at the school yard.

"Over there," Hank told Cora as he pointed to a spot in the trickling stream. "That's where Jake an' I found a pretty good-sized nugget."

Cora wrinkled her brow, her blue eyes glittering in the afternoon sunlight. Yessiree, she was the best-looking woman he'd seen in a long time. He'd thought that to himself yesterday morning, when he had moved some bookcases into Cora's shop, and then this morning, when he glanced through the Gold Nugget's front window and spotted Cora heading down the street. She'd worn a dress that fit tight from the waist up, and a hat all done up with feathers perched on her head. She'd looked mighty sharp, better than anything else on Main Street.

"Jake?" Cora said, looking confused. "Nugget?"

"Jake's the barber," Hank explained. "A friend, sometimes. Nugget . . . I mean gold. A gold nugget."

Her eyes sparkled more. "The gold you found in this stream?"

"Yep. About a year ago now."

"Did you look for more? Isn't there usually more in an area?"

"Usually. But streams around these parts are about panned out—most of the gold's been found. A person might find some real small nuggets, if he has years to put into lookin' for it. Prospectin's hard work."

She smiled at him. "Well, you and Jake must have worked very hard to find such a . . . a 'good-sized nugget.' "

"Mighty hard," he said, beaming at her. He liked impressing her.

They walked alongside the stream for a time, not saying a word to one another, just listening to the water trickle and the birds chirp. He sure was glad Michaela hadn't told Cora that he'd been a saloon keeper. That might've ruined everything. A respectable woman like Cora Reeves might not want anything to do with him if she found out something like that. And that'd be a damn shame. He liked her an awful lot.

Cora had packed a meal, and just past noon they'd headed out of town. Hank had led the horses and wagon, to a place not far from here, back down the stream. He'd helped Cora spread out a quilt, then he'd brought her wicker basket from the wagon. She'd unpacked it, laying out sliced beef and fresh bread, pickled cucumbers, and two helpings of cherry cobbler. They talked while eating, between bites. She told him about the traveling she'd done with her husband, helping him peddle his watches in different cities. Finally he'd settled down into his mail-order business, which right away did well.

Cora tilted her head back, thrusting her chin out. "This is what I've wanted. Peace . . . tranquillity. It's so quiet here. The water, the birds . . . the mountains." She looked at the snow-topped peaks, shaking her head in amazement. "Denver is in the mountains, but it's not so quiet there. It's becoming a crowded city. Even on the outskirts—wagons are always cluttering the roads going in and out of Denver."

"Colorado Springs is a lot busier than it used to be," Hank said.

"It's much better than Denver. Where are the hot springs?"

"A few miles from here."

She smiled again, and Hank felt his heart lurch. "We'll go see them another afternoon."

Another afternoon. . . . That meant she'd had a good time today and that she wanted to see him again soon.

"I've heard about them," she said, color rising in her cheeks. She stepped onto a stone, then onto another. She wobbled a little, enough that Hank reached out and grabbed her arm to steady her.

"They're a sight," he said. "Better be careful—those stones get slick."

He'd just finished warning her when her boots slipped off the side of the rock. She yelped as she slid. But Hank was there again, this time with both hands to steady her as she came down not two inches in front of him.

He had hold of the backs of her elbows. As she stared up at him, he couldn't get his senses together enough even to think about letting go of her.

Color flushed her face, starting at her nose and spreading

163

out. She was looking down, acting too embarrassed to look up at him. This was as close as they'd been since they'd met. She smelled sweeter than the air, and the air was pretty damn sweet up here in the mountains. But it was nothing compared to Mrs. Cora Reeves.

"How silly of me," she mumbled. "I didn't mean to—"

"Thought I'd give you a hand," Hank said, and he realized he was mumbling, too. "Didn't want you landin' . . . y'know . . . landin' on . . . on. . . ."

"My derriere?" She looked up as she finished the sentence for him, and smiled despite her embarrassment.

A grin spread across his mouth. "That's it."

"I'm most grateful."

She was *most grateful?* Damn if that wasn't a ladylike thing to say! He liked it, and that surprised him. A year ago, when he and Jake had found that nugget, he wouldn't have liked her ladylike ways. He would've thought she was uppity, the way he thought Dr. Mike still was sometimes. But he'd decided he wanted to clean his life up a bit, and because of that decision Cora Reeve's ladylike words appealed to him.

His mouth had gone dry. He nodded at her, acknowledging the gratefulness.

"Best be careful," he cautioned, releasing her elbows. "You could land in the stream if you fell."

Smiling, she tipped her head at him. "Would you fish me out?" She didn't move away. She stood right where he'd left her, just an inch or so separating them.

"Sure would."

She moved three steps to the left, away from him and the stream. She was still smiling, a smile that would make even the toughest man weak in the knees.

"Let's have another picnic again in a few days, an' I'll

show you the hot springs,'' he suggested, hoping his voice didn't sound too wobbly.

She nodded. ''All right.''

She turned away, began walking again. ''For now, I want to see more of this stream. Look, it twists around up there!''

Hank trailed her. Whatever she wanted . . . wherever she went, he'd follow.

13

By late that afternoon, Robert E. was far behind on his blacksmith work. He'd carved and whittled and sanded for two days, and finally he'd made a wheel almost exactly like the one he'd broken on Horace's velocipede.

He fitted the wheel on and pushed the pedals on. Then he stepped back to have a look at his handiwork.

He was proud of what he'd done. Now maybe Horace and Grace wouldn't be mad at him anymore.

He sure would like to ride the contraption down that hill again. But Grace had a sharp tongue when she was irritated, and he didn't especially want to irritate her today, not when he was just getting things right again. He'd fixed Mrs. Everly's henhouse yesterday evening. And today, the velocipede wheel.

He wouldn't ride the velocipede down the hill again anyway, even if Grace weren't still irritated at him. Horace had said he couldn't ride the thing again, and he didn't blame Horace much for that. He reckoned he might've reacted the same way if it had been his velocipede.

As soon as possible, he wanted Horace to know that he'd fixed the contraption. So Robert E. hitched a team of horses to a wagon and loaded the velocipede into the back of the wagon.

He led the horses through town, pulling them very slowly through all the traffic. He passed the clinic, and then the mercantile, and just beyond Loren's store he started down the hill that had gotten him into so much trouble the other day. Actually, the trouble hadn't started until he'd forgotten to turn with the curve in the road, something he never forgot to do in a wagon. Of course, a wagon wasn't nearly as much fun as a velocipede.

He drew nigh to Mrs. Everly's place, and Lord, if that tom turkey didn't look up from pecking at the ground to glare at him. Even after Robert E. passed Mrs. Everly's place, he felt the tom staring at him, wanting to peck a hole in his back, maybe somewhere else in his body. He half expected the turkey to come gobbling after him. If the tom did, he planned to give the reins a good hard shake, kicking up the pace of the horses. That was a mean turkey, and Robert E. didn't want to fuss with him anymore. He sure wouldn't let the thing attack him from behind, Grace or no Grace steaming at the bottom of the hill.

She was waiting tables when he approached. She looked up, raised her brows, and studied him as if she thought he was up to something else. She spotted the velocipede in the back of the wagon, and she nodded at him. Just a quick nod, but at least it was some kind of indication that she might not be mad at him forever. Since he'd fixed Mrs.

Everly's henhouse, Grace's irritation with him had calmed a little. Now he needed to take it from a low simmer down to cool.

Not far beyond the café he reined the horses and jumped down from the wagon seat. He unloaded the velocipede from the wagon bed and pushed it toward the telegraph office.

A man was coming out of the office. He stopped to hold the door open for Robert E., who thanked him. That would've been a trick, holding the door open while getting the velocipede inside. He didn't really think it was made to fit through doorways. He turned it several ways, then gave up and pulled it out.

Horace was stooped down behind the counter, rearranging packages whose owners he couldn't locate. His line of vision was blocked by the wall that separated the customer area from the package area. He heard Robert E.'s voice and straightened, catching his head on the corner of the countertop.

He winced, rubbing the sore spot, as he caught sight of Robert E. trying to fit the velocipede through the telegraph office's front door.

Horace's legs twitched. The velocipede was fixed. It looked good as new. He hoped it worked good as new.

"Just—just leave it outside," he told Robert E.

Robert E. heeded Horace's advice. Horace lifted part of the countertop and scuttled toward the doorway. He needed to have a closer look at the velocipede, at the front wheel— just to make sure everything was in order.

"I'm sure sorry 'bout that Horace," Robert E. said as Horace inspected his handiwork.

"You oughtta be," Horace said. He was still sore at Robert E. Not nearly as sore as he'd been the other day, when he'd rushed out of the telegraph office and caught up with Robert E. on that hill, but still pretty sore.

"Well, I am," Robert E. snapped. "I made ya a new wheel. Ain't that enough?"

Horace glanced up. Robert E. didn't want him to be mad anymore. But he'd have to see about that. "I'll have to see how it rides," Horace said.

Robert E. splayed out his hands. "Here it is. Ride it."

Horace straightened up quickly, huffing. "I don't wanna ride it right now. I'm tending the telegraph right now."

"Where's your boy?"

"He ain't here yet."

"It's gettin' on in the day. Shouldn't he be here real soon?"

Horace nodded. "Pretty soon. 'Bout an hour."

"Well, I ain't got an hour to stand around an' wait to make sure this thing works all right."

Horace squinted, not against the afternoon sun beating down on them, but at Robert E., trying to figure him out, why he thought he needed to wait around at all.

"You just wanna see me ride it," Horace said finally, grabbing hold of the velocipede's handlebars. "Not me— just anybody. You like it so much, get your own. I ordered it out of the *Denver Post*. I waited weeks for it, an' nobody's gonna take it over."

Robert E. scrunched his face at Horace, looking at him like he was crazy. "I ain't tryin' to take it over."

"Yes, you are."

Horace had his nose in the air now. He pushed the velocipede toward the front window of the telegraph office. He'd park it right here so he could see it from the counter. And he'd keep a good eye on it, too. No more hunching behind the wall that separated the two areas today. He had to watch over his velocipede.

"Get your own," Horace said again as he parked the velocipede. He turned and glared at Robert E.

Robert E. glared back. "I ain't never seen nobody be so partic'lar 'bout somethin'."

"I got my reasons."

Robert E. grunted. "I reckon."

He turned around and shuffled off, wanting to throttle Horace. He really didn't want to take the velocipede over. He just wanted to see how it rode, what with the new wheel and all. Horace could've ridden it around the depot once or twice. But no . . . just because he—Robert E.—wanted to see how it rode, Horace decided to be bullheaded. Horace was still mad about him breaking that wheel. He'd fixed it, but that didn't seem to count with Horace. Horace was still steaming.

Robert E. climbed onto his wagon and turned the horses back toward town. He had wagon axles and brake handles and more horseshoes to pound on back at his shop. And he reckoned that's what he'd go do—pound on those things real hard. Irritated as he was at Horace, he figured he'd get some work caught up mighty fast.

Back at the telegraph office, Horace went inside just as the telegraph began clicking. He hurried behind the low wall to tend the machine, and he wrote down the clicks and pauses as they came. He'd decipher them after the message finished. It was for Preston, from someone at the St. Louis Bank. Preston was a busy person. He sometimes received ten or twelve telegrams a week from people in different places.

Hans came, right on time, as always. Horace told him he planned to go ride the velocipede, and that he wouldn't be gone long. He'd started arranging the packages behind the wall in alphabetical order, and Hans could finish that if he wanted to. There never was a whole lot for the boy to do in the afternoons but sit and mind the telegraph. Mostly he sat at the desk and read. Horace didn't mind that—he figured reading was good for the mind.

Outside, Horace settled himself on the velocipede saddle for the first time. His legs were pretty long, and the saddle sat kind of low, which meant Horace was scrunched up. He'd have to remember to ask Robert E. if there was any way to raise the saddle.

Thinking of Robert E. suddenly reminded Horace that Robert E. hadn't said anything about how much he owed for having him put the velocipede together. He had to pay him something. Even as angry as he was with Robert E., he didn't expect his services for nothing.

Despite feeling scrunched up, with his knees not too far from his chest, Horace rode out a ways on the velocipede. He rode down toward Grace's café, where Grace eyeballed him like he might run into something the way Robert E. had. She shouldn't worry. He had no plans to fly down any hills and have his velocipede damaged again. He turned and rode back to the telegraph office.

The thing was fun to ride, and he hadn't had enough of riding it yet. He needed to practice riding it if he planned to deliver mail and packages and telegrams on the thing— which he did.

So Horace climbed back onto the velocipede, scrunched himself again, and pedaled toward the café again.

Grace and her girls were wiping down tables and chairs as he approached. Horace took his time, pedaling slowly, taking in the sights. Pedaling the velocipede was fun, but it took work. He didn't want to go too fast and tire himself out.

As he passed by the café area, he smelled something good—fried chicken and maybe cherry cobbler. Grace glanced up and waved at him, not looking scared that he might run into her tables. A few people sat having coffee. They paused to stare. The cook stared, too, from her post in front of the stove as she used a fork to turn something in a skillet.

Horace pedaled down the road that led out of town. Soon the café tables were a distance behind him. The velocipede tires grated over the wooden bridge that crossed the stream, the same stream that crooked around and cradled Colorado Springs in a half-circle.

The wind flapped Horace's ears and his collar, and suddenly he realized why Robert E. was so interested in the velocipede: it was fun to ride. A person could get some exercise, riding this thing every day. The velocipede rattled and squeaked, but only a little; it probably needed grease in places. He'd have to remember to ask Robert E. about greasing it.

The road curved and ambled, and Horace followed it. The few trees around town, kept up mostly to shade buildings and picnickers who didn't want to venture too far, gave way to thicker growth.

Soon the forest flanked Horace on both sides. And still he pedaled. He'd worked up some perspiration on his forehead. But he didn't care. He had his velocipede, it was all together in one piece, the front wheel was fixed, and now he was riding the thing, the way he'd wanted to do days ago.

A squirrel ran in front of him. Horace swerved, just missing the animal. He didn't have horses to rein, and he was going fast enough that if he put his boots down to the ground to slow the velocipede, friction might burn his soles. Suddenly he wondered how he was supposed to slow the velocipede. Luckily, he wasn't going downhill.

Horace ceased pedaling and let the velocipede coast to a stop. Then he threw his right leg over to the left side of the saddle and got down to have a look at the frame to see if there was a brake somewhere.

At first he was looking for a handle, like the one on a wagon. Even if there was one, he couldn't just pull it while he was pedaling along very fast. He'd go tumbling, pell-mell, and the velocipede might tumble with him. And no telling what he might tumble into. If he was in town, he'd have to wonder *who* he might tumble into.

There wasn't a brake handle.

Horace fiddled with the pedals, turning them back and forth, trying to see if maybe some kind of brake was rigged up to the pedals or to the front wheel. Turning the pedals either way just turned the front wheel either way, causing the velocipede to go forward and backward.

As far as he could tell, the velocipede didn't have a brake.

Wasn't that a fine thing! He'd have to be careful and not get to going too fast.

Of course, he might be missing something. He wasn't real smart about things like wagons and velocipedes. He hadn't even been able to put the velocipede together, just as he hadn't done too good a job of changing that wagon wheel a few years back. He'd have to ask Robert E. one more thing—if the velocipede had a brake. Maybe it didn't. Maybe that's why Robert E. had smacked into that hen-house.

Horace got back on the saddle and rode further. He was

careful to pedal slowly, not wanting to go too fast now that he realized the velocipede might not have a brake. He rode past the Sloans' place, then the Perkins' place.

By and by he began seeing fresh tree stumps. He saw more and more, and then he came upon a clearing. And there was Sully, perched atop an unfinished house, hammering.

"Hello, Sully," Horace called, having himself a good time.

Sully stopped hammering and peered down from the roof.

"Hello!" Horace called again, waving this time.

Sully put a hand to his brow, shielding his eyes from the sun. "Horace? Is somethin' wrong in town?"

"Nope." Horace was still pedaling, drawing closer to the unfinished house with each circle of his legs and feet.

"You got a telegram for somebody out here?"

"Nope." Horace grinned. His legs were tired. He'd have to turn back soon. He didn't know how far he'd gone—maybe two or three miles.

"What are you doin' out here?" Sully asked. Another man poked his head up through some rafters. Another newcomer to Colorado Springs.

"Ridin' my velocipede," Horace said as he stopped pedaling. This was as good a place as any to turn around. The velocipede slowed almost immediately. Horace put his boot down on the ground and stopped it.

Sully laughed. "I see what you're ridin'. I heard Robert E. crashed that thing into Mrs. Everly's henhouse."

Horace scowled. "Who'd you hear that from?"

"Dorothy. Yesterday."

"He did, but he fixed it," Horace said, scooting with the

174

velocipede as he turned it around. "How far do ya reckon I am from town?"

"A good five miles," Sully's companion said. "Name's Robert Blake."

Horace tipped his head at the man. "Good to know you. An' I'm a good one for *you* t'know. I'm Horace. I operate the telegraph. I get the mail from the trains an' coaches, too. Five miles? You really think we're that far out?"

Robert Blake laughed. "Guess you *are* a good one to know. Yep, you're five miles outside of town."

That information wrinkled Horace's brow. He felt tuckered out. But he couldn't afford to be. He was five miles from town, and he didn't have a horse to help get him there. He had to pedal the velocipede every one of those five miles.

He'd been pedaling along, enjoying the ride and the scenery, not thinking once about the fact that he had to pedal back. That however far he went, he had to retrace that distance when he turned the velocipede around.

"I went further than I should have," Horace mumbled to himself.

"What's that?" Mr. Blake asked.

Horace propped himself up on the velocipede saddle again. This time, when he settled his rear on the saddle, it smarted.

He winced. He might've bounced over one too many rocks on the ride out here.

"Nothin'," he called. "Reckon I'd better head back to town."

"Ain't that tirin', pedalin' that thing all this way?" Sully asked.

"You could hitch a horse up front," Robert Blake said. "Get yourself back to town that way."

They could tell he was tired. He must look it. They were teasing him now, and Horace didn't like that too much. He'd pedaled the velocipede out from town, and he could pedal it back.

"Nope," Horace said, and he started off, waving at Sully and Mr. Blake.

The velocipede bumped over rocks that wouldn't have bothered Horace an hour ago. Now he winced with pain every time his rear bounced up and down on the saddle. He wished he had more of a pad for his bottom.

He pedaled and heaved, and pedaled some more. He stopped and rested, sitting in the grass on the side of his hip, his rear was so sore.

After ten or fifteen minutes, he was back at it, pedaling and heaving, thinking town surely wasn't so far away now. But the road went on and on, and after a time he wasn't just wincing with each bump, he was yelping with pain.

He rested again. Then he pedaled again. Then rested again. Then pedaled again.

He'd never been so glad to see the buildings of Colorado Springs. When he passed the café this time, he was in sorry shape. His thighs ached, his rear ached, his head ached. He felt dizzy, and he'd never needed a drink of water so badly.

"Horace, you all right?" Grace asked, rushing to him. "You don't look good. You're face is red, an'—"

"Water," Horace said between quick breaths. He'd stopped pedaling and the velocipede had slowed. He wondered if he had the strength to throw his leg over the saddle and get off the velocipede. He was getting more and more dizzy, and now he saw spots, black spots, and his stomach felt sick.

"Just . . . need . . . drink . . . water."

Grace wasn't far from him now, maybe two or three

steps. "Horace, you look terrible. Come on over here an'—"

Horace didn't hear the rest of what she said. The black spots took over, widening out, and Horace keeled over. He passed out, his head coming to rest on a soft patch of grass.

At the clinic Michaela was disinfecting instruments and gathering dirty linen. Someone pounded on the door and called to her. The voice was female, and whoever it belonged to was in a panic. Which meant there must be an emergency somewhere.

Michaela unbolted the door and pulled it open.

There stood one of the girls Grace had hired several months ago to help at the café. The girl's complexion was light to begin with, but she appeared so frightened, her skin looked as pale as fresh snow. Her eyes were wide and wild.

Michaela couldn't remember the girl's name.

"What is it?" she asked, taking the girl by the shoulders. "Calm down so you can tell me." The girl was breathing so hard, Michaela wondered if she would be able to speak more.

"The telegraph man," the girl managed. She swallowed. "He fall . . . off . . . riding thing."

The girl had to mean Horace. Riding thing. . . . She must mean Horace's velocipede. Now *Horace* had had an accident on the velocipede? No wonder Boston required that people who wanted to ride velocipedes must attend a velocipede school first. Two accidents involving the same velocipede. . . . They couldn't be a coincidence.

"Stay here with the baby," Michaela told the girl. Katie stood with her arms over the fence, clapping two blocks together, entertaining herself. Michaela didn't know Grace's girl well, couldn't even recall her name. But someone had to stay with Katie; she couldn't run to the telegraph office with Katie on her hip.

The girl nodded, agreeing to stay with Katie. She looked about nineteen. Michaela hoped she had watched over a baby at least once in her life.

Michaela grabbed her medical bag and raced out of the clinic. She hurried across the street, carefully weaving her way between the many wagons and horses. A little way farther, she started down the hill. In the distance she saw Grace's café, with a small crowd congregated a few feet from an outside table. Horace's velocipede was lying on its side. Then she saw Horace lying on the ground. She lifted her skirts and ran down the hill.

By the time she reached the small gathering, Horace was conscious and trying to speak.

"He came ridin' along on that thing," Grace told Michaela. "Looked like he'd just climbed out of a grave! Tried to get off an' passed clean out."

"He didn't crash?" Michaela had to know if there was a possibility of broken bones.

"Nope. He was gettin' off an' he just passed out."

"He rode in from out yonder," someone said, pointing to the road leading out of town.

Michaela knelt beside Horace and visually examined him. His lips and skin were dry, and when he opened his mouth, trying to tell her something, she saw that his tongue and mouth were dry, too. She pressed her fingers to the side of his throat and discovered, not surprisingly, that his pulse was racing.

"He needs water," she told Grace, who hurried off.

"Rode . . . far," Horace rasped.

Michaela twisted her lips. "Mmm. Too far, I'd say.

You're dehydrated. Grace is bringing water. You'll feel better soon.''

Grace returned with a pitcher of water. She dipped a pewter cup into it and handed the cup to Michaela.

Michaela put her hand behind Horace's neck and held his head up so he could drink. He tried to gulp, but she wouldn't let him. She pulled the cup back. ''Slow, a few sips at a time. If you drink too much at once, you'll cramp and vomit.''

He sipped. They waited a few minutes, then he sipped again.

Three more times of doing that and Horace began to look better. Color returned to his face, and his pulse began to slow to a more normal rate.

The curious people who had gathered around him dispersed. Grace stayed, concern still written on her face.

Horace drank more, and kept the water down. Then he sat up and Michaela gave him a full cup. He drank the water as if he hadn't had a drink in weeks.

His eyes were wide when he looked at her, as wide as she had ever seen them—and in the past she had seen Horace angry, frightened, apprehensive. . . . Horace's eyes always widened when he experienced emotions. But they had never grown as large as they were now.

''I pedaled the velocipede all the way out to where Sully's helpin' build that new house,'' he said, grimacing and shifting from his back to his side.

''Horace!'' She was shocked. ''Horace, the Blakes' homestead is—''

''Five miles from town.'' He nodded. ''I know. I didn't realize how far I'd gone 'til Sully told me. Then I realized I'd have to pedal all the way back.''

"Take a canteen the next time you do such a thing," Michaela cautioned.

"That thing makes you an' Robert E. make bad decisions," Grace told Horace as she eyed the velocipede.

Horace pouted. "It was fun ridin' 'til I started back to town."

"You could have been more seriously ill," Michaela said. "Dehydration can kill a person."

Horace dropped his head into his hands. "I've got a terrible headache!"

"Another symptom, I'm afraid. You need to go home and rest. And you should continue to drink water."

"Thanks, Dr. Mike," he said, getting up slowly.

"Is Hans minding the telegraph this afternoon?"

Horace nodded, another slow move.

"I'll tell him you won't be able to return today."

"He can go on home," Horace said, creeping toward his velocipede. He looked like a crippled old man trying to get around.

Michaela looked at Grace, who shook her head as she watched him go.

"Horace, wait," Michaela said. "Please sit down. I'll go tell Hans. Then I'll come back and help you get home."

He didn't argue. He was too worn out to argue. He sat in a chair at one of Grace's tables. But as soon as he sat, his face twisted with pain and he bounced back up. He shifted and came down on his hip, and a look of relief smoothed his expression.

"Are you hurt, Horace?" Michaela asked, unable to help the question.

"Nope," he said quickly. "Just tuckered out."

She watched him for a minute, not sure that she believed him. Then she turned away, intent on going to the telegraph office and talking to Hans.

14

Brian stayed in town with Dorothy that night to help her finish her articles for the *Gazette*. Their common interest in writing had made them close, and Michaela thought the closeness was sweet. With everything that had occurred in and around town this past week, Michaela certainly understood why Dorothy needed help with her articles; she had a lot to write about. She also had trouble with arthritis sometimes, and needed Brian to help her operate the printing press.

Michaela arrived home before Sully. She was giving Katie her last bite of food when she heard a horse whinny outside. A few minutes later the front door opened and Sully walked in.

He greeted her with a smile and then a kiss. He had one hand behind his back. Seconds later, his arm came around, and he put the finished sign for the clinic in front of her.

It was perfect, with her new clinic hours burned carefully and precisely into the wood.

"Thank you!" she said excitedly, kissing him.

Sully laughed.

"Is this why you're late?" she asked, giving him a reproving look.

"What if it is?"

"It wasn't that important. You've had so little sleep lately."

"I recall sleepin' good last night," he said, suddenly looking sheepish. "Fallin' asleep with Katie on my lap."

Michaela laughed. "Seeing the two of you like that was priceless."

He bent and kissed Katie on the head. Then he wriggled her out of her high chair without removing the tray. Katie giggled, and smeared mashed carrots on his stubble.

"Where's Brian?" Sully held Katie above his head and shook her a little, making her giggle more.

"You'll have carrots from her stomach on you if you persist," Michaela warned. "Brian is staying in town with Dorothy tonight to help with the *Gazette*. He'll go to school from there tomorrow morning."

Sully played with Katie more, tickling her. He loved to hear her giggle.

"Remember Horace's velocipede?" he asked Michaela presently.

She nodded, guessing at what he was about to tell her.

"He rode to the Blakes' homestead on it this afternoon. Me 'n' Robert had a good laugh, watchin' Horace on that thing."

"I know all about Horace's afternoon excursion on his velocipede." Michaela went on to tell Sully about Horace's dehydrating himself during the ride and his collapse at Grace's café.

"Me 'n' Robert would've given Horace a ride back into town," Sully said. "He looked tired. We offered, but he wanted to ride the velocipede back."

"I don't imagine he'll ride it again for at least a few days."

"Why's that? Because he made himself sick on it?"

"Well, that. . . ." Michaela couldn't help a smile, and she bit back a laugh. She really shouldn't laugh at Horace. Dehydration could be a serious thing—life-threatening, in fact. "And I think his backside may be rather sore. When I saw him, he couldn't seem to rest his weight on it without wincing."

Sully grinned.

They ate supper and played with Katie some more. Later, Michaela dressed Katie for bed and Sully took the baby to rock her to sleep.

"I won't rock myself to sleep tonight, too," he told Michaela with a sparkle in his eye.

Michaela grinned. She knew what that sparkle meant. Brian was gone, Katie would fall asleep soon, and neither she nor Sully was exhausted tonight. As soon as Katie went to sleep, they would run to their bedroom. And, she hoped, a medical emergency wouldn't interrupt them tonight.

Michaela did the dishes and readied herself for bed while Sully rocked Katie.

When he was sure she was asleep, Sully put Katie down in her bed. Then he cleaned up over the washbasin in his and Michaela's bedroom while she lay on the bed and read the medical journal she had received today.

Soon he joined her there, peeking over the journal at her. He had splashed on the cologne water he kept for special occasions, meaning he *definitely* had plans for them tonight.

Michaela smiled—he was so obvious. She was nearing the end of a paragraph, so she held up her hand, indicating that she wanted him to wait, and read on.

He didn't make it easy for her. He kissed the fingertips of the hand she held up, then slid his tongue down her thumb, between her thumb and forefinger. He turned her hand over, and his mouth grazed her palm, his warm breath making her heart beat faster. He kissed her palm, then his mouth moved to her wrist, an incredibly sensitive spot—a fact he knew very well.

Michaela drew a quick breath, stumbling over the words she was trying to read. "I'm almost . . . finished," she said, her voice catching. "Sully!"

He grinned.

His tongue flicked over her wrist, and she gasped. She was done. She couldn't *possibly* finish the paragraph. Not right now, anyway.

He pushed the journal aside and slid his arm underneath her, pulling her close to him. He nipped at her jaw, becoming even more ardent, and Michaela tipped her head back.

"That wasn't fair," she whispered.

"Are you poutin'?" he teased, his voice low and deep, heavy with desire.

"Perhaps."

"Yes." His lips skimmed their way down to her neck, another intensely sensitive place.

Michaela slid her arms around his shoulders, enjoying his caresses. He definitely had snared her attention.

His fingertips danced up her arm, over her shoulder, to an even more sensitive place.

She arched her back, pressing herself against his hand. "All right, yes," she gasped.

He untied her shift, and his hands slipped beneath the material. A second later, Michaela gasped again.

She lifted his head, and her mouth found his.

He began moving against her, still caressing, kissing her, deeply, passionately, igniting fires.

Michaela was beyond rational thought. She followed the needs of her body, returning his caresses and kisses.

Over breakfast the next morning, Sully mentioned that Amanda Blake was interested in keeping Katie during Michaela's clinic hours. Michaela was glad to hear that. Sully seemed to trust Mrs. Blake, who had kept Katie the day Michaela stayed home. She certainly trusted Sully's judgment. Still, she wanted to meet Amanda Blake.

During church service, Michaela couldn't keep her mind where it was supposed to be. She looked at Reverend Johnson as he delivered the message, but heard little of the sermon. She recalled her and Sully's lovemaking last night, the tenderness of his kisses and touches.

She blushed and shifted around on the pew. She felt Sully glance at her, probably wondering what was wrong. But she didn't look at him. If she had, she would have blushed more. Then he would have wondered more. And she didn't want to discuss why she couldn't concentrate on the sermon. Church was a most inappropriate place for such a subject.

She managed to distract herself when she caught sight of Horace from the corner of her eye. He was seated one pew ahead of them and to their right. Now and then he shifted from his right hip to his left hip, never sitting exactly on his buttocks. Michaela felt sorry for him, but considering the nature of his soreness, how he had come by it, she had to stifle a giggle. Horace needed a saddle with thicker padding if he planned to ride his velocipede very often and very far.

After the service, Michaela and Brian walked around town, posting announcements of the town meeting to be held tomorrow night at the church. Sully, meanwhile, occupied Katie by walking with her in the churchyard.

Brian was quiet and seemed preoccupied. As he tacked an announcement on the post in front of the sheriff's office, Michaela asked if he had had fun with his friends yesterday afternoon. Brian had shown up at the clinic before closing time to ask if he could stay in town with Dorothy, and he had said nothing about whether or not he had had a good time with his friends and with Hank, learning to play football.

"Hank didn't show up," Brian said, a sour look on his face.

"Perhaps something came up at the hotel."

Brian's scowl deepened as he turned away, and Michaela smelled a conflict. She didn't know exactly what had happened yesterday, what had prevented Hank from showing up. But this seemed a bad time to ask Brian, so she didn't. Instead, she turned toward the mercantile, often the busiest place in town, where she intended to tack a notice on another post.

"I have to feed Matthew's goat," Brian said as she hammered. "I told him I would."

"Why do you have to feed the goat?"

"'Cause Matthew an' the goat don't get along. I'm the only one that can get along with Chester the Second."

"Chester the Second?"

"Yep. I named him that after I met him 'cause he looks like the goat Jack Archer used to have."

He told her how Jack's goat had been the first Chester,

186

so this goat was the second. He added that Matthew and the goat had had several tussling matches yesterday and the day before.

"Chester tried to tear up Matthew's office. So Matthew tied him up out back of the jail. Then Chester kept buttin' his head on the side of the jail so Matthew an' his prisoner couldn't sleep. Matthew tied him up like a calf ready for brandin'. That's how I found him."

"My goodness, a lot has happened with Matthew's goat!" Michaela remarked. Brian hadn't talked so much all day. The subject of the goat had made him perk up.

"So I untied him an' Matthew got mad. But then he realized how me 'n' Chester got along, an' he asked if I'd feed Chester every day. Wanna meet him?"

"Certainly. Who does Chester belong to?" Michaela asked as she and Brian walked to Matthew's office.

"Nobody's claimed him. He might end up just belongin' to Matthew."

"That wouldn't be good, considering that Chester and Matthew don't get along."

"I know," Brian said, as if he already had been considering that.

Chester didn't seem to be a disagreeable goat, or so Michaela thought when she met him. Matthew had brought dinner from the café. Seeing Matthew as he handed Brian a plate of food for the goat, Chester lowered his head as if he meant to charge Matthew. As soon as Matthew moved out of his sight, Chester was fine, raising his head and letting Michaela and Brian pet him. Brian fed Chester potatoes and carrots out of his hand. Meanwhile, Michaela walked away to talk to Matthew on the front porch.

"Seems you've inherited a goat," Michaela teased.

Matthew shook his head. He looked tired—shadows

hung under his eyes. "I'm never gonna get rid of that thing. Don't tell Brian, but I had to tie him up again last night— his legs together, you know, so he wouldn't butt the side of the jail. It was the only way me an' Skeeter could get any sleep. First thing this mornin' I untied him so Brian wouldn't know. Tonight's Dan's night to look after the jail an' Skeeter an' that goat, thank God. I'm goin' home to get rested."

Michaela tried not to smile, but she couldn't help herself. She apologized.

"I know, I know," Matthew said. "To everybody else, the situation here with that goat's funny. But it ain't to me. He's about to drive me crazy, an' that ain't even mentionin' how sore I am from wrestlin' with him."

Brian rounded the jail, his eyes bright. "He's all fed, Matthew. I'll come after school tomorrow."

"Thank you," Matthew said with such relief that Michaela almost laughed aloud.

Michaela and Brian returned to the churchyard, where they collected Sully and Katie, and started toward home.

Brian fell quiet again. When they were almost halfway home, he asked Sully if he could ride out to the Blakes' homestead after school tomorrow—and after he fed Chester—and help him and Robert Blake with the house.

"Chester?" Sully said. Then Brian explained Chester and Matthew's situation to *him*.

"Matthew had a goat in jail. . . ." Sully laughed. Then he cocked a brow at Brian. "Don't you have work at the Gold Nugget after school tomorrow?"

"I quit," Brian said.

Michaela and Sully exchanged stunned looks.

"Would you like to talk about *why*, Brian?" she asked. She knew he was angry with Hank for not showing up at the school yard yesterday afternoon. But certainly quitting at the Gold Nugget wouldn't help ease his anger with Hank. She recalled Hank calling at the clinic to ask her to not tell Mrs. Reeves about his former occupation. During that same conversation, they had talked about Brian attending Henry Hughes's funeral. Perhaps Hank had thought Brian wouldn't be in the mood afterward to learn to play anything.

"Perhaps Hank had a reason for not showing up at the school yard," Michaela said gently.

"Yep, he sure did—a lady friend," Brian said, staring to the side of the wagon.

Cora Reeves? Michaela wondered. She wanted to ask, but Sully shook his head at her. She agreed. Brian was angry at Hank today. In a few days, when he had had time to settle down, maybe he would be ready to listen.

Later, however, she told Sully that Hank hadn't shown up at the school yard yesterday. She and Sully were in the barn. He was repairing a harness. "And what was that about Hank and a lady friend?" Michaela asked, not really expecting Sully to have the answer; Brian's comment had baffled her, and she was trying to unravel it.

"I don't know," Sully said. "Hank's the one he needs to talk to."

"I agree. But he seems too angry to talk to him right now."

"He'll simmer down. Until then he can ride out after school, like he said, an' help with the Blakes' house."

"Hank deserves some sort of explanation," Michaela objected. "When Brian doesn't show up after school tomorrow, Hank will wonder where he is."

"He hasn't given Brian an explanation for why *he* didn't show up."

Michaela pondered that for a minute.

"That's what Brian is trying to do, isn't it?" she asked as the realization hit her. "He's trying to get back at Hank for forgetting about him. Sully, that's not right."

"Nope, it ain't. But you've gotta let Brian realize that, Michaela. He will, if you give him time—and the space to do it."

"You mean don't interfere?"

"I know you want to. But that's what I mean—don't interfere. Brian's got a good head on his shoulders. He'll realize it's wrong, what he's doin'—tryin' to get back at Hank. He's still mad right now."

Michaela wished she could talk sense into Brian. But maybe Sully was right. Brian eventually would realize that he shouldn't try to get back at Hank. The older Brian grew, the more she thought that Sully knew him better than she did.

Brian saved the scraps from their supper that night for Chester. Matthew had told him the owner probably hadn't claimed the goat because Chester was such a bother—or because the owner probably thought he or she would be in big trouble. But the owner wouldn't be, not really, not for Chester getting into Loren's vegetable bins. There was no ordinance against letting animals run loose in town, so all Matthew could do was advise the owner to keep the goat penned or tied. But Matthew might have some scalding words with the owner about all the trouble Chester had caused him.

"Do you suppose I can have Chester if nobody claims him?" Brian asked, glancing between Michaela and Sully.

Michaela had assumed the question was coming. She looked at Sully, who shrugged.

"He'd be your responsibility," he told Brian.

Brian smiled, as he had done every time the subject of that goat had come up today. In fact, he had smiled only when the goat was mentioned. Whenever something distressed one of her children, Michaela always felt tense. Brian's smile relieved some of the tension she had felt all day because she was worried about him. She would gladly help Brian take care of Chester if bringing the goat to the homestead would cheer Brian.

Horace's suggestion that Robert E. order himself a velocipede stuck in Robert E.'s mind. Like poison—because Grace sure wouldn't cotton to the idea, Robert E. thought all the next morning. No, sir, after he'd messed up the dinner business at her café, embarrassed her, and busted a hole in the side of Mrs. Everly's henhouse, Grace wouldn't like the idea at all of him ordering himself a velocipede. And then Horace had taken that crazy long ride to that new family's homestead and back, about killing himself. That evening Grace talked about nothing but how the contraption made people do some mighty foolish things.

Still, the urge to order a velocipede wouldn't go away. He'd had a lot of fun on the velocipede until he missed the curve in the road and ran into the henhouse.

He fixed a few wagons, then brushed down and fed the horses he kept in the stable. He shod Mr. Eisenbein's mare and fixed Tim Perkins's saddle. And while he worked and the day wore on, he thought more about what Horace had said about ordering himself a velocipede.

Why shouldn't he have fun now and then on something he'd enjoyed so much? If he rode the thing away from town, away from buildings and houses, what harm could he do?

He got tired of Grace's henpecking—sometimes it made

191

him do just what she didn't want him to do. He wanted one of those velocipedes. He was a hardworking man, and there was nothing wrong with him wanting to have fun. Riding a velocipede might not be Grace's idea of fun, but it sure was his.

Around three o'clock that afternoon, Robert E. went to the telegraph office, meaning to talk to Horace.

He didn't walk down the road that went by the café. No, sir—he went clear around it all, Mrs. Everly's place and Grace's tables. He cut probably a five-hundred-yard arch, glancing off in the distance every few minutes to make sure Grace hadn't spotted him. If he saw her look his way, he planned to hide behind the nearest tree.

At the Gold Nugget, Hank waited and waited for Brian to show up. He didn't expect Ben Hughes to make it to work for a while, just losing his pa and everything. But when four o'clock rolled around and Brian still hadn't shown up, Hank got worried and trotted over to the clinic.

Michaela had a new sign on the front door—seemed she'd decided to start new clinic hours. Hank didn't blame her, really. He'd seen the lines of patients outside the clinic every day, and he knew she hadn't been leaving for home 'til late most of the time.

He knocked on the door despite the new sign—and despite the one beside it that said *Closed*. Maybe Michaela was still inside.

She answered the door after the second knock. At first, she looked startled to see him. Her eyes flared a little. Then she seemed to gather her senses. "Hello, Hank. The clinic is closed."

Michaela usually wasn't so abrupt. She took Hank by surprise.

192

"I know," he said. "I ain't needin' medical advice. Brian didn't show up today. Just wanted you to know, in case somethin's wrong."

"That's Brian's business."

Hank thought it was a damn odd thing to say to him. He'd just told her that Brian hadn't shown up at the hotel, when Brian had shown up at the Gold Nugget pretty much every afternoon, Monday through Friday, for the last two months. She didn't think it was strange that he hadn't shown up today? She wasn't worried about Brian?

"I'm updating patient notes," Michaela told him. And then she said "Good day" and started to close the door.

Hank wouldn't have it. She knew something she wasn't telling him. He stuck his boot between the door and the frame, blocking her from shutting the door.

He narrowed his eyes at her. "What's goin' on, Michaela? Why're you actin' strange?"

She studied him, suddenly looking hostile. Michaela got fire in her eyes whenever she got her dander up about something. And her dander was up right now, that was for damn sure. Her eyes sparked at him.

"All right." She tilted her chin up and her head a little to one side, and Hank knew he was about to get blasted. He'd clashed with Michaela enough in the past to know when she was about to explode.

"Saturday afternoon," she said, "you promised to teach Brian and his friends to play foot ball. You told Brian to meet you in the school yard. You didn't show up."

Damn! He'd forgotten all about his promise to Brian. Not that he hadn't broken a promise or two in his life on purpose—he had. But he'd just out and out forgotten about this one. He and Cora had gone picnicking—while Brian and his friends waited at the school yard.

"He's tryin' to get back at me, ain't he?" Hank asked Michaela, pulling his boot back. "Tryin' to make me wait around."

She didn't say a word. Her head tilted maybe even more.

"All right, well, when he gets over bein' mad, you tell him he can come back to work."

"You tell him," Michaela said, and she shut the door in Hank's face. A second later, Hank heard the bolt slide across and lock into place.

Well, wasn't that just a fine thing! Hank scowled and kicked at the door but didn't hit it; he just went through the motion.

He didn't care. It wasn't like he *needed* Brian at the Gold Nugget. He could do the sweeping and the window washing himself. He could even get rid of the trash. Course, none of that would get done today, 'cause he was having supper with Mrs. Cora Reeves again this evening. He planned to spruce himself up and enjoy the pleasure of her company for another few hours.

Michaela stared at the door for a minute, her jaw hanging open slightly. *When he gets over being mad, tell him he can come back to work?*

Oh, really? No apology to Brian, no sensitivity to the fact that Brian was upset because Hank hadn't shown up at the school yard Saturday afternoon? No explanation that he thought Brian wouldn't want to learn to play anything after Henry Hughes's cemetery service? (*If* that was the reason Hank had not appeared at the school yard.) To think she had been prepared to defend Hank to Brian!

When she opened the door and saw Hank, she remembered Sully's advice about letting Brian take care of things between himself and Hank. Then Hank had put his foot between the door and the frame, and her temper had flared. It flared more when Hank acted like Brian didn't have a right to feel angry or, at the very least, disappointed.

She didn't know why she expected sensitivity from Hank. He had not displayed very much sensitivity in the time that she had known him.

She supposed that after he offered the boys the after-school jobs at the hotel, and then paid them so well, in the back of her mind she had begun to think that maybe Hank had changed. That his new occupation had improved his disposition toward people. That he had become more pleasant and agreeable, and yes, perhaps even sensitive. He had just shattered all those thoughts and hopes.

Shaking her head, she concentrated on finishing her patient notes. Katie was napping, and that was certainly a relief. Michaela could always get more done while Katie was asleep.

Once Michaela finished the notes and put away the patient files, she gathered up Katie and left the clinic.

She walked to Robert E.'s shop, thinking she would take the horse and wagon and go meet Amanda Blake. Sully would still be at the Blakes' homestead, probably finishing up for the day. The thought of surprising him made Michaela smile.

At the blacksmith shop, Robert E. went into the stable to hitch Michaela's horse to her wagon while she waited outside with Katie.

Soon Robert E. appeared with the horse and wagon. He held Katie while Michaela climbed up and settled herself on the wagon seat. Then he handed Katie up to her.

"Say, Dr. Mike," he said, his brow wrinkling. "You know Grace mighty well."

Michaela began situating Katie on her lap. "Yes, I do."

"You mind if I ask ya somethin'?"

"Of course not."

"Well, see . . . I'm thinkin' 'bout"—he glanced all around, as if wanting to make sure no one else was listening—"' 'bout gettin' one of those things like Horace's got."

Michaela glanced up. "You mean a velocipede?"

"That's what I mean."

She recalled Grace telling her about Robert E.'s race down the hill on the velocipede, how he had interrupted her business and embarrassed her . . . how later Grace had laughed a little at the thought of Robert E. racing down the hill. At the time Grace had told Michaela about the afternoon's events, she had wanted Robert E. to think she was still angry with him, although she wasn't all that irritated anymore over his race down the hill. However, Horace's dehydration after his jaunt to the Blakes' homestead and back had alarmed Grace. She had commented that the velocipede made people do crazy things.

"Whaddaya suppose Grace'll think 'bout that?" Robert E. asked, his voice lower than normal.

"I don't think she'll mind—if you make her a few promises," Michaela said. "Such as a promise not to race down hillsides. And a promise to take a canteen with you if you plan to ride very far."

Robert E. nodded, glancing down at the ground, a pensive expression on his face.

"You should talk to her about it first," Michaela told him.

"I reckon. It's just . . . she got so *mad* that day I rode Horace's contraption, I thought she'd bust!"

Michaela smiled, sympathizing with him. She had seen Grace in a temper, and it wasn't pleasant. "Talk to her,

196

Robert E.," she advised. "She'll be more agreeable if you talk to her."

He gave her a sheepish smile. "Thanks, Dr. Mike."

Robert E. didn't tell Dr. Mike that he had *already* ordered a velocipede. This afternoon, he'd gone to see Horace, who was being friendlier now that his contraption was fixed, and he'd ordered himself one. It was too late to talk to Grace about whether or not he ought to order himself a velocipede.

He'd ordered it, and then he'd come back to his shop, and he'd fixed this and that.... And all the while the thought that Grace might explode at him when she found out that he'd ordered the thing grew and grew in his head. By the time Dr. Mike arrived to pick up her wagon, the worry had swelled to *fill* his head. He thought he deserved something that he knew he'd have fun with. But he was worried that Grace would pitch a fit when the thing came in.

Maybe he'd give her a week or two—Horace had said the velocipede might not come for about four weeks—then he'd bring up the subject. Maybe while they were having a quiet night at home. Maybe while they were all snuggled together in bed. Maybe right after they got up in the morning, when she was fresh and felt real good—Grace was usually in good spirits every morning.

He *had* to talk to her about the contraption sooner or later. He couldn't just put it together after it came and then show it to her. If he did that, she really *would* bust.

15

There was a good turnout at the town meeting. With a pound of his gavel on the podium, Jake quieted the room. Then he called the meeting to order.

The meeting had been called, first of all, to discuss what to do about the problem of animals running loose in town, he said. The animals hadn't been a problem before, but they were now.

"They sure are," Michaela heard Loren grumble from the pew behind her. "They're eatin' my vegetables. Every day, I chase 'em off. Chickens 'n' hogs 'n' goats. It's gettin' to where I don't wanna put anything in the bins."

Matthew stood up. "I have a goat nobody seems to wanna claim. He was eatin' the corn in Mr. Bray's bins."

"How's that prisoner holdin' up, Sheriff Cooper?" asked Hal Archer, chuckling.

More laughter went through the pews—everybody knew

Hal was referring to the goat—and Matthew's face reddened. Michaela felt sorry for him.

"All right!" Jake pounded the gavel on the podium again. "We've gotta talk about this problem."

"I'd rather talk about the problem of not bein' able to get a haircut in a decent amount of time," a man said. Michaela glanced back and saw Roy Humphrey on his feet.

Jake scowled. "Tell you what," he said, pointing the gavel at Mr. Humphrey. "You open another barbershop, an' that might take care of the problem. I cut an' snip an' shave as fast as I can."

"That's an idea," grumbled Mr. Humphrey.

"Sure is," Jake retorted.

"Gentlemen," Michaela said, standing. "The loose animals are definitely a problem. They hurt Mr. Bray's business by forcing him to guard his vegetable bins."

"Yeah, an' they're leavin' dung on my walkway," Hank said, as he entered the church.

"Should we ask people to pen or tie up their animals?" Reverend Johnson said.

"Askin' ain't gonna do it." Hank responded from a middle pew.

"What about fines?" Robert E. proposed. "I don't mind chasin' animals out o' the blacksmith yard. But if I was tryin' to sell vegetables like Mr. Bray, or run a hotel, I'd complain, too."

Murmurs of agreement rose around the sanctuary.

"Fines may be the only way to handle the problem," Sully remarked.

"All right," Jake said. "Everyone seems to agree about the fines. How much?"

People looked at each other, unsure of what to propose.

"A dollar for chickens an' two for hogs," Matthew said.

"An' five for goats," said Hal Archer. "Let's not forget goats."

People laughed, and Matthew reddened again. Hal was having a wonderful time teasing Matthew about that goat. Matthew glared at Hal, who was holding his stomach, laughing.

"Five for cows, too," Hank said.

Jake nodded at him. "Anyone object to the fines?"

A few people did, but most didn't. The council members voted on the fines and then on the proposed amounts, passing both.

"It's up to you to enforce the fines, Sheriff Cooper," Jake said.

Matthew nodded, squaring his shoulders. He had a job to do.

Hal guffawed. "That is, if he can find out who the critters belong to."

Matthew glanced at Jake. What was he supposed to do if nobody claimed the animals or if he didn't know who their owners were?

"If people fail to claim their animals, we could sell the animals and put the money in the town treasury," Preston proposed, always perking whenever he smelled a way to make money. In this case, the money would benefit the town. But Michaela imagined that was all right with Preston. He had a financial interest in Colorado Springs, and he loved the fact that the town was thriving.

Jake raised a brow, as if he also thought that was a good idea. "Anybody object?"

Nobody did, and that proposal was passed, too. Any loose animals would be taken into custody by the sheriff, and any unclaimed animals would be sold, the money going

200

into the town treasury. Which was, of course, accruing interest at Preston's bank.

Hank and Michaela brought up the subject of people riding horses and leading teams too fast through town. Hank didn't always adhere to rules and laws himself, but he wanted an ordinance against racing horses in town. Michaela wanted an ordinance not just against horse *racing* but against galloping any horse through town, alone or harnessed to a wagon, buggy, or coach. Congestion on the main streets certainly made them hazardous. But people getting in a hurry with reins in their hands made the streets even more hazardous.

In the end, everyone agreed that anyone caught galloping a horse through town would be fined five dollars, which seemed to be the maximum fine citizens were willing to institute. Michaela thought five dollars was enough to discourage anyone who thought about ignoring the ordinance.

All in all, the meeting went well. There were a few grumbles as people filed out of the church, but all in all, everyone seemed satisfied.

Hank spent two afternoons washing windows and sweeping floors, two afternoons he could have spent with Cora. He actually had to turn her down when *she* invited *him* to supper on Thursday evening. She'd rented a small house a few streets over, and she wanted to treat him because he'd been so friendly to her.

Having to turn her down annoyed him, and on Friday, Hank hired a Chinese boy who came in looking for work.

He knew by Saturday afternoon that the boy wouldn't work out. The Chinese always did good work and lots of it, at least that's what Hank had observed and heard. But not this boy. The floors were still dirty after he swept them, and the boy washed one window in the time it would have taken Brian to wash four.

Hank supposed he could give the extra chores to his maid, along with her regular cleaning of the guest rooms. But the way rooms emptied and filled up so fast, she needed to keep her attention on them. Sweeping the downstairs floors and washing the windows wasn't enough of a job to warrant hiring *another* maid. Still, the chores were enough to occupy a person for two or three hours.

He wasn't sure what to do. He'd never been any good at apologies, but he was starting to think that maybe, just maybe, he ought to apologize to Brian.

Deputy Dan Cox minded the jail on Monday night of that week, and Chad Barge minded it on Tuesday night. Both nights the deputies had to tie Chester up after he began butting the side of the jail.

Wednesday was Matthew's night again, and when he approached Chester with the rope, instead of lowering his head and acting like he meant to charge, Chester backed away. Matthew wondered if Chester was starting to learn how things were—that if he butted the side of the jail, Matthew would come with the rope and tie him up for the night.

Thursday night, Matthew decided to mind the jail again and try something different. When Chester butted the side of the building, Matthew went out with the rope, as usual. Chester backed off. Instead of tying him up, Matthew turned around and left, the rope still in his hand. A while later, Chester butted the wall again, and Matthew went out with the rope again. The same thing happened—Chester backed off, so Matthew backed off.

They repeated that probably six times that night, and it

was a long night. But Chester learned. If he butted the side of the jail, somebody would come with the rope. By about four o'clock the next morning, he'd given up butting the wall.

Chad stayed at the jail Friday night. When Matthew showed up to relieve him the next morning, Chad said he hadn't had a bit of trouble from Chester.

After the town meeting Monday night, Matthew and his deputies had started enforcing the new ordinances. So far this week, they'd picked up a cow, two hogs, and four chickens. And so far they'd been lucky—they'd known who the animals belonged to. The owners grumbled about paying the fines. But Matthew didn't care, and he didn't sympathize. It was simple—if they didn't want to pay more fines, they would pen or tie up their animals.

Matthew got two rowdy men for racing their wagons along Main Street at about ten o'clock on Wednesday night. Only liquor would make men do something like that, Matthew figured—and sure enough, the men reeked. So he locked them up, let the liquor run its course, and then told them about the monetary contribution they'd have to make to the citizens for racing their wagons.

Matthew didn't know either man—both were new to the area. When one got smart and said he didn't intend to contribute anything, Matthew told him he'd sit in that cell until he did. And that's what happened. The man sat in the cell for three days before he agreed to pay the fine.

Meanwhile, Matthew and his deputies fined five more people for galloping horses along Main Street. Everyone knew about the new ordinances—they'd been posted around town and Dorothy had printed them in the *Gazette*—so Matthew and the deputies took a no-tolerance stance. If you galloped your horse, you had to make a contribution.

People grumbled and whined, but in the end they paid the fines. The town treasury grew, and one afternoon Matthew found himself grinning and wondering what sort of civic improvements could be made with the fine money. Colorado Springs might soon be able to afford lampposts and might even have the funds to pave the streets.

Katie's first two days with Amanda Blake were days of adjustment. She fussed off and on most of the first day, especially if Amanda took her outside the tent and Katie saw Sully working on the house. Sully ate dinner with her both days, and that settled her down for a while. On the third day, she didn't cry when he left her with Amanda and she wasn't as fussy throughout the day.

Wednesday evening, the Blakes came to supper at the Sullys' home.

Michaela liked Amanda Blake. She decided that soon after meeting her, something that came as no surprise. She trusted Sully's judgment. She simply felt better meeting the person who was keeping her daughter.

The Blakes had three daughters—Erin, Suzanne, and Sarah—and Brian seemed to get along well with them. Michaela could tell by watching Sarah that the Blake's eldest daughter had taken a fancy to Brian. And apparently he wasn't indifferent to her. He blushed three shades of red every time she spoke to him.

After supper they played a game called The Post that Brian and the girls had learned at school. They gathered enough chairs for everyone, minus one, and placed them in two facing rows. Brian was the post clerk the first time around, so he had no chair. Everyone chose the name of a city, and Brian wrote down the names. He would call the names of two cities that the post was going between. The players with the names of those cities must try to change seats—with him trying to take a seat before one of the players sat down.

It was a fun game. During the fourth round, Sully and Brian ran into each other while trying to exchange seats, and everyone had a good laugh.

Horace developed a summer cold. On Friday morning, he woke up with a stuffy nose and head and not much energy. And today of all days. He had given his bruised bottom time to heal—all week—and today he planned to start trying to deliver mail and messages on his velocipede. But now this cold.

He delivered a package to Dr. Mike at the clinic and several to Loren at the mercantile, dodging buggies and wagons and horses and people a lot easier on the velocipede than in his buggy. But pedaling the velocipede was work, and it wasn't long before he felt exhausted.

He decided to use his horse and buggy to deliver the rest of the mail and any telegrams that came in. When a body didn't feel good, there was something to be said for the old-fashioned way of doing things.

His hair tonic arrived the next morning. That afternoon Horace left the telegraph office to Hans and went home, planning to apply some of the tonic.

He sniffed it, curious about what it smelled like. But he couldn't smell a thing, his nose was so plugged up. He poured his palm full of the tonic and rubbed the liquid all through his hair. After he'd combed his hair back into place, he washed his hands thoroughly. He wanted to grow new hair on his head, not on his hands.

The cold tuckered out Horace so much, he sure would like to lie down and take a nap. But he had telegrams to deliver. After that, before he shut things down for the day, he had to check back with Hans to see if any more telegrams had come in and if they were urgent.

He went first to the sheriff's office, where he found Matthew seated on the front porch, watching Main Street. It was a sunny afternoon, and Main Street seemed quieter today than it had in months. Hank remarked about that.

"The town treasury's been growin'," Matthew said, grinning. "People have had to contribute here an' there."

At first Horace didn't know what Matthew was talking about.

"You know, when their animals run loose, or when they decide to gallop down Main Street."

"Oh," Horace said. The new ordinances, the fines. Matthew had been enforcing them. That must be why things had quieted down on Main Street.

Horace stepped onto the porch and nearly stumbled over a sleeping animal. It was Matthew's goat, tied to a porch post, curled up and looking calm as it slept.

"For a second I thought that was a dog," Horace said, jerking his head toward the goat.

"He's behavin'." Matthew looked proud of himself. "Me 'n' Chester the Second, we've reached an understandin'. I won't tie him up like a calf ready for brandin' if he doesn't charge an' butt."

"Chester?"

"Yep. He's got a name now. Brian gave it to him."

Horace was amazed at how calm the goat looked. He knew how much trouble Matthew had had with the temperamental animal. Everybody all over town talked about Matthew and the goat.

Matthew tipped his hat back as Horace stepped onto the porch. He twitched his nose, like it itched. "Nope. Like I said, we've had a few understandin's.

"I saw you on that velocipede yesterday. That's pretty smart, usin' it to deliver things. You didn't have such a bad time gettin' through all the traffic."

"It's easier than gettin' around in a horse an' buggy. Lots of people are wantin' one since they've seen mine," Horace said proudly, pulling Matthew's telegram out of the bag he carried over his left shoulder. "I ain't felt so good the last few days, an' pedalin' it is work. So I ain't rode it much."

"Have you seen Dr. Mike?"

"Not today."

Matthew was still twitching his nose. "No, I mean about not feelin' good."

Horace handed the telegram to Matthew. "It's just a cold. I'll wait a day or two. I'll go see her after that if I don't feel no better."

Matthew looked at him funny, scrunching his nose up now, like a person did when he smelled something bad.

"You wanna. . . ." Horace didn't know why Matthew was looking at him that way. "You wanna read that before I go? You know, to see if you wanna send anything back."

"Oh." Matthew glanced down at the piece of paper and opened it. "Oh, sure." He read, then he looked at Horace. "Nothin' back. Marshal just wants to let me know somethin'."

When Horace nodded at him, Matthew caught another whiff of whatever it was he'd started smelling when Horace came onto the porch. It smelled like a dead animal, a rotten one. Horace went down the steps, heading for his horse and buggy, and the smell drifted away.

Matthew was tempted to tell Horace that he needed a bath. But that would be rude, so he kept his mouth shut. Somebody was bound to tell Horace sooner or later. Matthew couldn't believe Horace hadn't noticed the bad smell himself. But Horace had a cold, and that would explain why he hadn't caught a whiff of the odor.

Horace drove his buggy across the street and stopped in front of the mercantile. Inside, Reverend Timothy Johnson sat at the little table Loren kept for coffee and conversation, although Loren hadn't had much time for either lately. The reverend was eating cheese and crackers, and pondering his better-than-average senses. He'd never had a problem with them, but since he'd gone blind, his hearing and his sense of smell were better than they had ever been.

He'd told Dr. Mike about his improved senses, that he could be in his room above the mercantile, where he and Loren lived, and hear things downstairs that he would not have been able to hear months ago: a customer talking in a low voice; Loren moving things around and *where* he was moving things around—on the eastern shelves or the western shelves, under the counter, near the small table where Loren and friends gathered for coffee now and then.

As for Timothy's sense of smell . . . he could be upstairs and know as soon as Loren began grinding coffee beans, or downstairs and know when Loren began chopping an onion.

Dr. Mike had told him that the other senses often made up for the loss of one. So if a person was blind, as he was, it wasn't so rare to have remarkable smelling and hearing.

Even after being informed that he wasn't unusual, the reverend was proud of his improved senses. He might not be able to see the brightest lamp in the world, but he could hear and smell things long before the average person did.

Today, minutes before the reverend heard Horace greet Loren, he smelled the most awful smell, something putrid. When the smell hit him, he fought to swallow what he had in his mouth.

Customers milled around the store. Mrs. Hall was here. So was Mary Tennessey. (The reverend had asked about her broken arm, and she had told him that Dr. Mike said it looked to be healing fine.) The reverend had heard numerous pairs of boots scraping across the wooden floor at nearly the same time Horace arrived, and he wasn't sure exactly how many people were in the mercantile. He never could tell about that because so many customers came and went.

Timothy Johnson didn't know where the smell came from, or who it came from. He just knew that it was bad. He grabbed his walking stick, stood, and picked his way to the staircase that led up to his and Loren's living quarters.

Behind the counter, Loren sniffed the air as he packaged flour and salt for Mary Tennessey. Something, or someone, didn't smell good. They smelled like rotten eggs. Maybe somebody had stepped in some dung and didn't realize it. If that was the case, they'd be out of here soon. Customers didn't stay long at the mercantile, not unless they were a friend of Loren's and wanted to sit a spell for a cup of coffee and conversation. And here lately Loren hadn't had much time for coffee and conversation.

Hal Archer and Horace drew nigh to the counter, and the smell got worse. It came from either Hal or Horace, that was for sure. Hal needed a bag of tobacco, and Horace had brought two lemons in from the outside bins. Both men laid money on the counter, thanked Loren, and walked off at about the same time. So no telling which one carried the dung on his boot. Loren was just glad when the men left.

16

The next morning Horace inspected his scalp. He didn't see any new growth yet. It might take time, maybe a week or two. Meanwhile, he'd put the tonic on several times a day. Anything to hurry the new growth along.

He wrapped the tonic in brown paper, not especially wanting to advertise that he was using it, and carried the package to the telegraph office.

He applied more tonic to his hair around noon. And when Hans showed up a few hours later, Hank took the package with him when he went out to deliver packages and mail from the morning train. He had several packages for Dr. Mike, four for Loren, one for Jake, and one for Hank. The package for Hank was about the same size as Horace's wrapped-up hair tonic.

Horace carried the hair tonic along with the package

or packages he was delivering. Once he'd had to shoo some kids away from his buggy when they'd decided to unwrap a few things meant for other people. He didn't want anyone, child or adult, to know that he was using the hair tonic. He felt self-conscious about using it, and he sure didn't want to get teased about it.

He delivered the packages in the order places were located—to the clinic, then to the mercantile, then to the barbershop, then to the hotel. Everywhere he went, people looked at him oddly and wrinkled their noses, like something was wrong, like something didn't smell good.

The cold still had hold of Horace and he still tired easily. So he ran out of steam pretty fast and didn't worry much over why people wrinkled their noses at him. He just wanted to get back to the telegraph office so he could sit for a while, maybe even lay his head on the counter and take a catnap.

Back at the telegraph office, he was getting down from the buggy when he realized something horrible. He picked up his wrapped tonic from the buggy seat, only there was black writing on the package. At first he wondered who'd written on the paper. He hadn't let the tonic out of his sight all afternoon—so how could someone have written on the paper?

They hadn't. When he looked closer at the writing, he read, "Hank Clag—"

Horace gasped. "Oh no! I gave Hank the wrong package."

He scuttled back onto the buggy seat and wasted no time getting across town to the hotel. He hollered to let people know he was coming through, and once he came two hairs away from colliding with another buggy.

212

When he finally reached the Gold Nugget—seemed like it took him forever—he jumped to the ground before the horse had stopped completely.

Henry Miller was minding the hotel's front desk. When Horace dashed into the hotel, Mr. Miller glanced up, a startled look on his face.

"Where's Hank?" Horace demanded.

"Why . . . Mr. Claggerty is in his office, I be—"

Horace raced off that way, not letting the man finish. He tore down the hall and pushed on the partly open office door.

Inside the office, Hank had propped his legs on one corner of his desk, frustrated again at the Chinese boy he'd hired to sweep floors and wash windows. This afternoon he'd had to sweep the lobby floor himself after the boy swept, then disappeared. Several windows were streaked—maybe the boy had used a soapy rag to wash them.

Shaking his head, Hank had torn open the package Horace delivered to him a short time ago. (He'd been glad when Horace left—Horace had an odor about him these days.) Inside the paper was a bottle of something.

"Princess Hair Restorer," Hank read from the front of the bottle. "Somebody's tryin' to tell me somethin'."

He ran a hand over his head, then pushed his fingers up into his hair. It felt as thick as ever. He didn't need help growing hair; he'd always done that just fine, and his hair didn't feel like it was thinning out anywhere. So it was pretty damn odd that somebody would send him something like this.

Maybe Jake had sent it. He was still mad about that fight Hank had had out front of the hotel with those men who were racing horses. It'd be just like Jake to send something like this to insult him.

Curious, Hank pulled the cork from the bottle and smelled the tonic. He jerked back. Whew! He wasted no time recorking the bottle. The stuff might grow new hair— but it smelled so bad it'd scare away women and anybody else that wandered by.

When his office door banged open, Hank swung his boots down off of his desk and tipped forward, holding the Princess Hair Restorer in one hand.

In came Horace. He skidded to a stop, reached over the desk, and snatched the bottle away from Hank.

Hank's head spun with bewilderment. "What're you *doin'?*"

"I gave you the wrong package," Horace said, his ears turning red.

Pause.

Hank shifted his gaze to the bottle Horace now held against his chest. "Is that yours?"

"Yeah. What about it?" Horace huffed.

"I was wonderin' if somebody was tryin' to tell me somethin'. Like I'm gettin' thin or somethin'," Hank said, running a hand over his hair. He leaned back in his chair, wanting to put some distance between him and Horace. The odor around Horace lately was too much.

But it was familiar.

Curiosity made Hank tip forward again and sniff.

Horace smelled like that putrid hair tonic.

Hank squinted an eye at Horace. "You usin' that stuff?"

Horace tilted his head defiantly. "Why?"

" 'Cause it stinks, an' it's makin' *you* stink."

Horace's jaw dropped open. He sputtered, "I—You— wrong package—It don't stink!"

That wrinkled Hank's brow. How could Horace think the tonic *didn't* stink? It smelled worse than two skunks spraying at the same time. (That had happened to Hank when he was a boy. He'd been messing around a creek one day, fishing and collecting rocks that were shaped neat. He'd run upon mating skunks, and he'd paid for interrupting them.)

"Horace, is your nose plugged up?"

"No."

"Yeah, it is. I hear it. Go home, blow your nose real good, then pop the cork on that bottle an' take yourself a good whiff of that tonic. Smell that stuff real good, then go take yourself a bath. Hell, Horace, if you wanna grow more hair, set yourself down with a bottle of whiskey."

"I will not!"

Hank heaved a sigh of frustration as he rose behind the desk. Always defiant Horace.

"Go on," Hank said, waving him away. "You can't stay here. You stink."

No one had ever told Horace that he stank. Since Hank was the one telling him, Horace knew he shouldn't let it bother him—he'd never thought much of Hank or Hank's opinions anyway. But it *did* bother him.

Horace left the office and shuffled down the hall. When he reached the front desk and Henry Miller, he crossed to the other side of the lobby and walked alongside that wall, as far from Mr. Miller as he could get. He didn't want to be offensive to anybody.

Several women came in, and Horace tried to stay as far from them as possible. But they smelled him anyway; they grimaced, looked at him, wrinkled their noses, lifted their skirts, and hurried off.

Maybe Hank was right. Maybe he did stink.

Outside, Matthew was waiting beside Horace's buggy. He leaned his frame against it, then straightened when he saw Horace emerge from the hotel.

Horace couldn't figure what Matthew was doing. But he found out soon enough.

"Remember the town meetin', Horace?" Matthew asked, unfolding his arms.

Horace scowled. He remembered.

"Remember that new ordinance about not gallopin' horses through town?"

"Yeah," Horace said quietly. He had a feeling he knew what was coming.

"You've got a week to make a donation to the town treasury," Matthew said. "Otherwise you get the pleasure of visitin' me at my office for a few days."

Horace gulped. Matthew would arrest him if he didn't pay the fine?

Well, he'd voted for the new ordinance about not galloping horses in town, and he'd voted in favor of the fine. Matthew was right and he was wrong, and Horace reckoned he'd make that donation as soon as possible.

"Have yourself a good day," Matthew said, tipping his hat and walking off.

After a few steps Matthew stopped and glanced back. "Horace, I hate to be the one to tell you—"

"I know," Horace said, hanging his head. "I need a bath."

"Yep."

A blush burned Horace's face again. He squeezed the bottle of tonic. It hadn't done much for him so far but get him in trouble. If it really did stink—and it must since, both Hank *and* Matthew had told him he needed a bath— he wouldn't use it again. He'd get rid of it.

Thank his lucky stars there was no ordinance against stinking. Otherwise, he'd owe *two* donations to the town treasury.

17

B y Monday of the following week, Hank hadn't seen Cora, as in having time alone with her, for several days. Not because he hadn't wanted to see her or because he'd asked and been declined. He'd just been too busy to ask. He'd waved to her from across the street whenever he went out for a quick smoke. Other than that, obligations inside the hotel had consumed his time.

Tuesday afternoon, he stepped outside to smoke and saw Brian headed toward his ma's clinic. Hank walked that way, ready to grovel if he had to. This thing with Brian had gone on long enough. It was time they talked.

He reached the clinic after Brian had gone inside. Most likely he'd get Michaela if he knocked. But he knocked anyway, hoping Brian would answer and he wouldn't have to face the mother hen again.

No such luck. Michaela answered the door. She saw

Hank and she didn't even greet him. She said, "The clinic is closed for the afternoon."

Hank offered his most charming smile. Of course, with Michaela, it didn't always matter whether or not the smile was charming. She usually could see right through him.

"I'd like to talk to Brian," he said in a friendly tone.

She stared at him for a good thirty seconds, as if she had to decide whether or not to let him do that. "All right," she finally said. "I'll get him."

She left the doorway. Hank heard low conversation, then after a minute Brian came to the door. He didn't say anything, but just stared at Hank.

That made Hank uncomfortable. He shuffled his boots on the porch a few times before he could get words to come out of his mouth.

"I didn't forget about you an' your friends on purpose, Brian. I got busy, then it went over my head."

"You had somethin' more important to do," Brian said, his eyes flashing.

"What was I doin'?" Hank really couldn't remember.

It was the wrong thing to say. He saw nerves twitch around Brian's eyes, like Brian was getting more irritated rather than having his feathers smoothed. Like Hank ought to *know* without thinking about it what he'd been doing that afternoon.

Brian finally reminded him. "You were picnicking with Mrs. Reeves."

Hank rubbed his jaw, as if he'd been hit. "Yeah. That's it. That's what I was doin'."

Brian started to close the door.

Hank put his hand up to the door to keep it from shutting. "C'mon, Brian. You ain't ever had your head clouded by a woman? I forgot. I know that doesn't sound good, that I forgot about you an' your friends, but I did.'' Hank winked at him. ''You get to likin' girls a lot an' you'll lose your head, you wait an' see.''

''I won't forget about promises I make.''

Hank studied him. Brian was just a kid, and he was trying to talk to him like he'd talk to another grown person. He didn't understand forgetting everything else when a certain woman came along.

''All right, all right,'' Hank said, losing patience fast. He talked slower now, being sarcastic. ''Maybe you won't. Maybe you'll be different than the rest of the male population of the world.''

''Maybe. I ain't comin' back to the hotel.'' Stubborn boy.

''I didn't come over here to ask you t'come back,'' Hank lied. He wouldn't tell Brian that that's exactly why he'd moseyed across the street when he saw him. No, sir. He was getting a different reaction to his attempt to apologize than he'd expected, and he had to save some pride. Walking over here, facing Michaela again and then Brian, had taken a lot of pride. He wasn't about to give up the rest of it by begging.

Brian closed the door in his face. Hank had to fight the urge to kick the door in. He yanked on his vest, reminding himself of the respectability that came with his new occupation. Then he turned and walked away, pasting a smile on his face.

Inside the clinic, Michaela rolled clean bandages and covertly watched Brian as he shut the door and returned to the task of crushing herbs. She had the dried herbs bound together with twine and labeled with strips of paper. The jars were labeled accordingly.

Michaela folded more bandages as Brian busied himself

219

with the pestle and mortar. He worked on a countertop just below the cabinet where she kept her medicines and herbs.

"So what did Hank have to say?" She was prying, and she ought to be ashamed—but she couldn't help herself.

Brian shrugged. "Not much."

"Will you be working for him again soon?"

"No."

His answers were short and to the point, which indicated that he didn't want to talk about Hank. He didn't look at her as he answered, either. It was an uncomfortable subject, and he still wasn't sure how to react or what to do about Hank.

Brian had continued to help Sully work on the Blakes' house. The house was nearly finished—the men were working on the roof today. Michaela had some catching up to do at the clinic, and she had asked Brian if he wanted to help her this afternoon. He had come over after school and hadn't been here very long when Hank knocked on the door.

Michaela let the subject go. She finished with the bandages and began wiping down the examination table and sterilizing her instruments. Sounds from the street drifted through an open window—wagons rattling, people talking, children laughing and shouting.

"Ma, do you reckon I can have Chester?" Brian asked, breaking the silence inside the clinic. "Matthew said he's got to sell him soon. He doesn't want to keep Chester for himself, an' he says the town can't keep feedin' him."

Matthew must mean that the money to buy Chester's food came from the town treasury—as it rightly should. The money spent to feed any prisoner came from the town treasury, and officially, Chester was still a prisoner. Brian sometimes collected scraps from home for Chester, but more often than not the Sullys' scraps went to their hogs.

"Doesn't Matthew have to sell Chester?" Michaela asked. "According to the new ordinance, Matthew must sell unclaimed animals and the proceeds must go into the town treasury."

"I already asked Matthew about the ordinance. He does have to sell Chester. But I've got the money to buy him," Brian said, pouring crushed leaves into a jar. "I've been savin.' "

"How much is Matthew asking?"

"Ten dollars."

Not much at all. At the town meeting no one had said anything about how much Matthew should charge per animal, or for what type of animal. Which meant he could charge whatever he wanted to charge. Ten dollars. . . . He wanted to get rid of that goat. And after all the trouble Michaela heard Matthew had had with the goat, she didn't blame him.

"That's reasonable," she said.

"Chester's been behavin' real good. Matthew says he doesn't butt the side of the jail at night anymore."

She wondered how Matthew had broken the goat of that. She didn't for a second think that the goat had simply stopped on his own. Matthew had broken the goat somehow and just hadn't said anything to Brian—she knew Matthew. Brian had gone softhearted over Chester, Matthew knew that, and probably hadn't wanted Brian to worry about how he was dealing with the goat.

"That's wonderful," Michaela said. "I don't mind if you buy Chester from the town. But you need to ask Sully, too. And as you agreed, you must take care of Chester. He'll be your responsibility."

"I will, Ma—promise." Brian's eyes had brightened

with excitement, changing from dull and evasive after his conversation with Hank.

Michaela was glad to see him cheer up. She smiled at him, at his sweetness in taking care of the goat, and now in wanting to give it a home.

"I love you, Ma," he said.

Her smile widened as warmth rushed through her. "I love you, too, Brian."

When Hank left the clinic, he went to the mercantile, where he asked Loren to order him more of those fine cigars. As Loren scratched out a note to remind himself, an engraved music box caught Hank's eye. He studied it, wondering if it would appeal to Cora. He didn't know if he should buy her a gift—she might think that was too forward of him. Ladies were funny about gifts from gentlemen. Anyway, buying her a gift instead of spending time with her didn't seem right.

"Oh, no, here comes Horace," Loren said, crinkling his nose. "He came in one day last week an' I couldn't figure out what the awful smell was. The next time he was in, I knew. You don't have to get real close to him to tell, either."

"I know," Hank said.

Mrs. Levins and Mrs. Sloan glanced up from their browsing, their interest perked. Both women were gossips, and everybody in town knew it.

"He's been usin' a hair tonic," Hank told Loren. "Something to help him grow new hair. Guess Horace figures he might be goin' bald. Imagine that, a bald Horace. That's scary."

Hank and Loren had a good laugh over that remark.

Loren sobered as Horace walked into the mercantile.

Horace's arms were loaded with packages. He glanced over the tops of them at Hank, a worried look passing over his face. Like maybe Hank would tell him again that he needed a bath.

Ordinarily Loren would have come around the counter and offered to take some of the packages from Horace. But remembering how Horace had smelled last week, he kept his distance behind the counter.

Horace plopped the packages down and dipped his head, greeting Loren. "Hello, Mr. Bray."

"Horace," Loren said, jerking his head.

"All those packages wouldn't fit in the bag you wear over your shoulder when you ride that velocipede?" Hank teased.

"No," Horace snapped, as if it wasn't a joke but something Hank didn't realize and ought to realize, as if all those packages not being able to fit into his bag was a matter of common sense. And it was, of course. Hank was jesting.

Hank scowled. "A little sensitive today, aren't you, Horace?"

"Maybe."

"Had yourself a bath yet?"

Horace reddened.

"You sure needed one. Loren here was just sayin' how you stank last week when you came in here."

"Oh, I didn't say that," Loren snapped, embarrassed that Hank repeated what he'd said.

Loren didn't want Horace to think he'd been talking bad about him. Loren had gone soft the last few years. He'd once been the town's grumpy old man, not especially liking anybody but Maude. Then Maude died and Loren became even more grumpy. Brian had come along, and Loren's heart must not have been that hard, because Brian had

223

melted it. A little boy had turned a grumpy, hard old man into a sensitive old man who did kind things every once in a while and who frequently made Hank walk off shaking his head.

"Yeah, you did," Hank said. "Noticed any new growth, Horace?"

"Shut up," Horace muttered, clenching his fists.

"A velocipede . . . now hair tonic. Are you tryin' to make a new an' improved Horace?"

The women had their noses poked clear over a row of pots and pans, inhaling every word Hank and Horace said. Fodder for the gossips. By this evening, they'd have it all over town that Horace the telegraph operator had been using a tonic that was supposed to grow new hair, that the tonic stank, and that Hank had told Horace he needed to take a bath—something Loren Bray agreed with Hank about.

Hank glanced at Loren, laughing, wanting to see if Loren was at least smiling. He never saw Horace raise his fist. Hank heard Loren say, "No, Horace, don't—" and then, *bam!* something slammed into Hank's jaw.

The force of the blow knocked Hank backward. He hit the counter, slid down, and slammed his head against the edge of the counter. He heard Horace say, "That'll teach you." He heard glass break, and a sound like a hundred pebbles clattering on the floor. Then Hank's world winked out.

Loren scurried around the counter. Hank groaned and moved his head, and Loren bent down for a closer look.

Horace hunched down beside Loren. "I didn't mean to hit him so hard. Just wanted to shut him up."

"Well, you did that, all right."

Mrs. Sloan and Mrs. Levins came close. They peered down at Hank, wide-eyed, obviously in shock.

Mrs. Sloan said, "I'll go get Dr. Mike." Then she hurried out of the mercantile.

"He ain't hurt bad, is he?" Horace fretted, peering down at Hank.

"Bad enough to be out cold. He'll be plenty mad when he wakes, too," Loren grumbled. "You might not wanna be here."

"I ain't leavin' 'til he wakes up an' I know if he's gonna be all right."

Teas leaves, hard candy, and glass littered the mercantile floor. Horace's eyes widened at the sight. Not only had he maybe seriously hurt Hank, he'd broken Loren's tea and candy jars and disrupted Loren's business.

"I'll sweep up the mess an' pay you for the candy an' the leaves," Horace said.

"An' the jars."

Horace gulped. "An' the jars."

That tonic had been nothing but bad news. It stunk, it had cost him five dollars for galloping his horse through town, and now it would cost him the price of Loren's tea, candy, and jars. Horace scowled. He couldn't really blame the tonic for his hitting Hank and messing things up in Loren's mercantile. He'd lost control of his temper, and he shouldn't blame anybody or anything but himself for that.

"The broom's behind the counter," Loren said.

Loren apparently wanted the mess cleaned up as soon as possible, and Horace didn't blame him. If somebody had punched somebody else and broken things in the telegraph office, *he'd* want things cleaned up as soon as possible, so he could get on with business as soon as possible.

Horace found the broom and began sweeping up the tea,

the candy, and the broken glass. Hank groaned again, and his eyelids fluttered. There might be more broken glass and other things to clean up after Hank woke up all the way. He'd be mad as a whole nest of bees. Horace figured he was in for a hard punch himself.

Mrs. Sloan returned with Dr. Mike, and right about the time the women hurried into the mercantile, Hank opened his eyes all the way and slowly sat up.

"You should lie back down, at least until I've had a chance to examine you," Dr. Mike told him.

"I don't need examined," Hank snapped. "I've been in a helluva lot worse shape."

Dr. Mike moved closer to Hank, looking concerned about him. "You might have a concussion."

Hank wobbled to his feet, ignoring her. He held on to the edge of the counter for a minute, then glared at Horace, who had stopped sweeping. Horace expected Hank to charge after him, and he was as surprised as everyone else when Hank stumbled to the door instead.

"You think he'll be all right, Dr. Mike?" Horace asked, more worried than he'd been about anybody in a long time.

She shook her head. "I don't know. He'll certainly have a tremendous headache."

Horace resumed sweeping, mumbling with each stroke of the cornhusk broom, "I've never hurt anybody. I can't believe I hit him. I can't believe he didn't hit me back."

"He deserved it," Mrs. Sloan said indignantly. Then she and Mrs. Levins left the mercantile without making a purchase.

Horace felt even worse about things now. He'd hurt Hank, he'd broken things, and he really had disrupted Loren's business.

•   •   •

Preston had discovered Cora Reeves, and he liked what he saw. A cultured lady (like Dr. Quinn, but she was taken) who enjoyed the theater and books and fine things, right here in Colorado Springs. Good fortune always seemed to come his way.

Of course, many of Preston's guests at the resort were cultured. But they weren't permanent. They stayed for several weeks, perhaps as long as a month. Then they went home. So while he met many young women who impressed him, he rarely spent time with them beyond his capacity as the resort's owner and manager.

To add to her personal appeal, Preston discovered Mrs. Reeves's plan to open a bookstore. He championed any improvement to Colorado Springs, anything that would add to the town's charm, anything that would enhance it. Enhancement meant more people, more tourists. And more tourists meant more money for the resort, since visitors to the town would inevitably flock to the resort.

When Preston visited Mrs. Reeves's partially furnished bookstore the next morning, she disclosed that several shipments of bookshelves and cabinets were due to arrive any day from the home in Denver that she had not yet sold. She hadn't a clue as to how she would get the many crates of different sizes from the depot to the shop.

"The telegraph man—I can never remember his name. . . . He has delivered smaller packages," Mrs. Reeves said. "But I cannot expect him to deliver these crates."

Preston volunteered his services. "I have numerous employees at the resort. When your crates arrive, alert me, and I'll send someone to pick them up and deliver them."

Mrs. Reeves clapped her hands together. "That's wonderful! Thank you so much!"

He beamed. Then he asked if she would like to tour his

resort sometime soon. She said yes, of course. Perhaps tomorrow afternoon?

Preston gave a little bow and said he would see her tomorrow afternoon. Moments later, when he left the little shop, he had a spring in his step. Today was a fine day—sunny, the temperature mild, just right—but tomorrow would be even better.

Hank had a bad headache for a full twenty-four hours after Horace laid him out.

He still couldn't believe it—Horace punching him like that. Horace sure had a harder swing than Hank would ever have guessed he had.

When Hank got up from Loren's floor, he'd wanted to hit Horace back—and everybody in the mercantile had known that, he reckoned, because they knew *him*. They knew he always hit back. But he'd been so unstable on his feet that a swing would have put him on the floor again. He wasn't going to have that. When he hit Horace back, he'd stay on his feet so he could look down at Horace and laugh.

The headache finally eased up, although his jaw was plenty sore. Hank decided that, busy or not, he needed to get away from town and from the hotel soon, or he'd go crazy.

The next morning, Hank visited Cora's shop to ask if she wanted to picnic with him that afternoon. Turning pink, she said she was committed for today. She didn't say what—or who—she was committed to. Just hearing that she was *committed* threw Hank for a loop. He felt awkward and didn't know what to say.

"The day after tomorrow?" she suggested.

He nodded.

She gave him a curious look. "What happened to you?"

Hank frowned. "What are you talking about?"

"Your jaw is blue!"

Horace had left him with a bruise, the dirty rat. No wonder his jaw was still so sore. This morning he'd noticed it was swollen, but not enough so that anybody ought to notice. But since this morning apparently it had decided to bruise up.

"I raised up behind the hotel desk and smacked myself," Hank said. He wasn't about to tell Cora about Horace punching him. With luck, no one would tell her the truth.

Hank remembered the two busybodies who'd been in the mercantile when Horace swung at him, and he felt uneasy with the lie. He knew those women, and he knew they'd started telling people what had happened as soon as they left Loren's store. Cora was bound to hear the story sooner or later. Still, he didn't change what he'd told her to explain the bruise.

"You must be more careful, Mr. Claggerty."

He wished she'd call him Hank. But Cora Reeves was too much of a lady to do that so soon after meeting him.

Hank returned to the Gold Nugget.

That afternoon he saw Preston arrive in a sharp-looking buggy. Preston went into the shop and reappeared a few minutes later with Cora.

Hank seethed as Preston handed Cora up to the buggy seat. Preston the rat had moved in, had snared Cora's attention while the hotel had occupied Hank's.

Now Hank knew he had a job to do: somehow, he had to impress Cora more than Preston could ever *think* about impressing her. And he wasn't sure how to do that.

He knew the person he should talk to, who might have an idea how to go about impressing a lady. But Michaela was sore at him because he'd forgotten about Brian and his friends. She was probably sore, too, because he hadn't wanted her help yesterday in the mercantile. She might not even want to talk to him. She sure wouldn't want to do him a favor right now.

He had to patch a few things up before he tried to talk to Michaela.

In his office, Hank dug through a trunk of old things until he came up with what he was looking for—a dried pigskin stuffed with rags and stitched up with heavy twine. He stuck it under his right arm and headed for the school yard, hoping to see Brian during recess. He wasn't sure when the teacher let the kids go outside and run around, but he figured recess might be around dinnertime. And he was right, he saw, as he approached the school yard. The little critters were scattered all over, sitting in the grass, eating their food.

When Hank approached Brian where he sat with a group of his friends, Brian sure didn't jump up to greet him. He just sat and stared at him, and Brian's friends did the same. At first Ben Hughes was the only one who talked to Hank. He said hi, and then apologized for not showing up at the hotel after school for the last few weeks.

Hank wasn't sure it had been two weeks altogether yet, and he wasn't interested in trying to figure up how many days had passed since the last time Ben had worked for him. Hank still felt bad for Ben that he had lost his pa. As soon as he'd heard the news, he'd known the loss would be hard for Ben, especially considering the way things had happened at the Hugheses' ranch, with Ben knocking over the lantern and all. Actually, Hank was surprised to see Ben back at school already.

"I don't expect you to come to work for a while."

"I'll be back soon, I promise," Ben said. "I've been lookin' after my ma an' the cattle."

"When you're ready." Hank glanced at Brian. "You've got enough friends here. Wanna take a stab at learnin' foot ball now?"

Brian studied him, working his jaw, looking undecided.

"That's why you're here?" Jack Archer asked, his eyes squinted suspiciously.

"That's why I'm here," Hank said.

Andy Blythe peeked around Brian. "How'd you know we'd be outside right now?"

"I didn't. I guessed."

Rick Humphrey swiped at the grass between his legs. "You forgot about us that one day."

"Yeah," said Jack. "You went picnickin' with your lady friend."

They were all sore at him, not just Brian. Hank plopped down on the grass. "I know, an' I'm sorry about that. Girls make you forget what you're supposed to be doin' sometimes." He let his eyes travel around the school yard, to the clusters of girls. Then he looked at Jack again. "Any of those girls ever make you forget what you're supposed to be readin' in school or what you're supposed to be writin' on your slate?"

Jack scowled at him. He grabbed a handful of grass, pulled it out of the ground, and threw it. "So what if some do?" he challenged.

Hank shrugged. "Ain't sayin' there's anything wrong with that. I'd say there's something wrong with you if girls *don't* make you forget what you're supposed to be doin' sometimes."

"Jack likes that oldest Blake girl," Charlie Hall said, a sparkle in his eye. "So does Brian."

That riled Jack. "Don't be talkin', Charlie! 'Member the day Miss Theresa caught you an' Susy Perkins whisperin'? She called you to the board an' told you to write out the problem the class was supposed to be cipherin'. You couldn't remember it to write it out for nothin'. All you could think of was Susy. You carried her books home for her that day, too."

"You see . . . ," Hank began. But he got no further because Charlie threw himself at Jack. Charlie could tease, but he didn't like to be teased back.

Charlie rammed his head into Jack's shoulder. Jack grabbed Charlie, and the boys rolled around on the ground. Hank grabbed the backs of the boys' shirts and pulled Charlie and Jack apart. "Hey, now, I didn't come to watch y'all fight. I came to teach y'all to play foot ball if anybody still wants to learn."

"I do," Paul Steerforth said.

"So do I," said Rick.

Andy and Ben wanted to play, too, and so did Gary Hamilton. Brian mumbled that he guessed he'd play, too.

They didn't have a lot of time, maybe only twenty minutes. But it was enough time for Hank to divide the boys into two teams. He taught them how to hike the ball, how to guard, how to pass, and how to score. The girls began gathering around, interested, and the boys worked even harder to learn the game.

They were hot and sweaty when Miss Theresa rang the bell to signal the end of recess. They all thanked Hank.

As the boys filed into the schoolhouse, Hank hoped Brian had had a good enough time that he'd mention the game to his ma tonight. If Brian did, then when Hank went to see Michaela at the clinic tomorrow afternoon, Michaela might be friendly to him again.

18

Hank waited on the clinic porch behind Michaela's other patients, who probably all had real symptoms, for what seemed like two hours. Actually, he waited slightly less than an hour.

She was all business when she ushered him into the clinic. But at least she didn't close the door in his face, refusing to see him. Hank didn't know whether or not she'd ever refused to see a patient, and he'd started to worry that if she hadn't—well, then, he might be her first.

"I'm surprised to see you, Hank," she said as she shut the door.

He limped slightly, favoring his right leg, as he made his way to her examination table.

"I've got this hitch in my leg since yesterday afternoon," he said, hoping Brian had told her about the foot ball game. He was careful to hike the left side of his body onto the table first.

She approached the table. "I see. . . . Where in your leg?"

"Where . . . ? In the thigh. It keeps tightenin' up." He'd had that happen before, actually, once when he'd sifted and panned for days and found nothing, and once when he'd helped a friend cut trees and drag logs for about a week.

"Hmm," Michaela said. "Sounds like muscle spasms. I should examine your thigh."

"Sure."

He lay back on the table, thinking she'd feel around on his thigh a little, then probably give him some of her leaves for tea, same as she did with almost everyone.

"You'll need to remove your trousers."

Hank's head whipped her way. "Remove my trousers?"

Michaela nodded. "So I can do a thorough examination."

He sat up. He wasn't going to take off his trousers. Maybe he should've told her something was wrong with his arm instead of his leg, or his calf instead of his thigh. That way he could've just pushed his trouser leg up for her.

"Supposin' it is muscle spasms," he said. "What would you do for somethin' like that?"

"Rest and warm compresses. But the tightening could be a symptom of something else."

He slid off the table. "I bet that's all it is, just muscle spasms. I'll try the rest an' warm compresses. What do I owe you?"

She shook her head. "Nothing. I didn't even examine you."

"But you recommended somethin' to help my leg feel better," he said. He pulled a silver dollar from his pocket and plopped it down on the examination table.

He made his way toward the door.

Once there, he turned back. "Since I'm here . . . I'm wonderin'. . . . You met Mrs. Reeves, the lady that's openin' the bookstore soon. . . ."

"Yes." She looked puzzled.

"What kinda things does a lady like that like, y'know, when somebody takes a shine to her?"

"You mean when she's being courted?"

"Yeah. That's it—when she's bein' courted."

Michaela smiled. "Walks, rides, flowers, music, dancing . . . attentiveness."

Hank grimaced. "There ain't much in the way of music an' dancin' in Colorado Springs."

"Nonsense. We've had socials and dances. Loren plays the harmonica. Jake plays the fiddle. The town's overdue for a dance. Perhaps I'll talk to Dorothy about planning one."

Nodding, he turned back toward the door.

"If Mrs. Reeves truly likes you, Hank, she won't care about your previous occupation."

An unsolicited opinion, but one that made sense. Hank thought of Michaela and Sully, how different they'd been when she first came to Colorado Springs, as different as night and day; she was a city lady and he was a frontiersman and trapper.

"Thanks, Michaela," he mumbled as he opened the door.

Sully and Robert finished the Blakes' house that day. Brian stayed in town after school to help at the clinic. He and Michaela planned to take Chester home with them today.

From time to time during the past week, Matthew and the goat had sat together peacefully on the front porch of the sheriff's office. So when Michaela and Brian arrived at the office to pick up Chester, she couldn't resist teasing Matthew about missing Chester after he left.

"Maybe just a little," he said, grinning.

At home, Michaela and Brian turned Chester loose in the barn. He wandered around for a while, looking confused. Then he poked his head between the stall rails, investigating one of the horses. The mare chewed a mouthful of hay while she stared back at Chester. It didn't take Chester long to lose interest in her.

He went out into the barnyard and chased the chickens while Michaela and Brian settled themselves on the top rail of the barnyard fence. It wasn't long before one of the three roosters craned its neck, flapped its wings, and charged Chester.

Chester jumped, backed up, then turned and ran into the barn. Michaela and Brian laughed so hard at the sight of Chester fleeing, they nearly fell off the rail.

Brian called to the goat four times, trying to coax him out of the barn. Finally Chester poked his head out and glanced around, looking like he wasn't sure whether or not he wanted to venture out again. He finally did, slowly and cautiously, watching the rooster for several minutes.

When Sully and Katie arrived home, Chester was meeting the hogs, poking his nose at them. The hogs ignored the newcomer until Chester butted his head against one of them. Then they both spun around, snorting and sniffing at him.

Brian jumped down into the barnyard and brought Chester over to meet Katie. The goat chewed on the hem of her dress and Katie cried, trying to pull the dress away from him. Michaela finally wrestled the material away from Chester while Brian scolded the goat and Sully laughed.

Brian brought several corncobs from the hogs' slop bucket, and Chester lost interest in Katie's dress when he spotted them. Brian dropped them in the barnyard and Chester began rolling them around and chewing on them.

Katie had nothing nice to say about her brother's new pet. She pointed at the goat and called Chester "Bad," which became her name for him for the next several weeks. "Dwess," she said to Michaela as she scowled and lifted the part of her dress Chester had chewed on. The material was wrinkled but otherwise undamaged.

"Mama . . . dwess . . . Bad!" She pointed to Chester again, so upset she couldn't form a complete sentence. Chester raised his head to look at her, and Katie cried and buried her face in Michaela's shoulder.

Brian and Sully laughed, and Michaela fought a smile as she took Katie away from the barnyard. Katie had had enough of the goat for one day.

Once inside the house, Katie carried on about her dress for the better part of the next hour. She scowled and pouted, looking down at her hem. She pointed at the front door and said, "Bad!" so many times Michaela lost count. Every time she did it, Brian and Sully laughed. Katie's indignation over the goat's trying to eat her dress really was comical, but Michaela stopped smiling about it after a while, wondering if Katie would ever calm down.

Michaela rocked Katie and told her that it was all right, the goat couldn't get her dress now. Katie kept trying to brush the wrinkles away. Finally Michaela heated the iron, took the dress off Katie, and smoothed away the wrinkles. Then she slipped the dress back on Katie and fastened its buttons.

"Is that better?" Michaela asked her daughter.

Katie grinned. "Better, Mama," she said, throwing her arms around Michaela's neck.

The next morning, before the Sullys left for the day, Brian put Chester out in the barnyard along with the other animals, not wanting him to be cooped up in the barn all day. Then he, Sully, Michaela, and Katie got in the wagon and headed to town.

At one o'clock that afternoon, Michaela went outside to turn the sign on the clinic's front door from *open* to *closed*. She glanced down the walkway, toward Matthew's office. When she saw Matthew sitting there, she waved, then started to walk back inside the clinic. Suddenly she froze in place, realizing what else she had seen—Chester sitting on the porch with Matthew.

She and Brian had taken Chester to the homestead yesterday. She hadn't dreamed that. And they had left the goat at the homestead this morning. She hadn't dreamed that, either. So how could Chester be sitting with Matthew on the porch of the sheriff's office?

Perhaps it's a different goat, Michaela thought. Perhaps Matthew had become so fond of having a goat around that he had missed Chester when she and Brian took him yesterday, and had decided to get himself another goat.

But as Michaela peered down the walkway, looking harder this time, she knew it wasn't a different goat. The goat sitting with Matthew was Chester.

She pulled the clinic door shut and walked toward the sheriff's office, curiosity quickening her pace as she drew close to the porch where Matthew and the goat sat.

She peered at Matthew, who grinned at her and shook his head, and she peered at Chester, who stared back at her.

"How did he get here?" she blurted when she reached the porch steps.

Matthew shook his head and pushed his hat back. "Ain't this somethin'? Me an' this goat fought like mad bulls for a week. Now he can't stand bein' away from me."

"How did he get here?" Michaela asked again.

"Don't know. I came out an' here he was. Chester thinks this is his home."

"We left him penned in the barnyard this morning. He can't be here."

"Well, here he is, plain as day. He found a way out of that barnyard. He can butt good an' hard. Maybe he busted down part of the fence."

"Oh, no!"

Michaela was imagining the hogs loose in the vegetable garden.

"Do you have a rope?" she asked Matthew. "Chester doesn't know me very well. I have to get him to the livery somehow. I'll tie him to my horse's saddle and take him home that way. I don't know how else to get him home. I don't have Brian to help me today."

"Dan's relievin' me soon," Matthew said. "How about if I bring Chester out to you after a while?"

It almost seemed as though Matthew didn't mind the surprise visit from Chester. In fact, he didn't seem to mind the thought of spending even more time with Chester while he waited for the deputy.

"That would be helpful," Michaela said. "I need to hurry home and make sure the hogs haven't eaten the vegetables."

"If they're loose, they have."

"That's what I'm afraid of."

Michaela hurried back to the clinic to lock the doors.

From there she hurried to Robert E.'s livery to collect her horse.

She galloped the horse nearly the entire mile to the homestead.

The barn came into sight, then the barnyard fence, and Michaela saw that the section that separated the barnyard from the fenced pasture was broken. Part of the pasture fence also was broken. Pieces of wood were scattered in the grass just beyond the barnyard and the pasture. The hogs and the cow were gone. But at least the garden hadn't been ravaged.

The cow might come back on her own at nightfall, when she was milked. *Might*, if she hadn't wandered so far that she couldn't find her way back. Some people tied bells around their cows' necks and let them wander in the woods to graze, finding them when it was milking time. But for several reasons, the Sullys kept their cow in the fenced pasture. If Sully happened to be gone trapping, Michaela and Brian didn't want to wander the woods after dark, listening for the bell. They had lost several calves to coyotes, too, and one cow to a bear. Since then, they preferred to keep their livestock nearby, where they could hear their cries if a threatening animal drew too close.

Michaela had planned to come home and scrub the laundry this afternoon—this was Wednesday, her wash day. But the hogs and the cow had to be found before nightfall. So she unsaddled and unharnessed her horse, and put it in a stall in the barn. Then she went into the forest to look for the animals.

A few hours later Matthew arrived at the homestead with Chester. Dr. Mike wasn't there, although her horse was unsaddled and in the barn. The hogs and the cow were gone, too, and Matthew figured Dr. Mike was out looking for them.

Matthew had looped a rope around Chester's neck and tied the other end to his horse's saddle. Now he tied that end around a stall rail, pulling it tight. "You've caused enough trouble for one day, that's for sure," he told the goat. "We're not so friendly that you had to break down the fences to come an' see me."

Chester didn't look worried. He plopped down on a pile of hay. He'd had a big day, breaking through fences and trotting all the way to town and back, and now he was tired.

"I bet Dr. Mike's tired, too," Matthew grumbled at Chester. Then he went to help find the hogs and the cow.

He searched for a while but found nothing, not even Dr. Mike. Then he heard her trying to coax something along— either the cow or the hogs.

He went in the direction of her voice and found her tapping one of the hogs with a stick, telling it to go home. The animal was being stubborn, turning circles around her.

Matthew picked up a stick and whacked the hog on the rear. It grunted and ran in the direction of the homestead. Matthew ran after him, setting him right when he wandered in the wrong direction.

At the homestead, Matthew ran the hog into the barn and closed the door. Then he went back into the forest to help Dr. Mike find the other hog and the cow.

Matthew and Michaela looked and looked. They encountered deer, rabbits, squirrels, and smaller animals that scurried through the undergrowth. Finally Michaela found the other hog taking a nap beneath a tree. She had run out of patience; she was hot and thirsty, and she still had a pile of dirty clothes and linens to wash. So she herded this hog back to the homestead, using Matthew's aggressive, more effective technique. When the hog moved away from her, not wanting to go anywhere, she whacked him on the backside. That started him running in the right direction.

She put the hog in the barn with the other animals, then she and Matthew spent another hour looking for the cow. She was totally lost, they finally decided, and returned to the homestead. They went straight to the well, and each drank several dippers of water.

Matthew worked on repairing the fences while Michaela scrubbed laundry behind the house. If the cow didn't return at nightfall for milking, she and Sully would have to buy another cow. The cow supplied their milk, cream, and butter. Sully would not be happy when he arrived home and heard that the cow was missing.

Michaela hoped Sully wouldn't insist on getting rid of Chester. Matthew had proven that Chester was smart and could be taught. A few days and nights of leaving the goat tied in the barn might teach him to leave the fences alone.

Sully, Brian, and Katie arrived home. When they saw the broken fences and heard that the cow was still missing, Brian felt bad. After all, Chester was his goat. Sully told him that it wasn't his fault, but Brian hung his head and worked hard to help Matthew mend the fences while Sully went to look for the cow.

She came back on her own just as the sun began lowering behind the trees. Brian saw her first, lumbering toward the barn. "I'm glad she needs to be milked," he told Matthew. "Otherwise she might not've come back."

Sully returned five minutes behind the cow, ready to give up on her. When he saw her, he smiled at Brian.

Matthew stayed for dinner. Michaela had roasted a chicken and made a bread pudding with lemon sauce—Matthew's favorite.

Sully had spent the last several days helping rebuild the Hugheses' barn, and that was going well, he reported. Ben had been at school all week, Brian said, but sometimes he still looked like he might cry any minute.

Matthew was surprised to hear about Hank and the boys' foot ball game; between Hank's hotel and his interest in Mrs. Reeves, he didn't know how Hank had found time to teach the boys anything. That impressed Brian, and he said he might consider going back to work at the Gold Nugget.

"Lately, I've seen Preston around town with Mrs. Reeves," Matthew said. "I think Hank may have some competition."

"I'm still amazed that Horace knocked Hank out. I couldn't believe it," Michaela remarked. "Nor could I believe that the blow didn't fracture Hank's skull."

"He's got a hard head," Sully said, and they all laughed.

Matthew nodded. "Ain't that the truth! You can bet Hank won't let it go. He's got to be in a temper over it."

Michaela shook her head. "Horace and Hank butted heads when Horace was courting Myra. That's the only time I've known Horace to completely lose his temper."

"Maybe too much has happened to him lately," Brian commented. "Robert E. breakin' his velocipede. Then Horace ridin' too far on it. Does that tonic really make a person grow hair, Ma?"

Michaela dabbed a napkin to the corners of her mouth. "Well, I haven't tested it, Brian. But if it really could, surely every medical journal in the United States would be recommending it."

"If it didn't smell so bad, Horace could keep usin' it an' find out. Maybe he could mix something with it that smells good, some cologne water or somethin'."

Matthew laughed. "Brian, don't give Horace any ideas.

243

He might fill the telegraph office or his house with tubes an' start concoctin' things, tryin' to find something that'll grow hair.''

Everyone laughed at the thought. Katie clapped her hands together. She said, "Hair," and rubbed her head.

Brian had taught her to point to her hair, her mouth, her ears, her nose, and her chin. Seeing her rub her hair reminded him that he wanted to show Matthew how much Katie had learned since the last time he'd visited the homestead, over two months ago.

"Where's your mouth?" Brian asked Katie. She grinned and pointed to her mouth. He went through the rest of it with her, asking her where her ears, then her nose, then her chin were. When he asked about her chin, she gave him a sly look and pointed to her ear again.

Michaela laughed. Katie was being mischievous. She knew exactly where her chin was—she and Brian had played the game a hundred times.

That afternoon, Hank took Cora out along the stream, going farther out this time, to the foot of a mountain.

She was thrilled, jumping down from the wagon before he had a chance to hurry around and help her down. She peered up at the peak, shading her eyes from the sun, taking in the different colors of the mountain—blues, purples, and pinks.

It was pretty amazing the way the sun made the colors appear. The mountain wasn't really all those colors. Hank had climbed Pike's Peak, and he knew the rock was just as gray up there, and the grass was just as green, as anywhere else.

At the foot of the mountain they spread the quilt she'd brought and opened the basket of food he'd brought. They pulled out cheese, mutton, a fresh loaf of bread, and a chunk of butter. Hank had added a bottle of wine from the hotel's cellar, and he pulled the bottle out, along with two glasses. He'd drink wine, although he didn't like it as much as other people seemed to. He'd thought it would go well with the bread and cheese, and that Cora might enjoy it, so he'd included it.

She did enjoy it, along with the food.

After they ate, they climbed partway up the mountain. They didn't go far—Hank didn't think that would be a good idea, without ropes and other equipment. If she wanted to climb the mountain, they could come back another day. She wanted to, she said, and her eyes were bright with excitement—and a little glazed from the wine.

Back near their quilt she found a patch of clover, and began looking for one with four leaves. They both looked, Hank getting down on his hands and knees and searching right alongside her. After about fifteen minutes she finally found a four-leaf clover, and she danced around, laughing, then held it up to show him.

The edge of one of the leaves was folded under her finger, and Hank reached out to straighten it. When he looked from the clover to her face, she wasn't laughing anymore. She looked straight into his eyes and smiled nervously. Then she turned serious again.

It was too sweet a moment to pass up. So Hank lowered his head and tasted her lips. He just brushed his mouth across hers, not wanting to scare her. But he'd wager his every penny that the brief meeting was the richest sampling of anything he'd had in his life.

Birds chirped and fluttered in the treetops. Nearby, the mountain showed off its colors in the bright sunlight. Her face glowing pink, Cora turned away, touching her lips. She wasn't mad, he could tell, just self-conscious and embarrassed.

"We should get back to town," she said, and he knew the afternoon was over. She needed time to think about that kiss, about whether or not she should have allowed it.

He had to stay fresh in her mind now—call at the shop often, maybe pick some flowers and leave them on the doorstep of her house, along with a note. Ordinarily he didn't think about about doing a silly thing like that for a woman.

But then he'd taken quite a fancy to Mrs. Cora Reeves.

19

Preston and several of his male employees from the resort delivered Cora's crates from the depot to her shop and to her house. There were so many crates, and some were so large, that they made five trips. Apparently Cora had decided to have some of her furniture shipped, too. The delivery took most of the morning, and by noon Preston and his men had to get back to the resort.

When it was all done, Hank strode across the street and found Cora looking lost among the many crates, not knowing where to start. Hank figured he had an advantage over Preston: Preston's resort was located several miles outside of town, while the Gold Nugget was located right across the street from Cora's bookstore. It took him a minute to get from the hotel to the bookstore, while it took Preston twenty minutes to ride into town. Which meant that Hank could drop in on Cora Reeves a lot easier than Preston could.

"Mr. Lodge had to leave," Cora told Hank. "He's so busy with his resort."

Ain't that a cryin' shame. "I'll help," Hank volunteered. She looked relieved.

"We'll need something to open the crates with. I'll be right back," he told her.

He went to his office in the hotel, and dug out a long-handled bar, curved at one end, that he used for just such things.

Minutes later, with the bar in hand, he poked his head back into her bookstore and began working on a crate.

"I thought you bruised your jaw by hitting it on something," she said, watching him pry at the top of the crate.

Now why would she say something like that? Had someone been talking too much? "I did."

"Preston said Horace Bing hit you."

"He did," Hank said, his eyes on the crate.

"Why did you tell me something different?"

"I didn't want you in the middle of my differences with Horace."

That was the truth. Hank still didn't like the fact that that weasel Horace had managed to flatten him. And why was she asking questions all of a sudden?

"Preston said you were teasing Mr. Bing about his hair tonic."

Preston talked too damn much. Hank popped the lid off the crate and moved on to the next one. "That's right. Horace was too sensitive about it."

"Mr. Bing seems sweet," Cora remarked, looking baffled. "He doesn't seem like the type of man inclined to violence."

"He was that day."

"He stayed and helped Mr. Bray clean the mercantile floor." Cora said that like maybe *he* ought to have stayed, too, and helped clean the floor.

Hank gave her a surprised look. "Horace about split my head open on Loren's counter. I wasn't in any kind of shape to help him clean the floor. I heard Horace paid Loren for the damage, too. He should have, seein's how he caused the trouble."

She raised a fine brow. "Teasing Mr. Bing didn't prompt him to hit you?"

"Maybe it did, but I'm not the one that raised a fist." Damn if women couldn't argue a point to death!

"And you don't plan to retaliate?"

"No," Hank said. But he did. Nobody socked Hank Claggerty and got away unmarked. His jaw was still sore where Horace had punched him—probably would be for the next week—and Horace had some paying to do.

"I certainly hope not," Cora said.

Now he was in a fine pickle of a mess. If he "retaliated," she'd be angry with him. If he didn't, Horace would get away with what he'd done—and that would be a rough drink to swallow.

He pried the rest of the lids off of the crates for her, then helped her unpack books and put them on shelves. Later, she could put them in the order she wanted them, she said. For now she just wanted them unpacked and on the shelves, so she could at least see what she had.

Before he left, he asked if she might need his help tomorrow afternoon, and Cora said that would be wonderful. Hank walked across the street, whistling as he went, sure he had the jump on Preston now.

. . .

Brian showed up at the Gold Nugget that afternoon, asking Hank if he wanted him to come back to work for him. He said he'd been mad because Hank hadn't shown up for the foot ball game the way he'd promised he would. Later, Brian had found out that Hank had picnicked with Mrs. Reeves that afternoon, and he'd worked himself into a temper.

Brian said (kinda quietly) that he'd taken a shine to Sarah Blake and that he might be tempted to forget a game of marbles with his friends if Sarah asked him to carry her books home for her or something.

"Course, that'd be a real long walk to her folks' place, then to ours," Brian said, considering it with a serious look on his face. "An awful long walk. I'd have to see if Robert E. would loan me a horse an' wagon."

. Hank couldn't help a laugh. "Yep. It'd be an awful long walk."

"Five miles there an' five miles back. Why, that'd take me half a day of steady walkin'." Brian looked amazed as he summed up the total mileage.

"What if Robert E. didn't have a horse an' wagon to loan you?" Hank asked, leaning down close to Brian. "Would you still do it?"

Brian twisted his lips this way, then that way, working his jaw. Finally, he said, "I'd have a hard time sayin' no."

Hank grinned. "You'd do your damnedest to carry those books, wouldn't you?"

Brian's face, neck, and ears turned red. "She's awful pretty. So is Mrs. Reeves, I reckon."

Hank nodded. "She sure is. Preston's movin' in on me, though, an' I ain't figured out what to do about that yet. I've got a jump on him, though—he's out at the resort an' I'm right here."

"Looks like she's got a lot of unpackin' an' arrangin' to do in that shop."

"She does, an' I aim to help her with it. So, yep, I sure could use your help here. Ben's, too, whenever he's ready to come back."

"I don't know about Ben," Brian said. "He's helpin' his ma a lot these days. The cowhands are still out there, but Ben feels like he's got to be at the ranch a lot."

"Well, you tell him the offer stands if he ever needs a job in town."

Brian set to work sweeping the floors, and Hank went off to his office in good spirits. He didn't always get along well with kids, and he was surprised the conversation with Brian had been so easy. They had something in common with the girl thing, that's why they'd talked so easily. He really had been distracted by Cora the afternoon he was supposed to teach the boys to play foot ball, and now that Brian had his sights on Sarah Blake, Brian was understanding how easily a girl could distract a boy.

The next morning Hank nearly bumped into Dorothy in front of the mercantile. He wanted ham and beans, and he knew Loren had some in cans.

Dorothy was coming from the opposite direction, scribbling (always scribbling) on her tablet as she walked. Hank had to put out a hand to stop her, otherwise she would have walked smack dab into him.

She glanced up, looking dazed. He'd pulled her out of the middle of whatever she was writing down.

"You ever walked into a post or a door or a wall doin' that?" he asked.

"Oh . . . Hank." The glaze cleared from her eyes. She thrust back her shoulders, suddenly looking irritated with him. "You oughtta leave Horace alone about his hair tonic."

That made him jerk back in surprise. He hadn't talked to Horace in days, not since Horace had punched him. He'd seen him around town, pedaling along on that contraption, but that was all. Horace had stopped delivering packages to the Gold Nugget, and Hank sent Henry Miller to pick up any mail or messages from the telegraph office. If he went himself, he'd be tempted to throw a fist across the desk at Horace.

Hank had started thinking that maybe punching Horace wasn't such a good idea. He was trying to build a better reputation for himself, after all, and reputable hotel owners and managers didn't involve themselves in scrapes. They sure didn't continue the scrapes. Continuing this one might hurt his business.

"I haven't said nothin' to Horace about his hair tonic in a good week," Hank told Dorothy.

"Horace has had a rough time of it these past few years," Dorothy retorted, still scowling at him. "Myra leavin' him, takin' Samantha away like that. Horace had to get used to livin' alone again. Maybe he's tryin' to feel better about himself."

"All right, all right, I hear you," Hank said, backing off. He couldn't believe Dorothy knew he'd teased Horace about the tonic. But then, remembering that Mrs. Levins and Mrs. Sloan had been in the mercantile when Horace punched him, yes, he could. Loren talked, too, more than he ought to, most of the time.

Dorothy had pull whenever she printed an "editorial opinion" in the *Gazette*. Hank didn't want to get on her bad side with this Horace thing, otherwise his business might suffer because of that, too. The respectable reputation thing again.

"I ain't gonna bother Horace," he told Dorothy.

"Good," she said, and then she marched off, her notepad and pencil still in hand.

Hank made his way into the mercantile, shaking his head.

Loren was out of the canned ham and beans. "I hear Grace has some goin' today," he told Hank. "Ever'body knows she makes some mean ham an' beans. Probably has some fresh corn bread at the café, too."

The café was a little too close to the telegraph office for Hank's peace of mind. But he wanted a bowl of ham and beans—and now corn bread—badly enough that when he left the mercantile, he headed toward the café.

Grace had what he wanted, sure enough. But she had a cold shoulder for him, too. Grace could be even more uppity than Michaela when she got her feathers ruffled about something, and they were really ruffled today. She brought Hank a cup of coffee to go with the ham and beans and corn bread, her shiny nose turned up to the sun, her eyes avoiding his. He jokingly made a stab at what might be wrong.

"Let me guess," he said. "You think I oughtta leave Horace alone."

She flipped her skirt, turning away from the table. "What Horace does is Horace's business. You guessed right—I think you oughtta leave 'im alone."

He glared at her as she walked off. "You know, Grace, if you're this rude to all your customers, pretty soon you won't have any customers!"

"You ain't a customer very often," she called back. "I figure I can afford to be rude to you."

Loren was right. Grace made some mean ham and

beans—and corn bread. But now Hank had lost his appetite. He was sick of this Horace thing. First Cora, then Dorothy, now Grace. Soon the entire female population of Colorado Springs might be beating his door down, demanding that he leave Horace alone.

"I ain't talked to him in a week!" he blurted, frustrated.

He shoved the bowl away and pulled money out of his trouser pocket. He tossed it on the table, then stomped off.

After a few nights of tying Chester to a stall in the barn, Sully tried leaving him out in the barnyard during the day again. He put the hogs inside for the day and tied a bell around the cow's neck, just in case Chester decided to butt through the fence again. The cow needed to graze, so he couldn't keep her in the barn all day. But this time, if she got loose in the forest, he, Michaela, and Brian could listen for her bell and maybe locate her.

Chester stayed put. He had scratches on the side of his face when the Sullys came home that evening, and he was avoiding the hens, moving to a different place in the barnyard whenever they came close to him.

"I wonder if Red attacked him again," Michaela said as Katie held tight to her—Katie still worried that Chester wanted to eat her dress. Red was the rooster that had attacked Chester during Chester's first day in the barnyard, after he chased the hens.

"Most likely," Sully remarked. He laughed. "He's sure stayin' away from those hens."

"He's all scratched up!" Brian said, worrying over Chester. He ran his hand over the scratches. "I'll clean 'em up for you, Chester, don't worry."

"Chesser gawt scwach, Mama," Katie said, peering cautiously at the goat.

Michaela smiled at the baby. "I know. Brian will wash Chester's scratches."

"That ain't the first hard lesson Chester's learned this past month," Sully said. "It ain't half as bad as Matthew tyin' him up every night."

"Matthew only tied him up one night," Brian said.

Sully and Michaela exchanged apprehensive looks. Matthew hadn't wanted Brian to know that he had tied Chester up for more than one night.

"Once Chester learns what he can and can't do in the barnyard, I'm sure Red will leave him alone," Michaela said quickly, changing the subject.

"It ain't like Red's the boss," Brian grumbled.

Sully laughed. "Nobody's beat him yet. He even wins when he fights with the other roosters."

Over supper Michaela told Sully and Brian that she had eaten dinner at Grace's Café today. There Grace told her that Robert E. had made Horace a new saddle for his velocipede. "It's made of sheepskin and it's padded," Michaela said, smiling. She gave in to a giggle while Sully and Brian laughed—they were all remembering the day in church when Horace couldn't sit squarely on his bottom because it was so sore, bruised from riding his velocipede for so long.

"Grace is proud of Robert E. for doing such a thoughtful thing," Michaela said. "I'm glad, because I think Robert E. may soon have a very big surprise for Grace, one she may not like."

Sully looked at her, waiting.

She lowered her voice, as if disclosing a great secret. "I think Robert E. ordered himself a velocipede." She told Sully about the day when Robert E. had asked what she thought Grace would think of him getting a velocipede. "I had the distinct impression that Robert E. had already ordered one.''

"What'd you say to him?'' Sully asked.

"That I thought he should talk to Grace.''

"I wonder if he did.''

Michaela shook her head. "I don't know. I was tempted to ask a few times, but I thought I should leave the subject alone.''

Brian had fallen quiet. Now he seemed deep in thought, pushing vegetables around in his bowl. Finally he asked Michaela a rather serious question: "Ma, have you ever had a patient make somebody promise to do somethin' they didn't really wanna do? When the patient knows he ain't gonna live, I mean.''

"You mean like a deathbed promise?'' Michaela asked. "A promise to carry on something for the patient?''

Brian nodded.

"Yes,'' Michaela said. "That happens frequently. It happened with your ma—she wanted me to take care of you, Matthew, and Colleen, and I promised her that I would. It happened with Ben's father, too. He made Ben promise that he would take care of the ranch.''

He pursed his lips, and she knew that Ben's promise was bothering him.

"You kept your promise, Ma. But supposin' somebody didn't?''

"I think a lot of deathbed promises are made to give the dying patient some final happiness. Not all are kept.''

"Ben's ma has plenty of ranch hands to help her,'' Sully told Brian gently. "Ben doesn't have to be a rancher.''

Michaela squeezed Brian's hand. "Ben should talk to his mother. Perhaps he expects more of himself than she expects of him.''

Brian glanced at her and Sully, and smiled. He nodded and said, "Thanks." Then he ate his stew, as if a heavy load had been lifted from his shoulders and he suddenly realized how hungry he was.

When it came to money matters, Preston wheeled and dealed and usually got his way. He was good at charming people until they got to know him better and realized that the only person in the world Preston was really concerned about was himself. He talked about town improvements, agreeing with Matthew that they should pave the streets and erect lampposts. But Matthew wanted the streets paved and lampposts erected for the comfort of the townspeople; Preston wanted the improvements for the sake of impressing tourists who undoubtedly would return to Colorado Springs for another visit in the future, and who might pass some good words to possible future tourists. In the end, almost all the tourists visited Preston's resort.

"Most of the time my resort is the only reason they come at all," he told Cora one afternoon.

By coming to Colorado Springs, to this settlement where the people were mostly friendly and open, she had escaped the big city stuffiness. She didn't like class separation, the rich from the poor, the educated from the uneducated. She liked Dr. Mike (as everyone in Colorado Springs called Michaela Quinn) because she had heard that Dr. Mike was from a wealthy Boston family—and yet that seemed to make no difference to the woman who had married a frontiersman who dressed like an Indian. Dr. Mike didn't consider herself better than anyone else.

Preston talked about building the resort up more. He talked about destroying the beautiful forests by cutting down the trees for lumber. Lumber means money, he told

Cora. And the more he talked, the more Cora knew he wasn't right for her.

Dr. Mike helped her make the final decision about whether or not she wanted to continue seeing Preston on a romantic basis, although Dr. Mike surely didn't realize it. She came around with her boy, Brian, one Saturday while Preston was in the bookstore, talking about his dream of a lumber business, going on and on.

Cora greeted Dr. Mike, who said, "I hate to interrupt. . . ."

Preston huffed, as if he hated her interrupting, too. But Cora was grateful for the interruption—Preston had been talking her head off.

"We're gathering donations for the immigrant families," Dr. Mike told Cora. "Anything at all—blankets, clothing, shoes. . . . We do this once a year. If there's anything you would like to donate, you can take it to the church or we'll take it for you."

"What a wonderful thing," Cora said. "I'm sure I'll find something."

Michaela smiled. "Preston, would you like to donate anything?"

"No." He glanced at Cora, perhaps saw that she thought he should—a man of his means could certainly help the less fortunate now and then—and he quickly amended that: "I'll have my men bring a few things."

How positively generous of him. He certainly wouldn't miss whatever he donated, and he wouldn't have to strain himself in getting the donation to the church. He'd have his "men" deliver the donation.

Cora had seen and heard enough. The next time Preston asked if she would have supper with him, she declined. At first she'd thought they might have common interests, she explained, but she couldn't agree with destroying forests for the sake of riches, or with drawing tourist after tourist to this quaint little town. She had come here for the serenity, to enjoy the beauty of the surrounding countryside and the peacefulness of the environment. Colorado Springs would grow as it already was, why not let it grow naturally?

She became friendly with Dorothy, who wrote and printed the *Gazette*. She had tea with her sometimes at the *Gazette* office, above which Dorothy lived, and sometimes they had dinner at Grace's Café.

Dorothy told Cora how she'd come to be in Colorado Springs after being accused of murdering her abusive husband. She'd started the *Gazette* with a broken-down old printing press in Bray's Mercantile, Mr. Bray being her brother-in-law. "Why, when I started it, the *Gazette* was nothin' more than a piece of paper with some awful printin'—and it wasn't very well written either," Dorothy said.

Curious, Cora asked if Dorothy still had any of those early issues. Dorothy blushed and said she was ashamed to say she'd kept every one of them, just because—well, no newspaper editor threw away the old issues. Newspapers did more than just record the weekly news in a town, after all. The more they aged, the more they became a record of history.

"I'd like to read the old issues," Cora told Dorothy. "I'd like to see how far you've come."

Dorothy's blush deepened. "Far. Real far."

So Cora and Dorothy went to the *Gazette* office, and half an hour later Cora left with a bundle of old issues in her arms.

She discovered all sorts of things. How Dr. Mike came by her clinic, how Matthew Cooper was hired as sheriff. . . . She read about the debate over whether or not the railroad should be built through Colorado Springs. And then a particular story caught Cora's eye. It was about a fight in "Hank Claggerty's saloon."

This issue of the *Gazette* was over two years old. But Mr. Claggerty hadn't been in Colorado Springs that long. Not according to him, anyway. He'd told her that he came from Missouri last year, and that he and Jake Slicker had started the Gold Nugget together.

Her curiosity aroused, Cora went through all the old issues again. She found numerous references to Mr. Claggerty, which lessened the possibility that the mention of his name in the article about the saloon fight was a misprint. The references also made her realize that he had lied to her—that he'd been in Colorado Springs a lot longer than he'd told her he had, that he'd never owned and operated a hotel in Missouri, but a saloon right here in this town.

Well, well! Mr. Claggerty had some explaining to do.

She visited him at the Gold Nugget the following afternoon. When she dropped several old issues of the *Gazette* on his desk, ones that were at least two years old and contained specific references to him, he inhaled deeply.

He'd been caught red-handed, and he knew it.

"I don't like being deceived, Mr. Claggerty," Cora said. She then told him they wouldn't be dining, picnicking, taking rides, or hiking together anymore. She couldn't avoid *seeing* him, of course, since their businesses sat on opposite sides of the street, but she certainly wished she could, at least until her temper cooled down. She detested being lied to.

He said nothing as she gathered the old newspapers and left his office, her skirts swishing along the quiet hallway.

In the lobby, Mr. Miller nodded to her and wished her a good day. Cora thanked him, and then she stepped outside into the bright sunlight.

20

Several of Michaela's patients had asked about making appointments to see her. The more Michaela thought about the idea, the more she liked it. Appointments would save patients long waits, and she would know how many patients she would be seeing each day. Except for emergencies, of course. No one could predict those. If an emergency occurred, she would have to postpone certain appointments.

The appointments worked well during the next several weeks. Everyone was happier with them than with the old system of having the patients wait turns on the clinic's front porch. And so she continued with the appointments. Along with set clinic hours, she was delighted to find something else that helped the clinic run more smoothly and that made life easier for her patients. Michaela began to think she didn't need to hire an assistant after all.

The Dry Goods Store opened on the other side of town, relieving Loren of some of his business. "I had more than I could handle anyway," he told Michaela.

Since she had observed his busyness at the mercantile many times during the past two or three months, she knew he wasn't just spouting words, trying to pretend that he didn't mind that another store had gone up in town. He really *didn't* mind. In fact, he didn't even view the Dry Goods Store as competition.

"I have time to do other things again now," he said. "Like take Brian fishin'." Which he did the very next day.

Another barbershop opened near the Dry Goods Store. The owner's name was McClure, and Reverend Johnson told Michaela that the new barber had a kind face and a nice word for everybody.

Within just a few weeks the lines fell to almost nothing at Jake's barbershop. Michaela saw Jake in the mercantile one day and heard him complaining to Loren. "Durin' the rush, I made some good money," he said. "Now that money's gone to the other side of town."

An improvement in your disposition would help, Michaela thought. But she kept the thought to herself as she gathered what she needed. She had Loren add the items to her account, and left with her lips sealed.

Jake struggled for a while. He halved the prices of shaves and haircuts, and he advertised in the *Gazette*. Eventually his business picked up again, but his shop still didn't have long lines. Mr. McClure's barbershop absorbed Jake's overflow.

During those weeks, Michaela hardly saw Hank at all. She heard through Dorothy (who had heard from an angry Hank after Cora Reeves read those old issues of the

Gazette) that Mrs. Reeves had discovered that Hank had lied to her about his past, and she wouldn't see him anymore.

When Michaela recalled the day Hank had come to the clinic complaining about his thigh, she felt sorry for him. She had guessed that nothing was wrong with his thigh, that he had come seeking only advice about how to court a lady like Mrs. Reeves. She also recalled Hank asking her not to say anything to Mrs. Reeves about his former occupation.

In the end, the fact that Hank had been a saloon keeper hadn't mattered to Cora—what mattered was that he had lied to her. A hard lesson learned. But then, she doubted that. Michaela knew Hank, and she knew he didn't absorb lessons well. He probably hadn't learned anything from his experience with Mrs. Reeves.

Horace delivered mail and telegrams with his velocipede every day now, and he let people know if they had large packages or crates at his office, so they could pick them up themselves. He had the padded saddle on the velocipede, and he could be seen riding up and down the roads leading in and out of Colorado Springs, mostly in the afternoons and evenings. He had rigged himself a basket on the back of the velocipede, and he used it to store packages while he pedaled. A thick cotton bag, the strap draped across his chest, held smaller mail and telegrams.

When Michaela picked up a large package from the telegraph office one afternoon, Horace told her that he had sent off at least two dozen orders for velocipedes during the last month. A lot of people, himself included, had ordered the two-wheeled kind.

"None of 'em are real easy to stop," Horace said seriously. "I'm worried people'll have accidents and hurt themselves."

"You know how to ride yours well," Michaela remarked. "I'm sure you'll ride the two-wheeled one just as well, Horace. Why don't you give instructions?"

His entire face wrinkled. "You mean teach people to ride their velocipedes? Me?"

"Why not? You're the best velocipede rider in town."

He beamed.

He was the *only* velocipede rider in town. But Michaela didn't have the heart to say that, and Horace either didn't realize that he was the only one or else he was too busy basking in her praise.

"That's an idea," he said.

Robert E. received his velocipede. Or so Michaela discovered when she went into town late one morning. She stopped at the livery to leave her horse for the day, and Robert E. was putting a velocipede together.

"See what I got?" he said with childlike excitement, his eyes bright.

"I see," Michaela said, smiling. Then she glanced at him apprehensively. "Robert E., did you talk to Grace about it?"

He sighed, still working on the front wheel. "Nope, I never did."

"She'll be surprised." And probably not pleasantly surprised.

"Reckon I'd better tell her sometime today," he said.

Before she finds out by herself, Michaela thought. But she kept the thought to herself as she led her horse into the livery barn. Robert E. followed and took the reins from her.

She thought about Robert E. most of the morning, about the fact that he hadn't told Grace about the velocipede.

Since Robert E.'s accident with Mrs. Everly's henhouse and since Horace's ten-mile excursion, Grace had made it abundantly clear that she didn't like the "contraptions." Michaela worried that Grace would fly into a temper when she found out that Robert E. had ordered himself a velocipede, and that Grace and Robert E. might even have serious marital problems. Sully would tell her to leave things alone. But she couldn't. She just couldn't.

So out of curiosity and concern more than hunger, she had dinner at the café that afternoon.

She found Grace in a temper, as she had feared she might. "I can't believe he ordered that thing behind my back!" Grace huffed.

Michaela urged Grace to sit down, although this was one of the busiest times of the day for her. But Grace had plenty of help now, and in the interest of her marriage, she needed to sit down.

"I know you were angry about his ride on Horace's velocipede . . . ," Michaela began.

"He could have killed himself!" Grace's eyes flashed. "He could kill himself on this one."

Michaela covered Grace's hand with hers and looked her friend in the eye. "I worry about Sully every time he goes hunting. Every time he goes to see Cloud Dancing. I can't tell you how *many* times I've worried about Sully since we were married. He wouldn't go hunting or to see Cloud Dancing if I told him I didn't want him to. But I don't— because I know that hunting and his friendship with Cloud Dancing make him happy."

"You make him happy, too," Grace objected.

"I know. But I'm only part of his happiness. Just as he's only part of mine. Robert E. didn't want to ask anyone's

265

permission about the velocipede. Not yours, not anyone's. Maybe this is his way of rebelling.''

''Why would he have to . . .'' Grace glanced away, looking worried and pensive. Maybe she was considering all that Michaela had said.

''I'm certainly no expert on marriage,'' Michaela said. ''But I saw Robert E. this morning, and I thought I should talk to you. I've worried all morning about the two of you.''

Grace sighed, then said quietly that she'd better get busy.

Michaela still worried about Grace and Robert E. She talked to Sully about them that night, and as she had known he would, he told her she should leave things alone. Well, she had done all she could do, anyway.

The next two mornings, when she left her horse at the livery, she practically had to bite her tongue to keep from asking Robert E. how things were with Grace. She spent her dinner hours preparing herbs and writing patient notes so she wouldn't have to take the files home with her. Which meant that she had no time to visit Grace at the café to see if she would say anything about how things were between her and Robert E.

By the third day, Michaela thought she would pop with worry and curiosity. Robert E. again offered nothing when she left her horse at his livery. He was whistling as he worked. But then, more often than not, Robert E. whistled while he worked.

She went to the café for dinner—and to see how Grace was.

As Grace approached the table, Michaela grew more worried. Grace looked tired—exhausted, actually—as if she had had little sleep. Perhaps because she and Robert E. had been arguing.

By the time Grace reached the table, Michaela was convinced that they had been, probably for the last three days.

Grace plopped down in the chair opposite Michaela, resting her elbow on the table and her chin in her cupped palm. "Hi, Dr. Mike," she said. "I feel terrible."

"Oh Grace, I'm sorry," Michaela blurted. "I should have insisted that Robert E. talk to you before he ordered the velocipede. Or I should have talked to you myself. I knew it would cause trouble."

"It sure has! A passel o' trouble." Grace narrowed her eyes at Michaela. "D'you know how much sleep I've had lately?"

"H-how much?" Michaela asked uneasily.

"Maybe four hours between the last two nights!"

Michaela closed her eyes and shook her head. She remembered when Robert E. had taken such a shine to Grace, how shy he had been about it, how sweet they had seemed together. They were Katie's godparents, and Michaela couldn't stand the thought of them having marital troubles. But Grace was stubborn and liked to "rule her roost," and apparently Robert E. had had enough. Ordering the velocipede without telling Grace had definitely been an act of rebellion on his part. The fact that he had mentioned nothing to Michaela about it for the past three mornings proved that he didn't intend to budge—he would keep his velocipede, whether his wife liked it or not. And apparently Grace didn't intend to budge in her dislike of velocipedes and her disapproval at Robert E. having one.

". . . rode that thing 'round an' 'round inside the barn an' then we did the same fool thing last night," Grace was saying. "Me in my shift an' Robert E. in his skivvies. Told each other las' night that, well, we'd take one turn 'round the barn, then we'd go in to bed. But that ain't what happened. Nope, it sure ain't. My tired head an' body's proof o' that today.''

Michaela's eyes popped open when she realized what Grace was saying. She stared at her in disbelief.

''Horses an' cows lookin' over the stalls at us like we'd lost our fool minds. An' we had. I *told* you I didn't like those contraptions,'' Grace grumbled, scowling at Michaela.

''You *rode* it?'' Michaela asked. That's what she had heard—Grace saying that she had ridden the velocipede with Robert E. *We* . . . Grace had said *we.*

Grace nodded tiredly. ''I sure did. That's what I've been tellin' you, Michaela. You ain't been listenin'?''

Michaela felt ashamed. ''Well, only partly. I'm sorry. You and Robert E. were riding the velocipede in your barn in the middle of the night?'' she asked incredulously.

''Just about *all* night. He'd take a turn, then I'd take a turn, then he'd take a turn, then I'd take a turn. Once we tried to take a turn t'gether an' we fell over into the hay-stack. An' we stayed there for a spell, too,'' Grace said. Suddenly her eyes were full of twinkles and naughtiness—and happiness.

Michaela put a hand over her mouth and giggled. She knew she was blushing; her face suddenly felt hot. ''You didn't!''

Grace giggled, too. She leaned toward Michaela and whispered loudly, ''We *did.*''

Michaela hadn't wanted to know quite that much about the state of her friends' marriage. She took a few deep breaths to compose herself while Grace giggled some more.

Grace finally contained herself, which helped Michaela do the same. Both women smoothed their sleeves and their skirts of imaginary wrinkles.

"I gather everything is fine between you and Robert E., then?" Michaela asked presently. "Despite the veloci-pede?"

"Everything's *grand*," Grace said, standing. "*Because* of that contraption. But Robert E.—he's got to let me get some sleep soon!"

She giggled again as she walked off, leaving Michaela shaking her head in wonderment. Grace and Robert E. had quite a story to tell their grandchildren someday.

Sully kidnapped Michaela on Tuesday of the following week. He was waiting on the porch when she emerged with Mr. Sloan, her fifth patient of the morning.

She wasn't entirely surprised to see him. This week he was helping to build another livery stable in town. She stood on her tiptoes and kissed him. He grabbed her by the hand and tugged her toward the porch steps.

"What are you doing?" she asked, baffled.

Grinning slyly, he pointed to the clinic's front door. Someone had posted a note beside the sign that listed the clinic hours. The note read: *Gone for the day. Emergency. Return tomorrow morning.*

"I didn't write that," she said, and when he laughed, she knew that *he* had written the note.

"Sully, why did you—"

"Because you're leavin' for the day. You have an emer-gency."

If there was an emergency, she didn't understand why he was grinning and laughing.

"I'll get my bag," she said.

He tugged on her hand again. "Nope. You ain't gonna need it where we're goin'."

269

She peered at him. "Sully, if there's an emergency, I need my bag."

"It ain't a medical emergency," he said.

The mystery was deepening, and she was beginning to lose her patience. "Where are we going then?"

He pulled her close to him and whispered in her ear, "Away for the day."

Her face heating, she smiled. But leaving right now was impossible. She had numerous patient appointments this afternoon. "Sully, I can't leave the clinic. I have patients to see this afternoon and—"

"They'll wait. If there's an emergency, someone'll ride out to the resort an' get Andrew."

She stared at him, still shocked, still feeling like she should stay.

"All right, Michaela. Reckon I'll have to carry you off the porch an' tie you to that horse."

He had two horses waiting just beyond the porch. Sully had planned this. Stuffed saddlebags dangled on the sides of the horses. Blanket rolls were tied to the backs of the saddles.

"This is ludicrous," she said, laughing. "You're kidnapping me."

"Yep, I sure am, Mrs. Sully. An' you'd best come peacefully."

"Sully. . . ."

"C'mon, Michaela," he said, pulling her down the steps with him. "Dorothy'll be right over to lock things up."

"*Dorothy* knows about this?"

"She sure does. Brian's stayin' with her after school."

"You might have warned me," she objected playfully as they reached the horses.

"An' you would've argued 'til the sun went down. Figured I'd make out better if I just showed up.''

She mounted one horse while he mounted the other.

They rode past the livery and out toward the church. Their horses clopped over the little bridge that crossed the creek. They passed the church, then the cemetery and the scattered tents of immigrants and newcomers to Colorado Springs.

Michaela smiled over at Sully but shook her head, still not believing she had allowed him to take her away from the clinic when she had an afternoon of patients lined up.

She told him that, and he simply shrugged. ''When would you have had an open afternoon?''

He had a point. She didn't answer the question because they both already knew the answer.

A breeze lifted Michaela's hair while the sun warmed her face. The trees thickened, and soon Sully turned his horse onto a path Michaela had traveled with him many times. Twigs crunched beneath the horses' hooves, and suddenly the air smelled sweet, like honeysuckle and wild rose.

Michaela spotted the rose vines and laughed when she saw that Sully was already leading his horse toward the vines. He knew her well, knew she would want to stop and collect some of the roses. They would wilt not long after she plucked them, but at least she could smell them now and then as she and Sully rode on.

She collected a handful of the roses and had Sully hold them for her while she remounted her horse. He handed the roses up to her, smiling, and she laid them in the pouch her skirt formed in front of the saddle horn. Then he remounted, too, and they rode farther.

They led their horses around boulders and through streams, around gatherings of trees and undergrowth that was too thick to pass through. When they started up the side of a mountain, Michaela knew where they were going. Sully had brought her here twice before when he had wanted to take her away from everything and everyone, when he had wanted to spend time alone with her, without distractions. They wouldn't travel all the way up the mountain—they couldn't, on the horses. They didn't have much farther to go.

Michaela heard the rush of the water long before she saw it. And when she did see it, the water hurrying over rock ledges and then over a bluff to form a waterfall, she smiled, because their place was as beautiful as ever.

The frothy water fell fifty feet or more to a large, bowl-shaped pool, probably formed by the water itself during centuries past. The pooled water glittered in the sunlight, and the surrounding trees moved gently in the afternoon breeze. In the distance, snow capped the higher mountains. The rising peaks appeared purple, blue, pink, even red in places as the sunlight played tricks on the eye.

Sully helped Michaela down from her horse. With his hands on her waist, he lowered her to stand right in front of him.

"We're both so busy, I figured we should ride out here an' slow down for an afternoon," he said. "Enjoy the scenery. Enjoy each other."

He kissed her, and Michaela lost herself in his embrace and in his arms. She caressed his jaw, then she slid her fingers into his soft hair. He smelled like pine and leather and sage, minty and earthy and pungent. When he lifted his head and smiled down at her, Michaela wasn't ready for their kisses to end.

He tied the horses to a nearby tree and unsaddled them while she sat on the grass and removed her boots and stockings. He was untying the blanket rolls some ten feet from the horses when she skipped over to the water, sat, and stuck her toes in the pool. The water was cold, as water that came down from the mountains always was.

"You'll have to build a fire if you expect me to get in this water with you," she teased, glancing at him over her shoulder.

He laughed. "I'll build a fire."

She threw a twig at him. "That's not what I meant."

He unrolled the blankets and spread them out on the soft grass. Michaela watched him, knowing there could be only one reason why he would spread the blankets on the ground like that.

He knelt on one of the blankets and held out his hand to her.

Michaela went to him and knelt in front of him, her hands on his jaw as she brought his face to hers.

She closed her eyes as his lips touched hers, and she listened to the rush of the water. His arms slid down to her waist and around, and they pressed her close to him. His heart pounded against hers as their kisses deepened.

What had her life been like before Sully? Confusion and frustration and lack of fulfillment. . . . They were one now, and she loved him as much as he loved this land.

He pressed her gently down onto her back and smiled at her.

"Kidnap me more often, would you please, Mr. Sully?" she teased.

"Sure," he said. Then he kissed her again.

Epilogue

Michaela and Brian sat on the top step of the clinic's front porch and watched the gathering of velocipedes and riders across the street. Wagons and buggies, drawn by horses, rattled by, although the traffic had thinned out considerably from two hours ago. It was nearing suppertime, and many people had gone inside for the evening meal.

They were waiting for Sully, Katie, and Colleen—all of them were going to Grace and Robert E.'s house for supper this evening. Colleen was home from school, and she had spent the afternoon with Andrew. Sully had gone to pick up Katie from Amanda Blake.

Things finally had calmed down in town, at the clinic and at the Sullys' home. Colorado Springs had had a growth spurt and everyone adjusted. Michaela did not have to hire an assistant; her patients had adapted to the new clinic hours, and Michaela had made herself adhere to them—for the sake of her health, sanity, and family. However, in the end, Sully had been right; Colleen had said she wouldn't have minded if Michaela had hired an assistant.

Horace rode his two-wheeled velocipede today, as he always did whenever he conducted class. Right now he stood beside his velocipede as he talked to his students and pointed first to the handlebars, then to the front wheel.

"He's got five people today, Ma," Brian observed. "That's the most I've seen him have at a time."

"He's loving it, too," Michaela said, smiling. Giving the lessons helped boost Horace's self-esteem. She was glad he had taken her advice about conducting the classes.

Three months had passed since Horace's three-wheeled velocipede had made its appearance in town, and now the "contraptions," as Robert E. and Grace still called them, were a common sight. Some had two wheels, some had three; some were decorated with ribbons and baskets, some with silk flowers, and some were plain. The velocipedes were an interesting addition to Colorado Springs, and a better mode of travel when a person didn't need to go very far. A healthier one, too. They were a lot smaller than buggies and wagons, and they didn't leave a mess.

Within ten minutes the street cleared even more. Horace had put his velocipede aside, leaning it against a post, and now he held another velocipede upright while Susy Perkins climbed onto the saddle. He encouraged her to pedal a little, which she did, and he continued to hold the velocipede upright while the wheels turned and the contraption traveled to the end of the street. He didn't dare let go yet; this was Susy's first time on the thing, and it usually took a person several days to get a sense of balance.

The velocipede slowed, and Horace turned it around.

Susy pedaled again as he held the contraption upright, and they rejoined their group. Now it was the next student's turn. Michaela had watched the classes before, and she knew Horace's routine.

"I can't wait 'til mine comes," Brian said. He had ordered himself a two-wheeled velocipede, and he was having a hard time waiting for it. He went to the train station every day during recess at school, and he checked at the depot again every afternoon, after school let out.

Horace took his second student out just as Colleen rounded the corner of the clinic and joined Michaela and Brian on the front steps.

"How was your afternoon?" Michaela asked, unable to help herself.

"Fine," Colleen said, and she kissed Michaela's cheek. "Very fine." Colleen's cheeks were rosy and her eyes shimmered. She was definitely in love. She would be home until school resumed in late October, and Michaela imagined that much of her time would be spent with Andrew.

Colleen nudged Brian. "Your velocipede still hasn't arrived?"

He shook his head, looking rather gloomy. "Nope."

"It will soon," Michaela said. She knew he felt like it *never* would. Waiting for his velocipede was like waiting for Christmas morning, only this was August, not December.

Soon Sully and Katie arrived in the wagon. Colleen took Katie, as she always did. Whenever she was home from school, if she didn't have Andrew by her side, she had Katie on her hip. She adored the baby.

"I think you two should get velocipedes," Colleen told Michaela and Sully, a sparkle of mischief in her eyes. "You could ride off into the countryside some afternoons. How romantic that would be!''

''That's an idea,'' Sully said, grinning.

Michaela laughed, nudging him with her shoulder. ''I don't think we could take velocipedes to the places where we like to spend romantic afternoons. Imagine us trying to pedal them very far uphill.''

''A definite disadvantage,'' Colleen remarked as Sully chuckled.

''I'm hungry,'' he said. Brian said he was, too.

''Eat, Mama,'' Katie said, reaching for Michaela.

Michaela rose, took the baby from Colleen, and pressed Katie's cheek to hers. ''Let's go see what Grace has on her stove.''

Minutes later, the family rode away in the wagon, just as evening shadows began stretching over Colorado Springs.

XENA
WARRIOR PRINCESS ™

__THE EMPTY THRONE__   1-57297-200-9/$5.99

A novel by Ru Emerson based on the Universal television series created by
John Schulian and Robert Tapert

In a small, remote village, Xena and her protégé, Gabrielle, make a
stunning discovery: All of the men in town have disappeared without
a trace. They must uncover the truth before it's *their* turn to disappear...

__THE HUNTRESS AND THE SPHINX__ 1-57297-215-7/$5.99

A novel by Ru Emerson based on the Universal television series created by
John Schulian and Robert Tapert

Xena and Gabrielle are asked to rescue a group of kidnapped children,
but when they find the kidnapper, Xena realizes that no one is strong
enough to defeat it. For who can challenge the power of the almighty
Sphinx?

__THE THIEF OF HERMES__   1-57297-232-7/$5.99

A novel by Ru Emerson based on the Universal television series created by
John Schulian and Robert Tapert

Xena and Gabrielle are framed by Hadrian, who claims to be the son of
Hermes, the Sun god. Is Hadrian good or evil? A god's child or a liar?

__PROPHECY OF DARKNESS__   1-57297-249-1/$5.99

A novel by Stella Howard based on the Universal television series created by
John Schulian and Robert Tapert

Xena and Gabrielle encounter a twelve-year-old seer with a startling
prophecy. But more danger awaits. Because according to the prophecy,
one of them will not return...

HERCULES

THE LEGENDARY JOURNEYS™

__BY THE SWORD
1-57297-198-3/$5.99

A novel by Timothy Boggs based on the Universal television series
created by Christian Williams

Someone has stolen the magical blade and it is up to Hercules to recover
it—though he may be in for more than just a fight with ambitious thieves.

__SERPENT'S SHADOW
1-57297-214-9/$5.99

A novel by Timothy Boggs based on the Universal television series
created by Christian Williams

Hercules and Iolaus, heed the desperate plea of a small village. A deadly
sea monster has been terrorizing the townsfolk, and only the great
strength of Hercules can save them.

__THE EYE OF THE RAM
1-57297-224-6/$5.99

A novel by Timothy Boggs based on the Universal television series
created by Christian Williams

It is called the Theater of Fun. Run by Hercules's friend Salmoneus,
the traveling troupe has dancing girls, jugglers, comedians, and a
first-rate magician named Dragar. But Hercules is about to discover
that there is a fine line between magic...and sorcery.

__THE FIRST CASUALTY
1-57297-239-4/$5.99

A novel by David L. Seidman based on the Universal television series
created by Christian Williams

Someone is posing as Hercules. Someone with superhuman powers of
trickery and deception. A certain cloven-hoofed god with a bad attitude...

Copyright © 1998 by MCA Publishing Rights, a Division of MCA, Inc. All rights reserved.
